M000316309

THE BRIGANDS

PARRIS AFTON
BONDS

NEW YORK TIMES BESTSELLING AUTHOR

THE BRIGANDS

THE TEXICANS · VOLUME ONE

NEW YORK TIMES BESTSELLING AUTHOR

PARRIS AFTON
BONDS

LAGAN
PRESS

an imprint of
OGHMA CREATIVE MEDIA

OGHMA

CREATIVE MEDIA

Lagan Press
An imprint of Oghma Creative Media, Inc.
2401 Beth Lane, Bentonville, Arkansas 72701

Library of Congress Cataloging-in-Publication Data

Names: Bonds, Parris Afton, author.
Title: The Brigands/Parris Afton Bonds.| The Texicans #1
Description: First Edition. | Bentonville: Lagan, 2019.
Identifiers: LCCN: 2019942401 | ISBN: 978-1-63373-539-2 (hardcover) |
ISBN: 978-1-63373-540-8 (trade paperback) | ISBN: 978-1-63373-541-5 (eBook)
Subjects: BISAC: FICTION/Romance/Historical/American |
FICTION/Romance/Action & Adventure | FICTION/Romance/Western
LC record available at: https://lccn.loc.gov/2019942401

Lagan Press trade paperback edition November, 2019

Jacket & Interior Design by Casey W. Cowan
Editing by Mari Mason & Kelly Sohner

Dedicated to Carol Sue Holland Mason,
Laughter, Light, Loving

On their father's side, my sons are descendants of the settlers of Robertson's Colony, established in Texas in 1834 under Mexican grant. Until recently, the Bonds still possessed acreage from the original land grant. I always knew that, for my sons, I had to tell this story about the Texicans.

—Parris Afton Bonds

1

SAN FELIPE DE AUSTIN
STATE OF TEJAS Y COAHUILA, MEXICO
OCTOBER 1835

Some things were just not fated to be, Don Alejandro de la Torre y Stuart reflected wryly. Not that he believed in fate—or anything else for that matter—but possession of his birthright, by damn, would not be numbered among the ill-fated.

At midmorning, he met with his long-time acquaintance at the printing office in San Felipe. The office was the political center of the colony. In Alex's opinion, it was the most wretched settlement on the Brazos River, consisting of five stores, two raucous saloons, and twenty or so squalid houses.

Side by side, the two men—each craggy featured and well above six feet and three inches, with the acquaintance nearly three decades older—idly rifled through the office's pigeonholes. These were filled with notices from the colony's impresario, Stephen Austin. Land titles, by-laws, and other legal documents were available for sale to the hordes of would-be colonists descending on Tejas.

Tejas, the Caddo Indian word for friendly—what a bloody joke. Nowhere in the world was there more murder and mayhem and malfeasance.

The unique aroma of printing ink filled his nostrils. The blasting sound from the backroom press reassured him that they would not be overheard.

The older conspirator selected but one publication from the rack—*General Regulations Relative to the Colony*. After adjusting his sword, Sam Houston sat down and laid his wide-brimmed white hat on the pine table.

"I'm here, Alex, because President Jackson asked me to come. Without being specific, Old Hickory apparently desires me to collaborate with Tejas's mostly American contingent. He wants Santa Anna's control sabotaged."

"Hell, that's no secret."

"The President also wants the operations of a spy amongst the colonists— a certain Chaparral Fox—sabotaged."

Alex cut Sam a scoffing look. "Chaparral Fox for a codename? What pomposity."

"Nevertheless, he, or she, seems to know the movements of our militia, the contents of our dispatches, and more. That's why I wanted this one-on-one meeting."

Despite the colony's struggle to gain its independence from Mexico, something of a cause célèbre in the States, Alex hardly considered himself one of those colonists, most of whom called themselves Texicans. "I agreed to meet with you, Sam, only because I have a single inviolable intention, and it does not imply I will side with either those rebels or Santa Anna's forces."

Houston rubbed the back of his sun-cooked neck. "Ahhh, yes. You've lodged enough complaints about your hornets' nest of a problem—proving your legal right to your brother's estate."

"And, lest you forget, all the land surrounding it."

"But gaining legal rights to an almost century-old Spanish Royal Grant ain't gonna be easy, son."

"I am more aware than you think. I mean to remove that hornets' nest—as you so eloquently put it—and its stingers too. Within days, I shall meet with the Mexican land commissioner in Matamoros to substantiate the validity of my family's grant." Fashioning a cold smile, he added, "By hook or by crook."

"What do you know about the land commissioner? This Cavett Magnum fellow?" To any onlooker, Houston appeared to be reading the broadside he had picked out of the rack. "How did the American ever arrive at such an elevated position with the Mexican government?"

"By marrying a Mexican heiress. The man also speaks passable Spanish. An attorney from Connecticut with excellent family connections, he appears to have moved impressively through international circles before settling in Matamoros a year ago. Magnum may or may not be sympathetic to your Texican's desire for independence."

Leaning closer, Houston put down the broadside he appeared to be studying and lowered his voice to a whisper only Alex could hear over the roar of the printing press. "*Our* desire for independence, Alex. Right here and right now. I am aware I am imposing on our years of friendship, but with Mexican government spies everywhere, I need a loyal ally—*you*—in southern Tejas."

Fingertips brushing his day-old stubble, Alex stroked his jawline, pondering. For his own protection, he wanted to leave secrecy and intrigue behind him. Years ago, as Anglo-Spanish, he had served England. Now his heartfelt goal was to serve only himself.

Even so, he meant to accord his friend at least the respect of listening to his plan. "What precisely would such an arrangement entail?"

Houston's craggy features, looking a little worse for wear, assembled into a triumphant grin. "Hell, I knew you couldn't refuse me."

He grunted an exasperated breath. "Get on with it, Sam."

"Presumably, someone has infiltrated the central Committee of the Texican Provisional Government, operating from right here in San Felipe de Austin. So, take advantage of Magnum's connections. He's on the Texican's Independence Council in Matamoros. Get him to endorse you and join it. Keep an eye on its members. Find out who's reliable and who ain't. And keep me informed. Not only of what you learn, but what you may suspect, however unlikely that might sound to you."

He suspected Houston was still mourning the conclusion of a disastrous marriage. With some irritation, Alex conceded he had yet to recover from the conclusion of his own disaster.

What could he have been thinking, undertaking yet another marriage? At twenty-five, with his already wide experience, he should know better.

After an hour more of strategizing, Alex left the printing office. Houston set off for the Texican rebel encampment that had just begun a siege of San Antonio de Bexar, Mexico's Department Headquarters for Tejas and Coahuila.

Mounting his horse, Alex began the long ride back to Matamoros, the Rio Bravo del Norte *presidio* he had recently won in a card game, and straight into that hornets' nest awaiting his arrival.

LONDON

Rafaela Carrera rolled the nib of her quill between chilled fingers. The chill was not just from the Thames fog that seeped inevitably beneath her boarding school's doors. Alas, there was no credible way for her to delay signing the marriage contract forwarded by her father from Guatemala, where he dominated the English rum trade.

Behind her, the scarecrow-thin headmistress garbed all in black exhaled an agitated breath. "What can you ever be thinking, my child? Sign that contract! Now!"

"I am not a child. I am eighteen."

"Just barely." The old woman spread wide, age-knotted fingers. "Your classmates would weep to have thrust upon them your good fortune of marrying a Spanish nobleman."

"Don Alejandro de la Torre y Stuart may be Sixth Lord of Paladín, but he resides at the very bottom of the peerage pole."

Her childhood in Spain was, at best, a misty recollection of memories. Even so, she knew enough about Madrid high society—its best circles and salóns and its etiquette—to understand the finer points of peerage.

The headmistress raised a sparse brow. "Nonetheless, he is also regarded as a *hidalgo* of Old Spain's aristocracy—"

"—only in that backwater Spanish colony they call Tay-has."

"And you are no great—"

"—beauty."

She laid her pen next to the inkwell. "Tis said Paladín gambled away his English birthright, that he kills on a whim and whores away his nights. Worse, that daily, the Baron practices his life as a devout voluptuary. Hardly the brand of husband with whom I would ever wish to create my own family."

Family. That illusive ideal.

"For all that, he nevertheless possesses an aristocratic title, whether or not it is at the bottom of the peerage pole." The headmistress waggled an imperious forefinger under Rafaela's prominent nose. "*That* you may not cavalierly dismiss, my girl."

"All this foolishness, only to add to our family tree a title for which my father would actually sell me—body and soul!"

Either she bowed to her father or considered an even more-proscribed life than the present one at the boarding school—forced to work as a governess, domestic, or in the burgeoning textile mills of England's industrial Midlands.

"It is not as if his Lordship's estates are on the other side of the world from your father's in Guatemala—Mexico and Guatemala are neighboring countries."

She was barely acquainted with her too-distant father, though she possessed an even more distant relative somewhere in America on her mother's side.

Family.

To Rafaela, it was only a whispered word, sounding like a mysterious incantation on her own lips. Family ought to promise security, contentment, even occasionally joy—or so she inferred from her classmates.

Pushing back from the headmistress's writing desk, she paced, combing tense fingers through the knot of hair at her nape, loosening light brown waves. She crossed her arms, deep in frantic thought.

For the second time, her father was trusting her well-being to a swine—this last one the most notorious profligate in recent Anglo history—the Sixth Lord of Paladín.

She turned back to the writing desk. Nudging aside the Mexican map of the Matamoros region, she tapped a forefinger onto the next-to-last paragraph in her father's letter. "Not only is Lord Paladín receiving four-thousand pounds to wed me, he will also receive a square league of virgin land in the Tejas province of Mexico that will become mine after we marry."

The headmistress's vaguely defined eyebrows peaked. "What of it?"

Dry eyed, Rafaela rounded on her. "Virgin land in exchange for a virgin bride? Well, *Madame* Headmistress, I am no longer a virgin!"

Her pronouncement dropped the old headmistress's jaw. For once, Rafaela found herself smiling at her despoiled state. She seriously doubted that even the sybarite Lord Paladín would be delighted with that salacious fact.

FIVE POINTS, NEW YORK CITY

Sitting on the front stoop, Fiona Flanigan ignored the nose-wrinkling stench of boiled cabbage that drifted from the open windows of the Five Points tenement. She squinted into the waning evening light, trying to make out the words of a two-week-old notice in the newspaper.

Spectacles, spectacles... my kingdom for a pair of spectacles. Better yet even, to have sustenance. Something, anything, to eat today.

The overpowering reek originated in Madam Margie's kitchen. The crumpled newspaper she was trying to read had once wrapped madam's discarded fish bones. Fiona was scanning the last of the special notices in the *New York Morning Chronicle's* September edition when her eye caught the advertisement.

Seeking Industrious and Law-Abiding Irish-Catholic Male Immigrants and Widows Who Head Families: Interviews being held for colonists willing to live in San Patricio, in the Mexican state of Tejas y Coahuila.

Its subtext, *"... own a large tract of virgin land,"* elicited from her a rush of yearning. Land!

The too-familiar screech of a Beaufort whistle jerked her attention away from the advertisement. She looked up to see two constables sprinting down the street toward her very stoop. Bloody hell! This time, Madam Margie's whorehouse appeared to have become their target.

Fiona bounded off the stoop, flung open the front door, and dashed up the stairs. On all three floors, she shouted warnings at each room she sprinted past.

"Nab that doxy!" hollered a strident male voice from further behind her.

From too close behind, she could hear the huffing and panting, could smell the stale stink of her other pursuer's beer-tinged breath—at the same time she could feel the jarring thumps of her own heart. A big male hand clutched at her shoulder, only to rip away its muslin sleeve.

She was trapped in the darkened hallway....

Unless she ignored the peril of the open window at the end and its three-story drop into the courtyard.

THE NEXT DAY—HER STOMACH still rumbling hollowly from lack of food and her arms and hands, gouged by landing in a fortuitous bramble bush, still aching—Fiona dipped a quill pen in the inkwell. Her pen hesitated. Was her innate impulsiveness about to land her in a far different variety of brambles?

After the Battle of Kinsale, Ireland, in 1602, victorious English armies denied the vanquished Irish any means for gaining an education or engaging in political representation by voting. Even worse, the British government overseers would not allow the Irish to own any land anywhere in Ireland.

But, according to the newspaper notice, within the Tejas portion of the Mexican state of Tejas and Coahuila, each and every colonist was guaranteed a square league of land. 4,428 acres to be precise!

Wryly, she grinned at the preposterous image of herself as owner of more land than an English Lord. A territorial paradise was what that notice in the newspaper promised her. No tax collectors. No courts. No dispossessions. Best, there would be no hangings and riots against the Irish, who even the lofty-minded Voltaire considered an "inferior" race.

Inferior?

The word inferior implied more than she could force herself to swallow. During her own childhood, despite being denied an education by the ruling English, she had relied on schooling herself from the books she had managed to sneak from the library of the grand mansion where her own mum was a scullery maid—or to purloin the less prominent ones.

Most often, her books had been French novels, not the Greek classics. Even so, she had found delight in discovering varieties of nuance and coloring among the words she stored in her mind. Just like people, she realized, words could imply many varied and even contradictory meanings.

At nineteen, she was alive, which was more than she could say for the rest of her family. Life back in Ireland had been hard enough, and in America it was only a little better—newspapers were full of articles about the violence and depravity consuming the Five Points area where she lived and worked.

To survive even minimally in America, she accepted that she must work for next to no money. However, and obviously to herself, that harsh choice was not turning out to her advantage.

Would her life be better in Mexico? She knew nothing about that country, spoke no Spanish, was not even a confirmed Roman Catholic. Even worse, she certainly did not meet the notice's requirement for "… a widow with family."

Considering her own needs, she reminded herself—better the American devil she knew than the Mexican one she had no clear idea about. But Holy

Mother of Jesus, her ill-fortuned past had gotten her this far, had it not? Not bad at all for an "inferior" Irish lass.

Her lower lip caught between her teeth, she laboriously scrawled her signature on the emigration contract as a "widow with child."

Done!

Now, the one and only thing she needed before that schooner set sail for Tejas—a child.

2

"What will ye do, Alex, should ye discover your betrothed is as ugly as sin?" Niall Gorman grinned as he moved his white pawn one square forward.

"Ahhh, but you of all people know how sinning makes my black heart flutter." Alex captured his hired hand's pawn.

The two men were sitting on benches at one of the long boards of the Calle Real Café. Lounging close by their table were shopkeepers, government officials, lawyers, clerks, and craftsmen, idling away their time in the only coffee house in all of Matamoros.

Discounting its walls, decorated with exotic local taxidermy, the coffee house was much like others in London, with its shaved wooden floors, wain-scoted walls, candles on every board, and an occasional spittoon.

There was one more significant difference from London coffee houses—a well-thumbed directory of Matamoros prostitutes could be found on each board, from which patrons could choose "companions."

Alex set aside the newspaper he was reading, also well-thumbed. The September 1835 final edition of *El Mercurio del Puerto de Matamoros.* Its Serbian publisher, conversant in more than a dozen languages, had been deported after he was found guilty of participating in a plot against Santa Anna, Mexico's new dictator.

Because of so many similar plots, especially those arising in the Mexican state of Tejas and Coahuila, Fort Guerrero was under construction in Matamoros. Even now, at this early hour of morning, stonemasons were at work building fortifications meant to protect the city.

Matamoros was beginning to look like other walled European cities, as well as some of the seaports he had trolled during his tours of British military duty—Havana, San Juan, Cartagena. "I do believe your king appears to be in check, Niall."

Conceding with a slight shrug, the Irish Traveler nudged his king onto its side. He took another sip of strong Mexican coffee before speaking. "A gold escudo says your Lady Rafaela Carrera will refuse to occupy your bed before ye are wed."

A slow, derisive smile rearranged Alex's stern features. "You do know that I never lose—at chess, at faro, or with women?"

He was awaiting the return of the Negro he had paid to bring word of the arrival of his betrothed's ship from England. Even though Matamoros was almost thirty miles from its port on the Gulf of Mexico, the landscape around the city was so flat that the masts of most incoming vessels could be seen from the city as early as a half hour before they reached the port.

That half-hour waiting period allowed Alex some time to work on President Jackson's request from Sam Houston. Although Alex appeared to any onlookers to be dawdling over his cup of coffee, beneath half-open lids his eyes were scanning, and his ears were eager to intercept relevant and potentially vital bits from nearby conversations.

"Maybe ye do not ever lose, my friend, but with your latest shenanigan, exchanging your title for four-thousand pounds' sterling, I have to wonder which of you is the greater fool—aye or the Lady Rafaela Carrera?"

"You are the winner of that contest, Niall Gorman. You are the greater fool for letting yourself fall in with the likes of me—because some day, you will surely find yourself adobe-walled before this peccadillo of ours can ever be concluded."

A HARSH, CUTTING WIND SCUTTLED dark gray clouds overhead, whiplashing the Gulf of Mexico's choppy waters against the flimsy pilings of the Port of Matamoros.

One hand anchoring her cottage bonnet, Fiona turned her back on the miserable shanty port, a frontier town replete with gambling houses and brothels—all places with which she had become far too familiar back in Five Points. Anxiously, she watched the lighter ferrying passengers from the English brig toward shore.

The eleven immigrant families, her voyage companions aboard the *Albion*, had already decamped to one of the nearby taverns to seek warmth and hot drinks. The schooner was supposed to have put in at Copano Bay, but a storm forced it to weigh anchor farther south, at the Port of Matamoros.

At her elbow, a filthy hand tugged at the tattered sleeve of her shabby wool coat. "Fiona, 'tis fookin' freezing!"

"Mam, remember?"

Ten-year-old Liam O'Brien looked nothing like her. But skinny and malnourished as he was, he could pass for seven—and, maybe, pass for her son.

His freckled skin, the sole feature they shared, stretched across his cheekbones like parchment. His knobby knees protruded noticeably from his high-waisted pants. Instead of her lamentable orange-red mass of hair, he flaunted straw-colored, cork-screwed curls that begged for a cutting.

"Mam," he muttered, his skeletal shoulders hunched about his ears, his hands chaffing the threadbare sleeves of his brown jacket. "This San Patricio colony canna come soon enough."

After tending five siblings back in Galway, how had she ever mucked up her life with a kid like Liam? "Only the saints can possibly let us in on when that might be."

"I'm hungry. Tired, too." The boy shrugged his canvas haversack off one shoulder and flopped it down onto the deck.

"As am I. But so are the rest of the travelers." She sighed, weighted by the enormity she had undertaken. "And we have yet to travel the hundred-fifty-odd miles between us and me land grant."

"Well, clam it. This voyage was all your big idea."

"And this—this conniving—we are about to do is all yuirs." Had she even a halfpenny to spare for their bill of fare, she would not be stooping to this.

She had first noticed Liam in an alley behind one of the almshouses off East 14th Street. He had been wrestling with an older kid to snare some of the rank garbage the boys had found. Liam had a quick wit and even quicker fists.

Within days of his parents' Coffin Ship docking in New York, both of them, Irish immigrants, had died from the typhus. She had snagged the scruffy orphan off the streets of lower Manhattan by persuading him to become her "son."

Reluctantly, probing her coat pockets, she produced a shriveled orange she had filched from their schooner hold. Hunger was knotting her own stomach, and inside, she felt as shriveled as the orange. Growing up in a family with too little to eat, she had been the runt of the litter. To this day, the stink of rotten potatoes sent her stomach into spasms.

"Eat now." She offered the orange to him. "'Cause I don't know from where our next meal will appear." At that very moment, even imagining a cup of hot tea, swirling the color of mocha with thick cream, was threatening her generosity.

Liam easily snatched the dimpled, brown orange between his dirty palms. He peered at it with disgust before tossing it into the foamy waters.

"Are ye daft?" she yelped into the salt-scrubbed wind. Her own mouth was watering as she glimpsed the bit of orange bobbing in the wake of the approaching ferry lighter. Years before, she had skimped on her meals so her younger brothers and sisters could eat, and this grimy ingrate of an urchin threw food away?

Liam's jack-o-lantern grin punctuated a too-small, nearly angelic face quite bedeviled by his hardship. He fished from somewhere within his threadbare tweed jacket a Spanish gold doubloon and held it aloft. "The boatswain wilna miss it."

She exhaled her exasperation. "'Tis the clink ye will have us in before we even make it to the San Patricio Colony."

"If'n we make it at all. You heard them talking in the tavern about them Indians raiding around here." His skinny shoulders hunkered again about his ears and his shiver was only partly owing to the fierce norther wind.

"Ah, cut yuir carping." Futilely, she tried to brush her own wind-tossed hair from tangling around her neck. "Those tales of Indians were old drunks' tales they told ye just to scare us."

At the tavern, she too had overheard alarming tales about the Tejas territory—that the half-starving San Patricio colonists were bullied by former Mexican soldiers and ruffian cattle rustlers. That the Mexican general at Matamoros had ordered troops to a place called Gonzales, causing a stand-off with Texican rebels over some old cannon.

The rebels had even hoisted an inflammatory flag emblazoned, "Come and Take It." And now those rebels were laying siege to San Antonio de Bexar, the capital of the province.

What had alarmed her more was overhearing a conversation about the new land commissioner for the entire province. "... say the American is holding up land titles because of unprovable disputes and land speculation."

"Matamoros Fever, it's called."

Oh, lordy. She was beginning to have doubts about her hare-brained scheme, not that most of her earlier adventures were so well thought-out. All right then. She had come here for land, and, by God, she would find a way to claim her rightful measure of it.

Catlike, she knew that somehow, she always managed to land on her feet. She had been hungry and homeless before. She would survive now, one way or the other.

According to Liam, the "other" way was about to present itself.

When the lighter's hull thudded against the dock, shuddering the weathered pilings, Fiona almost lost her balance. Only to be present for the ferry's docking had she and Liam braved the biting cold. From among this group of disembarking passengers, Liam was certain some way could be found to acquire enough wherewithal to finance the perilous days confronting them.

Her shrewd, exacting glance swept over the brig's cluster of passengers. These people were definitely not like the tavern's impoverished colonists. The passengers represented class... and some of them, obvious wealth.

However, none of them looked to be easy marks.

She noticed a dry goods drummer with his trunk of wares, followed by a stocky man with bulldog features and an intimidating hickory cane. Next, a muscle-bound man toting a large cast iron bench anvil, a blacksmith by trade, strode across the plank. Then deboarded a young preacher, distinguished by his white clerical collar and tabs.

Each one of them were unworthy of her risk.

Discouraged, she half pivoted, then spotted a young woman barely old enough to be out of knee-length pinafores, crossing the dock's rickety planks as if she owned the world—or at least the league of land Fiona meant to acquire for herself.

The girl was inordinately tall, wide of shoulder, and narrow of hip, so long as one ignored her jutting bustle. Her light brown hair whipped free of her fashionable beaver hat and momentarily veiled her pale features. Except for her chin—that aspect lifted imperiously. Her gaze locked rigidly forward, the young woman swept toward Fiona and Liam obliviously, as if they were among the deckhands scrambling to help unload trunks and crates.

Liam yanked at Fiona's sleeve. "That one. She be our mark."

Now that their risky moment had arrived, fierce tension clamped Fiona's jaws tight. Seconds later, as the young woman passed them, Liam stumbled onto the train of her flounced skirts, causing her gait to shift to keep her from tripping and falling. Her swans down reticule purse swung off her wrist to plop on the deck beside her feet.

On cue, Fiona performed the part Liam had assigned her—in the blink of an eye, she dipped her hand into the purse, coming away with a fistful of English pounds, which she thrust behind her back.

"I believe this is yours, me lady." She returned the handbag with her free hand.

"Thank you." A vertical line separated the young woman's dark brows above the bridge of her patrician nose. "I appear to have lost my sea legs."

Fiona detected a desolate look shadowing the young woman's features and was at once smitten by her own shame and guilt.

She slammed tight the iron door of her conscience. Her intense relief at pulling off their caper would have made her faint, if her hunger did not. The sensation of the heavy coins watered her mouth at the imagined aroma of pork sizzling on a spit. With that thought in mind, her eyelids lowered in guiltless bliss.

Her relief was interrupted by a long-fingered, leather-gloved hand that enveloped her much daintier fist at the small of her back. Her gradually focusing eyes glanced up from the rapier at the man's waist—up, up, up, past a black silk cravat swathing his throat. Heading farther upward until she encountered the darkest, emptiest gaze this side of Hades.

"Pardon me, sir?" she managed haughtily, as if he were mistaken. If she had learned nothing in Five Points, always take the offensive. Never explain. Despite those earlier lessons, she shivered, more from this man's scowl than the cold. Willingly, she would have traded a week in gaol to possess his sumptuous fur-lined cloak.

The way he held her fist, still thrust behind her, was hurting—and he knew it. He smiled and released her. When he doffed his top hat, the wind whirled though his unruly charcoal hair. His narrow face was framed by equally black strips of whiskers curving just below the apex of his high cheek-bones. He looked far too harsh ever to be termed "handsome."

He lowered his head beside her ear. "Lord Paladín. You had best be careful with your money. This frightful wind might just snatch it away from your cold hands." He murmured that advice in a gravelly voice, sharp with its sarcasm. "But if the wind does not, there are surely countless unscrupulous people who surely will."

––––––––––

DURING THE LONG CROSSING FROM Liverpool, although Rafaela had contemplated hurling herself off the brig's bow, almost being toppled off the wharf by a little rapscallion was hardly the grand gesture she had in mind.

And the rescue by the man who reprimanded the rapscallion and young woman with him was little better. After the man introduced himself as her intended, she reconsidered her earlier grisly vision. Drowning herself in the marshy dregs of this run-down waterfront might not be at all that unpleasant.

She felt as if he saw straight through to the core of her flagging spirits. Hers were not so much virginal qualms as instant distrust of this man. Of all men.

An almost illusory aspect, lurking amid the severe stamp of his Castilian features, suggested a hedonist. Perhaps that conclusion could be attributed to the curl of the lips, resembling those of the late Lord Byron's—except that this Lord was rumored to be quite as notorious, and possibly even more scandalous, than the poet himself.

She had been hoping that when the time came for their marriage ceremony, Lord Paladín might have dropped dead from apoplexy or been mortally wounded in a duel by some cuckolded husband.

Being a practical young woman, however, she was forced to acknowledge that her father would only offer her another even less impressive baronet or viscount to ensure, yea, even to justify, his intention to purchase nobility for her family. Lord Paladín's mother was a descendant of the royal House of

Stuart, by way of an illegitimate son, which was the reason this Lord Paladín had been reared mostly in England.

If only fate had not thrust her into this far-flung Mexican arena inhabited by, she already knew, the two worst men she could conjure—her disreputable fiancé and that foul American who had robbed her of both her virginity and her net of independence.

She placed her palm upon Paladín's proffered arm. "Shall we, my…" Her voice cracked as she drew a deep, cold breath to regain her mastery. "… Lord Paladín, shall we conclude at once this marriage ceremony?" A part of her wanted to get the misery of the marriage over with as soon as possible, while another part dreaded its travesty.

He moved his head besides hers, close enough for her to detect his cynicism, cutting as it did through even the most frigid wind gusts. "It pleases me that you are eager, my lady." His mockery was unmistakable.

Oh God, he is worse than the rumors. Even his voice sounded like a dull saw attacking an iron oak tree.

Illogically, as he ushered her up the coarse planks toward the top of the bluff, she now found herself holding back. She realized every step she took was carrying her ever closer to sealing her own destiny. "Do we not require witnesses for our nuptials, my Lord?"

"My foreman awaits us at the landing—he can serve as one. Your lady's companion will stand for the other." He searched behind her.

Temporary relief soothed her predicament. "Apparently, Mexico held little appeal for my lady's companion. During our New Orleans anchorage, she decided to forego the ultimate leg of the journey."

Rafaela wished devoutly she could have done the same. "Alas, without her…." She shrugged, raising gloved palms in apparently regretful resignation that the ceremony would not take place immediately.

"Ahhh, but we do have another lady's companion for you right here, do we not?"

As he stepped to one side, Rafaela watched him grip the elbow of a wisp of a young woman who was trying to pass them on the shaky, narrow plank walk. The same girl who had recovered her reticule. "I understand you are looking for *honest* work, Miss....?"

"Er... ah, oim uhh, Mary. Mary Murphy."

She looked toward the urchin behind her, then, seeming to have arrived at a decision. "Aye... me and me son *could* use a bit of work. To tide us over, of course, while we are awaiting approval of our own land grant. Completely *honest* work, it must be, ye understand."

"We could?" the boy's rank disbelief reddened his chalky cheeks.

"I quite understand, Miss Murphy, I assure you," Lord Paladín's rigid mouth scarcely changing into a form that could ever be termed a smile or even, possibly, pleasant. "Let's say that honest work would include, among other chores, that of a lady's companion."

He turned his inflexible attention back toward Rafaela. She hung back, again trying to divert his intention. "I am quite certain you will appreciate, Lord Paladín, my position. In truth, I must insist that we refrain from marrying until... well, until my father arrives to give me away. You see, I... umm, I have already written to him, inviting him to our nuptials."

One crescent-shaped brow lifted. As he spoke, his voice, harsh and grating—well-suited to his disposition and features—dropped into a parody. *"In truth?"*

She flushed. Fingers fidgeting with her reticule drawstrings, she somehow managed, "Oh, yes, naturally, I wrote to my father before our ship sailed. It could be weeks before he arrives." She was an unpolished and uncertain liar because she constantly intended and expected she would always tell only the truth.

He leaned close to her. "Fair enough, my lovely fiancée. The intervening weeks will provide me all the time I wish to woo you."

Decorum, as well as relief at her reprieve, should have prompted her to reply similarly, that she too was looking forward to their courtship. But when she glimpsed his lips, she could not ignore the churlish curl to them.

Her own mouth tightened into silence. Her betrothed was toying with her, she realized, much as a cat batted a helpless mouse, teasing it until its death arrived.

At last, nudged by the wind at their backs, they all reached the landing above. At the cobblestone road, a man wearing a jaunty beige beret was gentling their traveling coach's span of horses. She caught only the briefest glimpse of the hired hand's features—a thick mustache, a broken nose, and an unsettling stare.

Only after a moment's reflection did she realize it was pity she glimpsed in the man's eyes. Oh, God. This place, this new life, was becoming worse, moment by moment.

Lord Paladín extended his hand once again. She forced herself to place her gloved hand in his and climbed into the coach with its sheltering warmth.

Glancing at the young woman and her son, who were settling against the coach's squab seat across from her and Lord Paladín, Rafaella could only envy them. If settle in this alien place she must, she wanted a genuine family. A family of her own.

Only definitely not with this odious man.

3

Ignoring the coach's spring-poking squab, Fiona leaned forward to peer by the waning light of the blustery afternoon at Matamoros. On the south side of the Rio Bravo del Norte, it gave her a tiny pulse of hope.

Maybe this Tejas was not the hellhole it was said to be by the dock-side tavern's patrons. Palm trees, swaying in the cold wind, ringed fortified walls blistered by years of tropical sunlight. Moorish-style cathedral domes rose above the city, adding a romantic, Old World dimension to it.

Then, to her disappointment, their aged coach lumbered on past Matamoros, crossing by a bobbing ferry to the north side of the Rio Bravo, then journeying a few miles farther along the palm-canopied River Road.

Her next disappointment was not a word that fully justified what she felt at beholding Lord Paladín's "residence"—an abandoned red-tile roofed mission and collection of outbuildings in various stages of neglect.

"*Presidio* San Francisco de la Espada is named for its *compañero*—the bell tower, you will note, resembles a sword hilt."

Stock still, her discouraged gaze took in the bell tower. She shivered, then, covertly, crossed herself. Against the setting sun, the tower appeared less like a sword hilt than God Almighty Him self's very finger. The middle one.

The foreman was unloading baggage from the coach, and she collected herself, hurrying to catch up with Liam and Paladín's betrothed. Still stiff from the carriage ride, they all stumbled a bit, following the Lord into the compound of the dilapidated mission.

Inside its pitted and patched stucco bulwarks that blocked the winter wind, a flower garden and grape arbor had run riot. The tiles of a bone-dry fountain were cracked and plagued by weeds. Paladín led them into a court-yard's arched portico and past a few rooms in tumbled ruins, others with fallen-in ceilings. At last, they reached their own rooms.

Lady Rafaela Carrera was given what had to be a friar's cell, containing a narrow bed with a warm-looking coverlet that Fiona coveted. The young woman appeared relieved when Paladín, bowing in farewell over her hastily extended hand, advanced no farther than the doorway. Obviously, the aris-tocratic young Spanish woman was not thrilled by her betrothal, and Fiona heartily empathized.

Farther along the quadrangle, she and Liam were separated. He was lodged in a workshop, smelling richly of sawdust.

"I shall have Niall round up some cots from the soldiers' barracks."

"A candle?" Liam's voice quavered.

"On the carpenter's workbench." Paladín directed a questioning brow at her.

"Me son likes to read late at night."

She doubted the kid could read and realized she knew little more about Liam than only that he had been a trapper boy in Ireland's coal mines. Sitting alone in the dark with only a sputtering candle, the trapper boys opened and shut wooden doors to circulate fresher air through the tunnels.

She accompanied Paladín back into the quadrangle. Studying him from behind, she noted he carried himself like a soldier, and fairly reeked of disci-plinary authority. A quality that was not at all encouraging.

Passing a few other rooms, they reached what had to have been the candle-maker's, still redolent of wax, dried lavender, and roses. She actually sighed. A room of her own…. She had always shared a bedroom, either with her siblings or with the ladies at *Madame* Margie's.

About to retreat into the tiny room, she was halted by the raised arm of her formidable host, barring her way. "Not just yet, Miss Murphy. We still have to resolve the matter of that money."

She tilted her head, smiling faintly and fixing him with her most artless expression. "Money?" The evening shadows danced around them, the chilly air dense, perfumed nevertheless by the citrus of the river valley.

"Oh, you know," his stringent gaze was studying her, as a collector's did a curious specimen, "those pounds you acquired so readily at the dock."

Bluffing and blustering would get her nowhere with this man, that was obvious. Her heart was ricocheting in her ribcage. "You'll call the bailiff?"

"You could always work off your pilferage." He appeared to muse. "You know, some sort of deposit on your gratitude."

Why had she not seen this coming? And the cad was betrothed, no less. "Lord Paladín," she strangled out, "I lived in a whorehouse in New York before I came to Tejas, so I know enough of men to know I would never service a piss post such as yuirself." She dug into her coat pocket, grabbed and hurled the coins at him.

His smirk altered the ridges that created his cheekbones.

At once, she lamented her foolish impetuosity. That damnable pride of hers had once again cost her. Knowing she would be banished from the *presidio*—and how would she and Liam fend for themselves through such a cold night—she could only hold her ground and glare up at him from her modest stature.

He appeared unimpressed by both the coins that lay at their feet and her outrageous statement. He clicked his tongue. "You mistake me. I had only thought you might render yourself useful by candle making here in your quarters when not attending to *Señorita* Carrera."

He moved close enough that she felt the whisper of his warm breath. "However, given your professed occupation—if you find me so odious—we might arrange for you to pay off your theft, should you prefer, by servicing instead our Frederick or Niall or one of…."

"Never!"

His amused smirk turned to an investigative scowl. He lowered the arm blocking her entry. "For a whore, Miss Murphy, you appear a mite too reticent."

She winced, all too aware she had brought his skewed opinion upon herself. "Not at all—only a mite too selective."

He grinned. Then his gaze slowly measured her from the toes of her worn shoes to the half-brim of her untied bonnet. "Ahhh, the whore speaks as if she were of genteel birth." He nodded at the coins scattered on the flagstones. "Better collect the money and restore it to Lady Carrera's reticule. If you do not, I shall be among the first here to collect your services in compensation."

As his departing back turned from her, she muttered, "On yuir grave."

He was already strolling along the colonnade, when she heard his chuckle. "Never you mind the details, Miss Murphy. It will be on your back or any way I choose, should I so desire."

THE FAMILIAR ODORS OF OLD leather, horse manure, and fresh straw permeated the *presidio* stables, as much in disrepair as the rest of the *presidio*. One stall door tilted outward, suspended only from the bottom hinge. A huge gap in the mud-brick wall was evidence that a kick from an ill-tempered horse had dislodged the stones. A patchwork of mesquite-staked roof admitted a beam of musty early morning sunlight.

At least the saddles and tack were pegged, and the curry combs and dandy brush were stowed in an open trunk. Rafaela was an experienced rider. In truth, she had few other gifts, certainly not those expected to amuse a drawing room such as singing or playing a pianoforte.

Whistling as he worked, the hired hand pitchforked hay into a stall. To her eyes, he appeared to be an artist's painting, all in russets and browns.

His leather overpants, without a seat or crotch, had been weathered into a scuffed rawhide. His well-worn buckskin gauntlets were a deep mahogany, his blousy muslin shirt was dyed light hazelnut brown. Even his thick mustache was a deep brown—as was the hair escaping from beneath his beige beret. Around his neck, he wore a loosely knotted rusty red neckerchief.

With his back to her, he worked economically, using precisely only the effort his task called for. His body, compact like a wrestler's, stretched, hoisted, and tossed hay and manure. Between his legs, a ring-tailed barn cat purred and stroked its fur against his brogans before padding away.

Certainly he already knew she was studying him from outside the stable doors because, without looking, he asked, "Something you wanted, my lady?"

His crooning voice sounded other-worldly to her. Despite feeling some trepidation, she stepped inside the stable.

"Come closer. I will not eat ye."

She felt her cheeks flush. Still not certain she was making the correct decision, she went around the unhitched coach, crossing the hay-strewn floor to stand a few cautious paces behind him. "Umm, could you tell me your name again? I apologize, I do not recall…. "

"Niall." He turned to face her, his gauntleted hand braced on the pitchfork handle. "I am Niall Gorman of Donegal."

If her academics served her correctly…. "I trust your name was not chosen for the notorious Niall of the Nine Hostages, one-time High King of Ireland?"

"Nay. 'Tis Gaelic for passionate. And ye are Alex's intended, the lady Rafaela Carrera. Ye come wanting something, my lady?"

His offer, in an Irish brogue thick as a London fog, was clearly not a polite inquiry, and she almost lost her nerve. The large pistol holstered at his right hip offered her no reassurance. Despite her misgivings, she decided.

"I… I was hoping you might help me."

"That so?" Pitchfork upright in his left hand, he stepped toward her.

While matching her own height, his physique was clearly more powerful. They were alone, out of earshot. Doubtless, she had placed herself in some peril. Once again, she was completely alone with a man. The first time had been ruinous for both her body and her dreams. Despite that, she resolved to carry out her plan.

She drew the flaps of her fur hooded black capote closely, as if that could ever stop an assailant. "I hope you can help me find refuge in Matamoros. Until I can arrange passage… away from here."

His heavy-lidded eyes, punctuated by squint lines and slanted slightly downward at the corners, sparkled at her. "Now why would I ever do that?"

She was poised between terrified flight and dangerous confession. The latter won out. "Because, when I arrived yesterday, I thought I noticed pity for me in your expression."

Hearing that, he raised his chin and threw back his head with a bellow of laughter coming from deep in his chest. Eventually stopping, he stared at her. "Sure enough, that was pity ye saw… only not for ye. For Paladín."

She forced herself not to look away. Stepping back, she stumbled over the cat, which scampered off. At once, his free hand grasped her forearm, saving her from falling. She felt her full skirts intertwine with his leather chaps. "Pity… for Paladín?"

"For my own taste, my lady, no two people could be more mismatched. There are only two types of people. Participants… and observers. And ye are an observer."

The way he pronounced the latter type made the word sound more objectionable than liar, thief, or whore. It labeled her coward. His insight, the fact that he could classify her so easily, curdled her pride.

She straightened to her full height. "An observer? As I stand before you, asking you to help me take action?"

"My point exactly, my lady. Ye are risking nothing by your own self."

Gall rose in the back of her throat. "I do recollect the Gormans of Donegal were considered Irish Travelers. Minstrels, horse traders, vagrants—"

"Wanderers, we Irish Travelers are. Not vagrants."

Releasing her arm, he raised his gloved hand—smelling strongly of leather and straw—and she tensed. But he merely moved a strand of hair that had strayed away from the elaborate knot at the back of her neck, replacing it gently onto her collarbone. With the back of his finger, he rubbed her lock with an almost fierce absorption.

She was struck dumb.

His slow smile was seductive. "Besides, I can't say as I have ever wandered astray, but I was once befuddled for three days."

She could not help but smile back. But when his eyes met hers, she defended her position, continuing, "—ne'er-do-wells, one and all of you Irish Travelers."

"Oh, aye, my lady. We Irish Travelers are all that you say and more that can be termed dastardly in our world. Yet we have a long and mostly honorable lineage, as well. We were the Druid priests shoved out of Ireland by your Christian church. We were Gypsies and Spell Casters."

"I do not believe in spells."

A spark flared in the dark vivid blue of his eyes. Considering her carefully, he paused, tilting his head. "Shall I cast a spell on you, my lady?"

"Better not to." She pressed her lips together against sudden mirth bubbling in her throat and narrowed a headmistress's stern gaze at him. "Instead, shave off that outlandish mustache!"

"If it's refining me that is your goal, that'll only happen in donkey years, my lady."

"As will your casting a spell on me!" Pleased with her volley, she smiled superiorly and sashayed out of the stables.

WHEN SHE SAW THAT LIAM was not in his room, Fiona began to fret. Given his predilection for five-fingering, he might well be making off with all the chapel's silver, pewter, and gold—in the form of flagons, plates, and candlesticks—he could stash in his haversack.

She already knew too well that their host, Don Alejandro, was no man to trifle with. His feral eyes guaranteed he had made a pact with the devil, that he was a man capable of immense depravities.

But, oh my, that beguiling mouth of his could well seduce a saint.... Aye, perhaps even the Virgin Mary herself. His departing comment last evening had evoked in her a forbidden curiosity. A curiosity never aroused by the sights and sounds—or groans and moans—at *Madame* Margie's.

She disliked him all the more for raising those kinds of provocative thoughts. Then there was his smile, scornfully devastating.

Escaping the chilly courtyard with its forlorn plants, shrubs, and trees, she reentered the flagstone colonnade. Its arched hallway looked deserted, so she was tempted to search for the kitchen instead. She was certain she might be tempted to barter her soul for a mug of steaming morning tea. If she did that, doubtless Lord Paladín would likely order with alacrity a pot for her.

Alas, the possibility of tea would have to wait until she found Liam.

As hazy as was her memory of the labyrinth of hallways, surely the main one ought to take her to the center of the mission. Outside the padre's quarters, the door was open. She paused.

Inside, her startled glance noticed only part of the quarters—an enormous four-poster bed and a commode. Wait, no, the commode looked—surely, not. Surely, it had not once been the chapel's holy stone altar?

If so, Paladín was also a sacrilegious blackguard who thought nothing of desecration.

"... see to it that you do." His commander-like voice echoed out into the hallway.

She ducked into the closest concealment offered—a musty confessional—and banged her knees against the kneeler. "Joseph, Mary, and Jesus!"

"Aye, milord." In Liam's reply, she sensed resentment, and then she heard the door close.

She waited until the boy was alongside the confessional. After yanking him through its curtain, her palm squelched his yelp. "Hush! Did that devil catch ye stealing?"

"Devil? If you mean the Lord Paladín, that he is. The devil's got a pistol that'll blow—"

"I said hush." She gripped his bony wrists. "I see ye're wearing a guilty look, Liam O'Brien. So, what did ye steal?"

"I took nothing, I swear. He was just giving me duties. I'm to scrub all the privies and then help someone named Winnie in the kitchen."

"Ye'll be sure to wash yuir hands in between the first and second chores. Oh, and once ye're in the kitchen, find me a cup of tea. With cream, if they have it. Now listen to me, did ye not say ye had once shoveled manure in a livery? Can ye saddle a horse?"

Even within the dimness of the booth, his small features were indignant. "To be sure."

"Good. Then tomorrow morning, early, find me a horse and saddle it for me. A swayback nag would be all the better. Something like Don Quixote would ride." No need to admit she scarcely could.

"Don Quixote?"

"Never ye mind. Just have a horse saddled for me early tomorrow morning."

His alert eyes narrowed in suspicion. "So, ye are planning to leave?"

"What? Leave a plum position like this one? Not at all. I am off to the land commissioner's office in Matamoros, but I should be back long afore noon. I will not be missed."

"Indeed, you will, 'Miss Murphy.'" Paladín's voice filtered through the confessional's curtained latticework.

She gasped, her stomach plummeting.

"But wait, 'tis Miss Flanigan, is it not? Miss Fiona Flanigan?"

Beside her, she heard Liam gulp. "Fiona, he wormed it out of…."

"Hush!"

Just how much of the conversation between her and Liam had Paladín heard? Besides, how had he even gotten into the adjoining confessional without her hearing him? But then did not those legendary creatures, vampires, glide? She should never have read *The Vampyre*.

Unconsciously, her fingers clutched her necklace's shamrock locket that she considered, if somewhat foolishly, her good luck charm. Against the power of this man's arcane charm, it would have to be more like an amulet that protected from harm.

"Run along, lad."

With undue haste, Liam scuttled through the curtain. She turned back to the wooden-laced grid just as its sliding door revealed a shadowed face.

"Do ye always bring out the worst in humans?"

"My Lord, if you please. I prefer to think I bring out their best, Fiona."

She could not let his calm frazzle her. "I never did give ye leave to call me by my given name," she said, only just remembering to add, "me lord."

"You are quite correct. But all servants are addressed informally."

Clearly, he was trying to impose "her place" upon her. Still, she had not come all the way to Tejas to be reminded of her social standing. All right, perhaps for a brief time, but only if that suited her purpose of claiming her land grant.

"I do delight in employing the familiarity of your given name, Fiona. As I mentioned, I would rather believe I bring out the best in everyone. Furthermore, bringing to the light the darker aspects of another's soul, those places one desires deeply to hide, is another goal of mine."

"Is that yuir devil's version of the Biblical advice that 'the truth shall set ye free?'" Pausing for a few beats, she drawled, "me Lord."

He paused, as if her question had caught him off guard. "Of course, freeing you from your fears, if you will. Now tell me, what are you afraid of Fiona?"

"Not one thing." In the confines of the booth, his unique personal scent of fire and storms and raging rivers was dizzying.

"Come now, we all are afraid of something."

"If so, what are ye afraid of, me Lord?"

She heard his scoffing snort. "Right now? Why, that I might never experience the enchantment of bedding you."

She could not stop her sharp breath of shock. "Ye... ye are an amoral man!"

"No, just freely immoral. Pleasure, Fiona, is always equated with guilt. Equated with hell itself. By reason then, all candidates for heaven must forego pleasure. So, I would never deprive you of heaven... but would you deprive yourself of pleasure?"

She knew her jaw had dropped open. Cautiously, she sought to untangle his question from its confusing skein of beguiling words. "I have no wish at all to deprive meself of heaven... me Lord."

His chuckle was unexpected, coming from his cast iron countenance, and it faded as he left the confessional, where she remained, too stunned to move.

The act of human coupling had never elicited from her more than a passing curiosity or a rolling of her eyes at the ridiculous postures of the prostitutes and their clients. Groping, sweating messiness. And yet, his evocative exchange with her had aroused a bit more than her curiosity.

After a good five minutes of sorting out wayward thoughts and trying to regain moral footing, she finally composed herself enough to leave the booth.

She was confronted by a pleasant looking older woman with apple-red cheeks and fly-away gray-brown hair. Her more than ample torso was circled by a white linen apron. This apparition could only be Winnie.

With a tsking sigh and a slightly salty smile, Winnie proffered a terra cotta cup and saucer. The steamy, delicious aroma of cinnamon and cream, with chocolate and some unfamiliar spice, wafted toward Fiona.

"Master Alex told me I'd find you here, miss. 'Tis Mexico's rendition of hot chocolate." She shook her head, raising her Wedgwood blue eyes toward heaven. "He also told me to tell you that what is in this cup is an...." Her jowls quivered, and her lip scrunched as though reluctant to voice the last word, "... an aphrodisiac."

For a fleeting second, Fiona thought about smashing the cup on the slate floor, but she longed to taste the Mexican confection. She would have grinned ruefully at her dithering except—if she was unable to resist the hot chocolate, how could she possibly resist a far more potent Paladín?

4

WELLINGTON BOOTS PROPPED ON THE sword-nicked desk, Alex stared above his pyramided fingertips at Niall. "You, of all people, know fully well I am a self-professed sensualist."

"What I do know is ye are a certifiable lunatic." Niall sidestepped one of the many boxes of books Alex had yet to unpack.

"Why? Because I am committed to marrying Rafaela Carrera?"

With the rolling gait of a born horseman, the Irish Traveler paced the *presidio* office of the former Spanish commandant. "Certainly not. 'Tis because ye seem intent on seducing that Irish girl."

At that, he took off his cap and spun it onto an antique bronze statue of a Hindu couple locked in a blatantly erotic embrace. He plopped down onto an equally venerable leather-backed armchair. "For the love of God, Paladín, think how your loose behavior could jeopardize our position...."

"Come on, Niall, God and I do not love each other. Do spare me your high-flown morality. You yourself can hardly refute sniffing around the lady Rafaela's skirts."

Stunned, Niall had the good grace to blush. "Never ye mind me. At least

I can control meself. But ye, waylaying that Mary Murphy this morning right in the confessional, of all places.... That 'tis carrying your lechery just a little too—"

"Her name's no more Mary Murphy than mine is Saint Francis of Assisi. Liam is not her son, either. The lad confessed that he is part of a plot she concocted to claim land."

Sighing, Niall clasped his hands behind his head, stared up at the dark-timbered ceiling, then glared at Alex. "You realize our own plans will suffer, and if we are not careful, the good citizens of Matamoros will tar and feather us. We need them on our side."

Alex produced a vinegary smile. "Have you not heard birds of a feather flock together? Niall, there is nothing the righteous citizens of Matamoros desire more than participating in one of my so-called orgies—without their actions getting noticed or suffering consequences, of course."

Nevertheless, he could not ignore his foreman's opinion. Indeed, mayhap he was losing his mind. Too many months concentrating on holding on to what was his with no dalliances for relief.

He never gave up what was his. Besides, he had spent far too many months plotting with Houston and Austin, who had just been released from prison in Mexico City, to waste a careless toss in the hay with that Irish hoyden.

Of course, he suffered not for means of release. Did not Matamoros abound with brothels, should he ever require their availability? Among the fortified city's international circles, more than a few refined female citizens were already glancing his way, including the English parson's curvaceous divorced sister, Mrs. Charlotte Madison.

She had skin like peaches and cream, with thick, butter-yellow hair that softened somewhat severe features. After her husband had abandoned her, she had followed her brother to Tejas. That good woman spoke her mind. While she was a force to be reckoned with, she might well prove to be an accomplished lover after she overcame a few of her religious taboos.

There was also the sophisticated young French widow of a high-ranking officer in the Mexican army, Therese del Valle—a beautiful *and* adventuresome vixen.

Alex's title in the booming River City was a major attraction. However, vanity and false modesty were never among his many sins, although the pursuit of willing and even hesitant lovers most certainly was.

As for seducing Fiona? Why should he even bother? She was both a prostitute and a gifted schemer. While wholly lacking in character, as he also was, something about her eluded him. He had been unable to define accurately all the elements that made up this Irish troublemaker. Regardless—or perhaps because of—her obvious flaws and background, what a fascinating study she was.

The image of her in the confessional captivated him—with her overly affected innocence, her complexion mottled with child-like freckles, and her hair, whorling from beneath her lace cap, an altogether uncommon shade of red. That shade was probably as fake a color as her four-leaf clover locket was cheap.

Still, something about her reaction to his seducement soured the pleasure he had anticipated in baiting her. A caution, she was.

It was his future wife to whom he ought to be paying court. Even all the gods realized Rafaela Carrera was only passably pretty—with her too prominent nose, breasts that were far too modest, and eyes and hair coloring that were, to be generous, nondescript. But she was well enough bred to comport herself adequately as his baroness.

He glanced at the letter he was penning to her father, inviting him to be present at their wedding the following month. His panicky fiancée, despite her declaration that she had written her father, was obviously outright lying.

Knowing old man Carrera's eagerness for acceptance into the higher elevations of British society, Paladín also knew Carrera would get himself to Matamoros even before this month had passed.

Propriety dictated an early wedding. If nothing else, Fiona's presence as Rafaela's companion would add the thinnest veneer of propriety for only so long. After that, Matamoros tongues would begin to wag.

Not that he cared one whit about what happened after the wedding, which involved a fair exchange—her dowry paid the back taxes on his brother's land grant, and a title would brighten the remaining days of Hector Carrera.

Though Carrera's grandchildren would maintain the title, which would mean Alex's consummating their marriage vows. His time in India suggested Tantric sex was always a pleasant diversion, but the education of a virgin called for effort hardly worth the trouble. Duty before pleasure?

If he must.

Then, too, the wedding served another purpose—his opportunity to mingle among the many guests and, at Houston's behest, ferret out the identity, if possible, of someone known only as the Chaparral Fox.

Switching his attention back to Niall, he asked, "Why am I wondering if there is something you are not telling me? Surely you did not charge in here to berate my penchant for dissipation."

That young Irishman, with his finite sense of justice, may be unlettered and may have many things to learn, but he was, indeed, a quick learner with the ability to watch and then to act accordingly.

"Well, do you want your betrothed to bolt—with the Irish lass right beside her? Because that is what is afoot."

"Not, at least, until I have married one and bedded the other."

At that coarse remark, Niall's fingers twitched toward his pistol—the new Colt revolver that could outdo any horse pistol and stop an elephant in its tracks. Maybe, too, it could help stop the Mexican enemy at their door.

Alex had lodged the fiery Irish Traveler at the Espada *presidio* for that reason—and, as a side benefit, to help restore to livable conditions its quarters.

Then too, Alex grudgingly conceded, he might have hired Niall because he recognized in the slightly younger man's eyes the same raw aching he himself was feeling—a rootlessness and vague dissatisfaction with the world.

Niall's reaction to his taunt about Rafaela and Fiona revealed what Alex already knew or suspected. His foreman was definitely lusting after Alex's future wife—whether the younger man recognized that or not.

Well, his friend and aide could diddle the oh-so-proper Rafaela Carrera as often as he wished, so long as he was not lusting after her dowry, too. That belonged to him… or it would as soon as they took the vows of holy matrimony.

Holy matrimony. What a contradiction!

———————————

AT THAT SAME MOMENT, RAFAELA was shuddering, tugging closer her lamb's wool shawl. "He is a glacially cold one."

"Aye, that Valmont is. Arrogant, suave, and a manipulative sexual predator, but don't ye think by the end of *Les Liaisons Dangereuses* that the depraved Valmont's softer, more caring side becomes apparent through his love for *Madame* de Tourvel?"

She and Rafaela sat in the miserable garden with its blowsy roses, discussing novels they'd read. Sunlight had long ago bleached most of the turquoise paint from their bench's splintered slats. One of the trees, an ancient lime, had spread its gnarled roots until they had buckled part of the garden's adobe brick path.

Thin, wintry sunlight intensified the garden's faint, almost intoxicating scents of desiccated orchids, hibiscus, and wild thyme. In the subtropical climate, the plants should have been thriving but for lack of care and a long drought, according to Frederick, who appeared to be Paladín's steward of sorts and the cook—Winnie's—husband.

While Fiona was in the garden, dutifully comporting as a lady's companion, she was counting on Liam to restore the pilfered pounds to Rafaela's reticule—provided the rascal didn't hold out some money for himself. If Fiona learned that he had, his ears would be suffering from a severe boxing.

"No." Rafaela's expression was wretched. "I was not talking about the novel's Viscomte de Valmont. I was talking about my fiancé, Lord Paladín."

Fiona could not but agree about Lord Paladín's cold temperament. Yet, when she was in his presence, she felt ignited—felt her skin flushing with heat. Saints forbid that she was as doomed to surrender to his carnal conquest as had been the ill-fated *Madame* de Tourvel to Valmont's.

Rafaela's kid-gloved fingers fretted with her bonnet's ivory ribbons, her voice sounding deeply dejected. "Lord Paladín sold his title to my father for an outrageous sum—my bridal dowry of four thousand pounds. The word I heard in London is that Paladín has gambled away his inheritance and murdered God knows how many innocents."

She managed to temper her shock. She watched a horned lizard soaking up December's sunlight on the fountain's stone rim. "Aye, if that is the case, it would seem Lord Paladín is, indeed, a mercenary soul."

Rafaela rubbed gloved palms together, as though to create warmth. "I cannot marry him. I simply cannot endure the thought of... of intimacy with him."

That was all Fiona could think and worry about. At least the prostitutes in New York had sold themselves for something tangible. Holy Mother, the sooner she could lay claim to her own land and vacate *Presidio* La Espada, the better for her.

She glanced at Rafaela. Notwithstanding the haunted look in the young woman's brown eyes, up close, she was quite pretty. Her aristocratic nose, creamy skin, and long, doe-like lashes all evidence of genteel features. "Why do ye not leave then? Tell Lord Paladín ye've had a change of heart?"

Rafaela's soft laughter was derisive. "Does he seem the kind of man who would take no for an answer, Fiona?"

She could no longer stand the riot of neglect in the courtyard. She left the bench to kneel beside the garden bed, pulling a weed here, twisting off a dried stem there. Her Maker had planted the love of land deep within her soul. "Then leave without it. Without his consent."

"Lord Paladín might relinquish me if he retained my bridal dowry of four thousand pounds, but my father would never countenance that. He is determined to have Paladín's title added to our family tree." Her voice lowered. "I sought out Lord Paladín's hired hand, Niall Gorman, for help getting as far as Matamoros. But he laughed me out of the stables."

"That took courage on yuir part. Niall looks to be a sociable creature, but, toting around that huge pistol of his, I would wager him to be the kind who takes no prisoners."

"Despite that disreputable broom of a mustache, there was something in his eyes... something friendly, something... gentle, I thought. Something kind." Rafaela sighed deeply. "But I was wrong."

Fiona yanked at a recalcitrant root. "'Tis the seemingly 'kind' ones that'll do ye in every time." She spotted an arnica plant among the scraggly mint and grinned to herself. It was like finding fairy dust on one's pillow.

"Yes, the kind ones just trade on your trust, then leave."

At the utter desolation she heard in Rafaela's voice, Fiona looked over her shoulder and saw the heartache behind the long-lashed eyes. Aye, she could spare this entitled young woman a mite of sympathy. Despite her wealth and her position as landed gentry, she, too, had suffered. "What ails yuir heart? Besides yuir looming marriage to this dastardly devil?"

A small smile briefly displayed her dimples. She shrugged. As if by doing so, she made her pain inconsequential. "A too-clever-by-halves lawyer. He took advantage of my naiveté years ago—an age-old story retold time and again, alas."

Fiona was grateful she had, at least, never been foolish enough to fall in love. Oh, infatuation she had experienced, the Earl of Grantham's son being one. But never that unassuageable yearning that she could not escape, that yearning that would abscond with her heart. No man was worth that.

"I'm sorry for this situation in which ye find yourself, Rafaela. I have found in talking to the sisters-in-the," she cleared her throat, "to other female friends, that a man needs to be needed and a woman wants to be wanted. Is there no one, no friend or family who might want ye—who might want to take ye in?"

Rafaela's graceful finger toyed with the ribbons of her half-brim bonnet, but Fiona did not miss the slightly forlorn downturn of her lips. "A maternal aunt in Savannah, Georgia, I believe. She never liked my father, and I doubt she even remembers me."

"Ye might want to contact her. Family is everything. Well, family and land, that is."

"I envy you. At least, you have a loving family—you have Liam. I do hope you will stay here for a while, Fiona. The girls at my school were always coming and going, none staying beyond a boarding year or so."

"How long were you there—at that boarding school?"

"It seems like forever—a goodly eight years, at least." Her gloved hand squeezed Fiona's dirt-smudged one. "I would simply love for you to be my friend, Fiona."

She flinched at her deception. She felt dreadfully rotten, even more so for having stolen the young woman's money. "I do not know how long I will be here. I will be riding to Matamoros tomorrow morning—to hurry along the title approval of me land grant."

"Paladín's letting you ride one of his horses?"

"Oh, bloody hell, no. I am stealing it. Or appropriating it, ye might say. And grabbing onto the pommel is a better description than 'riding.' I know little about horses. Afraid of them devils, in fact."

"I love horses, Fiona. They are such noble animals. And I am an expert whip. Could I help you in some way?"

"Aye. Keep your intended busy tomorrow morning, so he does not realize I have gone."

A wry smile transformed Rafaela's wan features into an incandescence, with enchanting dimples Fiona could only but envy. Her own features were as common as weeds.

"As intimidating as I find my fiancé, I'll manage to engage his company at breakfast."

"I was wrong about ye, Rafaela."

"What?"

"At the docks, I had judged ye a snob. Too preoccupied with yeself to deal with mere mortals like me."

Rafaela wrinkled her nose. "In truth, I am most terribly shy."

How preposterous. How could this woman who had everything possibly be shy? She returned Rafaela's hand squeeze. "When I come back from Matamoros, Liam and I will do our best to make sure you are rarely left alone with Paladín until you—and Liam and I—find a way to leave."

Discounting the luck of the wretched Irish, Fiona fervently could only pray she would not find herself alone with him again either.

————————

FROM A CHIPPED PORCELAIN BASIN on his barrack's pine chest, Niall washed his face and hands in the chilly water. A room could have been found for him within the mission itself, but he preferred to be closer to the company of horses than to humans.

Besides, he could keep a more protective eye on the *presidio* from the vantage point of the barracks. Mexican bandits, deserting soldiers from Fort Guerrero—most of them convicts—and lately a more fearful foe, the Comanche, were raiding ranchos and isolated homesteads.

Matamoros's cantinas, grogshops, and billiard parlors gossiped that the raids were most likely being provoked by one of the many land speculators intending to drive off colonists in hopes of reselling their claims.

He was not among the many United States immigrants who had upped and written on their cabin door GTT—*Gone to Texas*. Besides, why anyone would want land in the Rio Bravo valley, the birthplace of the flea, he could not imagine.

Neither could he imagine anyone being tied down by ownership of tangibles like land and houses and coaches. Apparently, his employer, Lord Paladín, thought the land was well worth it, having crossed an ocean five months earlier to claim his.

Finished with his ablutions, Niall checked his revolver and made his way into the mission. Inside the dining room, the other four were gathered around a long wooden trestle table with Paladín at its head. Candlelight made the tabletop look as if it had been rubbed to satin by the hands of a century of *padres*.

Something in Niall craved both the rustication of his past and the refinement afforded by Paladín's lifestyle. Niall pulled out a chair next to the kid noisily slurping the pork stew the Mexicans called *pozole* and accepted the plate Winnie brought him.

Across the table, Fiona was consuming with equal gusto bites of the roasted pheasant he had bagged early that morning, but he could tell she was also intensely absorbed by the exchanges between Paladín and the lady Rafaela.

Paladín's face displayed speculative cordiality, his fiancée's, uneasy politeness.

The Baron swallowed some wine. "As your father's prospective son-in-law, my lady, I am dispatching a missive of my own, inviting him to our wedding. Are there any other guests you would wish me to invite?"

She blanched, though Niall thought it would be difficult for the young woman to be any less colorless. Her visit with him in the barn shot to the forefront of his memory. The last thing he needed was her starry-eyed dependence upon him.

"When?" she breathed.

Paladín smiled coolly over his wineglass rim. "Four weeks from Friday. I thought New Year's Day would be an auspicious day for us to begin our life together."

Rafaela's eyes widened, reminding Niall of a nervous filly.

"Aye, there is a guest she would wish to invite. Her aunt in Savannah."

All heads swiveled toward the Irish woman. With her shock of autumn-pumpkin hair and a face sprinkled with freckles like gold guineas, 'twas no wonder she amused Paladín. But this cheeky recklessness was a candle for Paladín to snuff out easily, should he become bored.

Niall's sister, Bridget, had been just such a firefly—flitting here and there. Four months ago, she had deserted their clannish family, running off with a man outside the Irish nomadic society—a Kentucky militiaman. Taking Bridget with him, the Kentuckian had headed for Tejas and cashed in on the

800 acres of land awarded to volunteers in the Texican army being formed by General Houston.

Something in Niall's temperament that some would term protectiveness reared its misguided head. "Your aunt might not be so willing to risk coming to Tejas for a wedding, my lady." He helped himself to a ladle of *pozole*.

Her eyes, the color of caramel, remained fastened on him.

"Santa Anna, Mexico's dictator, is said to be gathering an army of six thousand. Marching right through Matamoros to quell uprisings farther north."

"But those rebellions would be, as you said, north of here."

"Your aunt would be wise to heed his advice," Paladín nudged aside his empty wineglass. "A few months ago, Santa Anna defeated a rebellious militia in the state of Zacatecas, which had declared independence. After two hours of combat in Zacatecas, Santa Anna's Army of Operations took three-thousand civilian prisoners, then killed everyone."

Fiona's spoon halted halfway to her mouth. "Those rebellions being staged north of here—will their conflict with Santa Anna affect the land grants of us settlers and immigrants?"

Niall shrugged. "Who knows how the legalities will play out in the state of Tejas y Coahuila?"

What he did know was that, while Paladín might want to keep his brother's land, he himself wanted to leave as soon as he accomplished what he had come for. Not even a lily-white woman of refinement could hold him here.

"We can expect the worst from Santa Anna." Paladín had one arm hooked casually over his chair's top rail. "As reprisal for the Zacatecas rebellion, he rewarded his soldiers by allowing them two days of rape and pillage."

"Such is war," pointed out the young Irish woman with a mere shrug.

"True, but even when merely traveling, it is reported he sends aides to kidnap the prettiest women solely for his own pleasure. I would imagine he also plans to bring the state of Tejas y Coahuila back under Mexican control with the same display of brute force as he used on Zacatecas. Are you willing to risk such an ending as compensation for hanging on to your land grant, Fiona?"

"Land is everything! It remains long after you and I are dead."

Niall noticed a fleeting spark of interest glimmer inside the blackest depths of Paladín's eyes that left as swiftly as it had appeared.

"Precisely my point," Paladín drawled somewhat languidly.

5

FIONA SLIPPED AMONG THE OUTBUILDING shadows before entering the dusty stables to search among the darkened stalls. Dawn would not arrive for at least fifteen minutes, and the stables were illuminated only by the fading wintry moonlight poking through the gaps in the roof.

When she spotted the saddled horse, she sighed with relief. Liam had come through for her.

At this predawn hour, no one but she was up, not even Winnie—and the least likely to be awake would be the indolent Lord Paladín himself.

Right now, she had only the wee problem of how to mount this huge, dark brown animal, which looked suspiciously more like a warhorse than the nag for which she had hoped.

She glanced around the stable, hoping to spy a stepping stool, and grimaced with disappointment when she did not. Cautiously, she entered the saddled horse's darkened stall and even more cautiously approached the very tall animal.

"Good girl… or boy." She could not make out which gender her mount might be. Tentatively, she reached out to pat its muzzle. The thing nickered, ears pricking upright. "Shhhh!" She stepped closer. "I only want to straddle ye for a wee while."

Just then, from behind her, a deep-toned corrugated voice broke the quiet. "And what a delight that would be if you were referring to me."

Startled, she whipped around. Paladín was leaning casually beside the open stall door.

In the dim light, his black eyes sparkled. He wore shiny riding boots, tight breeches, and a tweed jacket. Plus, of course, that formidable rapier at his left side that gleamed like Excalibur itself. The slender weapon was a mark of gentlemanly status that accorded its bearer the right to engage in feats of honor, though Fiona doubted seriously that Paladín was either a gentleman or that he possessed even a shred of honor.

She swallowed hard, wondering what had happened to her pluck. "What are you doing here?"

"The real question, Miss Flanigan, is what are *you* doing here? For some time now, I have been under the assumption that Raj is my horse."

"I was only borrowing it. Raj. Borrowing Raj." Her breath frosted the air.

As he stepped into the stall, he closed the gate behind him. "For?"

His recalcitrant horse began sidestepping nervously. She grabbed its bridle and was almost jerked off her feet. With a death grip, she clung to its strap. "Uhhh... why, to post a letter for me lady Rafaela."

"Ahhh, yes. No doubt to her beloved aunt—in Savannah, is it not? So, our warnings last night did not convince you of the peril here?"

He was her peril.

"Here, allow me to assist you into the saddle."

"Oh, no. No, I can mount this... steed on my own."

His grin was spiteful and a bit mean. "Then by all means, proceed."

The horse stared at her with huge, glaring eyes, its nostrils flaring. Please be nice, she silently entreated Raj, though Thunder Bolt or Fire Ball would likely have been more apt names. Carefully, she slipped a kid boot into the stirrup trying to hoist herself upward—only to fall flat on her bum.

As the breath gusted from her lungs, she scrambled to her feet—before Paladín could take one step closer to her—brushed off her skirts and adjusted her bonnet, trying desperately to catch her breath again.

He raised a querulous brow. "You are certain, are you, that you want to attempt this on your own?"

She backed a step away from him. "Aye."

Hastily, she grabbed for the pommel and with a mighty effort actually hauled herself into the saddle this time. She would have remained astride, too, except Raj had other ideas. The horse reacted by rearing, sliding her off his backside with a smacking thump that reverberated through her whole body, vibrating every bone and tooth.

At once, Paladín clamped her upper arm and jerked her away from the beast's prancing, death-dealing hooves. He pulled her close against his chest. "Do you find pleasure in taking dangerous chances, Fiona?"

Her palms were braced against his chest. Surely not flesh, but what felt to her more like iron lay beneath her mittened fingertips. "Well, I do find occasional pleasure in taking calculated risks."

"My Lord," he reminded.

"Me Lord."

"Then you will be taking one with me this morning." He lifted her easily into the saddle, shocking her by mounting behind her.

Gulping hard, she twisted around to stare up at him, her bonnet's brim clipping him in the jaw. "Then ye be going with me to post me letter?"

"It would seem you and I have a common interest in something besides my fiancée—land."

God take Liam and his runaway mouth!

"Your damnable brim is peskier than a horsefly." His fingers captured her bonnet's frayed ribbons and worked to loosen them. "As it happens, unlike yourself, I have an appointment this morning with our land commissioner."

His face was so close she could see the faint shadow of stubble his early morning shave had missed. She also detected an amber glint amidst the sooty blackness of his pupils, which doubtlessly was the precise hue of the fires in hell.

After removing her bonnet, he reached around either side of her, knotting its ribbons on the pommel. "Just relax against me. I assure you that you will enjoy our long ride all the more."

"I sincerely doubt that."

"My Lord."

"Me Lord." *Odious man.* She sat stiffly, refusing to settle back against the expansive wall of his chest.

After the sun rose, it warmed the chilly morning only slightly but illuminated a billowy fog along the River Road. The tops of cottonwoods, willows, and palms marked the Rio Bravo's meandering path. Otherwise, thorny chaparral stretched limitlessly, a land well-guarded by catclaw, briars, and Spanish bayonet.

To her disgruntlement, her employer was quite clearly a superb rider.

"I told you to relax, Fiona."

"I cannot. 'Tis not proper."

"And propriety is important to one in your... profession?"

Thankfully, he could not see her eyes, which she rolled in frustration. "Whatever do ye want from me?"

"Simple. To take your breath away."

Those husky words almost did exactly that. She jerked around to look over her shoulder at his arresting mouth. "And just how far does that desire of yuirs extend? When ye are taking my breath away."

"Oh, you mean literally, my dear?"

She tore her gaze away and faced forward once more. Ignoring his question, she chose to ask him one of her own. "Does the fact that ye are affianced to Miss Rafaela Carrera mean your word has no honor left in it... me Lord?"

"Long ago I learned that I need only keep my word with myself. Lie to myself, and I know I have lost my way."

From the cedars she heard the cooing of a mourning dove. "And which way is that?"

"Why, that is easy—to always have my own way. But mine alone. If nothing else, I am completely self-indulgent."

"Then ye have, indeed, already lost yuir way, me Lord."

He laughed. "You do make the passage of time more bearable, Fiona."

At that, he freed an arm to wrap around her waist. At first, she was acutely aware of being supported by him, by his chest, like the back of a throne.

Gradually, she became viscerally aware of his personal scent—apricot leaves and sandalwood—when he more logically should have smelled of hades' brimstone. Eventually, she became aware of something else. Paladín's privates appeared to be growing larger. When she shifted away, she heard his low chuckle.

"Oh, something disturbing you, Fiona?"

"Aye."

"Why, you should be accustomed to this—a man's arousal."

"Inured," she equivocated.

Just then, a man in a furry forage cap stepped out from behind a palmetto thicket and Paladín reined in sharply.

In the crook of one arm, the man cradled what had to be a firearm ancient as a blunderbuss but still as dangerous. He pointed it at them. "Dismount."

"May I assume then," Paladín drawled, his hand settling on his rapier's hilt, "you want the horse and not our lives, Lazarus?"

"A fine piece of horseflesh you have, Lord Paladín, so I'll be taking that from you as well. And don't 'cha be thinking of going for your sword. It'll do you no good. I can blow you both out of the saddle—or you can dismount first. Whichever."

The two brigands seemed to know one another. Goose bumps sprang onto Fiona's arms, and her mouth tasted of clay.

"Then may I ask your leave to give my beloved one last kiss?" In disbelief, she heard the mirth in Paladín's voice, then felt his large hand gliding gently toward the small of her back.

The highwayman jerked his weapon's wavering barrel toward Paladín's head. "Shut your clap and git down—"

An ear-shattering blast staggered the robber. One eye socket pumped blood as he dropped to his knees and fell face forward into the dirt.

Fiona stared, horrified. Her ears were ringing, her nostrils full of the acrid stench of sulfur and lightning bolts.

Paladín tucked his derringer back into his coat pocket. "I do dislike being delayed." He spurred Raj on down the River Road.

Determined not to let him discover what a quaking coward she was, Fiona managed offhandedly, "I believe ye mean 'waylaid.' So, ye knew that highwayman, did ye?"

He chuckled, as if he had just squashed a roach, not killed a man. "Played cards with him at Lady Letty's Saloon. Another of the 12,000 saved or unsaved souls of Matamoros's pestholes—and more than likely one of the Chaparral Fox's hirelings."

Obviously, Lady Letty's was a house of ill repute, among other things. No surprise there. She did not pursue that direction any further.

"And Chaparral Fox?"

"Someone in our area who's a bosom buddy with Santa Anna."

She glanced back over her shoulder at the splayed corpse. "Ye would leave that man—Lazarus—without even a burial?"

"Better he bereft of a burial than we."

She shivered, but not from the cold. "Have ye no feelings?"

"I should hope not."

"I believe ye do. Do ye not feel better by provoking others?"

"Some are hardly worth provoking."

Yet I am? She was determined not to utter another word and began straining rigidly away from him again.

He laughed quietly and tugged her back against him. Fortunately, the towers and spires that marked the oasis of Matamoros soon appeared, ending for the moment his provocations.

Salt marshes and *resacas* scattered around Matamoros's perimeter had been converted into tree-shaded lagoons. The dusty road crossed a handsomely constructed causeway spanning a complex of the Rio Bravo's estuaries, where some inhabitants were already washing clothes in the early morning sunlight.

The highway leading into the city proper was now teeming with ox-carts and wagons bearing supplies and produce. Once past the iron gates of Fort Guerrero and its imposing armory, gardens flourished amid brick and frame European-style houses with elaborate metal balconies and garrets.

A few late-night patrons, having undoubtedly soaked themselves in alcohol, were now departing the gambling houses and bordellos. A barking mongrel chased Raj's hooves all the way to the plaza, bowered in trees. Foreign flags identified English, French, American, and other consular offices.

Dominating the east side of the plaza, a magnificent cathedral rose above the other buildings, with its weather vane-topped steeple, but the neighboring Customs House—a gray two-story clapboard building—was Paladín's destination.

Its impressively carved wooden door was already open for business. After Paladín dismounted, he held out his hand. "Give me Lady Carrera's letter—the Customs House does double duty as the post office."

Hesitating at first, she finally reached inside her woolen coat and retrieved one of the two missives, handing it over. If she had not needed a place to stay so badly, she would hightail it to the Land Commissioner's office herself and leave Paladín to cool his heels.

"Do not even consider leaving without me. There would be hell to pay when I returned."

"Why, the thought never crossed me mind."

"My Lord."

She grimaced. "Me Lord."

She went to retrieve her bonnet, the great beast she sat astride snorting warningly. Cautiously retying her bonnet's ribbons under her chin, she glanced around.

The plaza was bustling with people. A trade and ranching center, a political hub, and a fortified city with a military garrison, Matamoros—at the mouth of the Rio Bravo—was said to compare to New Orleans on the Mississippi and to New York on the Hudson.

However, here, Matamoros alone commanded the gateway to the frontier. Already, Fiona was calculating how she could make her land grant profit from the city's flourishing commerce…. Of course, there was the wee matter of her land grant being approved.

Cash crops, she was thinking. They would reap the most profit from her land grant. More than one crop. Never concentrate an income on a single crop solely, like potatoes. Corn. Maybe cotton and rice. In the interim before sailing, she had done her research and learned those crops all thrived in this subtropical climate.

A few minutes later, he was back. Looking at her with his calculating expression, he took hold of the bridle. "Hmmm, you obeyed me. Why?"

"Being prudent." Noting his raised brow meant to remind her, she sighed and added, "Me Lord."

Afoot, he led the horse around the tree-shaded plaza to the Land Commissioner's stucco and plaster one-story building. After he helped her dismount, he kept his hand at the small of her back, propelling her inside the musty office.

"Miss Flanigan," he said to the man crossing to greet them, "meet Cavett Magnum, our esteemed Land Commissioner."

She did not know what she had been expecting the Land Commissioner to look like, perhaps a stately diplomat, but certainly not the middle-aged man with the dancing eyes and appealing smile.

"Miss Flanigan, companion to my fiancée, is here to accelerate the approval of her land grant, and I am here inquiring as to the exact amount of taxes that appear to be due on mine."

"You never mentioned you were engaged, Baron. But then, you always do play your cards close to your chest." The Land Commissioner winked, as he executed a half bow. "Cavett Magnum, at your service, Miss Flanigan."

Of medium height, with curly light brown hair receding slightly above each temple, he possessed inordinate good looks that suggested to her a merry genteelness. Magnum turned back to Paladín, taller than he by several inches. "Ahh, yes. The matter of your late brother's overdue taxes. I will be delighted to help you both. Come with me, please."

He led them past the counter and a desk occupied by a clerk, his quill busily scribbling in a ledger. They continued past him to a separate office. Taking a seat behind the desk, Magnum indicated two chairs opposite him. She perched on the edge of hers while Paladín sat back, as if he were King Solomon on his throne.

"As you can see, since accepting the land commissioner's position, I have been overwhelmed." Cavett Magnum grinned, spreading his palms toward the clutter. "Copybooks of Spanish and Mexican laws, scrolls of royal orders, inventories, dispatches, petitions, decrees...."

He turned to the shelves of cubbyholes behind him and withdrew a heavy legal binder. After fingering through several pages, he smiled. "Yes, here it is... two-hundred and thirty owed in taxes against your brother's land grant, Paladín."

The man turned curious eyes toward her. "Now, if you'll give me your deed, Miss Flanigan, I'll look it up."

She withdrew the folded deed and presented it. He perused it, his ruler-straight brows drawing together in an almost single line. "I'm somewhat confused. There must be a mistake."

"And why is that?"

The Land Commissioner looked up, glancing from her and back to Paladín. Magnum drew a deep breath. "Miss Flanigan's deed claims ownership to the same league of land— er, that is, the land grant just west of San Patricio... as that of your late brother's."

"That's impossible!"

"I am quite sure the King of Spain would have found that impossible as well, were he alive," Paladín pointed out in a deceptively mild voice for all its serrated timbre, "since Carlos III awarded my family the original Spanish land grant back in 1767."

"Yes, an impossible situation," Magnum agreed. "Truly, I understand the issue here. As I hope you are able to, Paladín." With a sigh, he nodded at the stacks of documents littering his desk and the cabinet shelves behind it.

"The successive transfer of ownership from Spanish to Mexican to Anglo produces a veritable tangled history of land titles, taxes paid and unpaid, and dispossession and new ownership. Achieving clear title is expensive—it's a lengthy and knotty process with new laws cantilevering over older ones."

"As well as a process quite profitable to land speculators with their fraudulent land grants," Paladín commented dryly. "And would-be colonists like our Miss Flanagan suffer the consequence."

She glared at him. "'Tis yourself who may be sorely disappointed, me Lord."

Cavett glanced from her, to Paladín, and back. "Well, naturally, this will take time to resolve. I must write Mexican headquarters in San Antonio de Bexar. Since that bureau administers the Department of Tejas, only it can provide clarification of this duplicating document, this *testamonio*—which I must emphasize that, without the authorized signature, is no more valuable than script."

"What?!" Fiona managed. "That canna be!"

"I agree this situation is deplorable, Miss Flanigan." Magnum's quill pen scratched information taken from her deed. He folded it and placed it atop the binder. "However, once headquarters reports back determining which of your documents is the legal one, only then can I seal it with the requisite approval stamp."

"Quite deplorable." Paladín rose.

"My wife will be delighted at the prospect of a regal wedding here in Matamoros." Cavett came to his feet as well. "Will both you and your fiancée be attending our soiree tonight?"

"We look forward to it."

The Land Commissioner's earnest gaze returned to Fiona. "We're honoring the newly appointed general of the Texican army who's visiting, and we do count on your attending as well, Miss Flanigan. Our home is just around the corner."

Once outside, she suffered once more Paladín's hands, lifting her into the saddle. He guided Raj out of the tree-shaded plaza, bustling with shoppers, strollers, and traders.

Once more, she sat stiffly, as far from Paladín as possible—which was less than a thimble's length. The big animal's prancing might make her nervous, but it was considerably less nervous than the scoundrel who was bracing her between his arms.

"That land belongs to me."

"Without a signed and sealed document, only a *testamonio*, you have no land," he pointed out in a sociable tone, all the while controlling the feisty horse with his thighs and a single hand managing the reins loosely.

"I will die before I ever give up my claim."

"Then die you most likely will."

RAFAELA WAS COMMITTED TO KEEPING her promise to Fiona to keep Lord Paladín occupied that morning, but he was nowhere to be found. When he didn't appear for breakfast, she sought out Winnie in the kitchen.

The cook, who appeared to command a position of both familiarity and authority, was dolloping honey from a pottery jar onto corn tortillas, then sprinkling the heady smelling cinnamon. Before Rafaela could even inquire as to her fiancé's whereabouts, Winnie looked up and smiled.

"Master Alex said to serve you and the boy breakfast."

The boy. Liam. She had almost forgotten him.

Winnie wiped plump hands on her flour-dusted smock. "I have dispatched him to the old granary to collect some eggs, if a coyote has not breakfasted on the hens first."

"But Lord Paladín, where can he be?"

The elder woman looked over her thick shoulder and, with a sigh, turned her comfortable, lived-in features on Rafaela. "Only the Lord and Lucifer know."

Asking Winnie to delay breakfast, Rafaela continued her search for the Baron. After a while, it led her to the soldiers' barracks and the fiery strumming of a guitar. The dusty, time-scarred quarters contained a dozen or so cots in various states of disrepair, some weapon storage racks, and a single, decrepit pine chest.

Niall Gorman was sitting on a cot. His back against the stone wall, one knee drawn up to brace the neck of his guitar, his head was dipped toward fingers now tuning the strings. The gray ring-tail cat was curled asleep beside his stocking feet, one with a hole in its heel. His burnt sienna hair was sleep-tousled, falling forward to blend with his mustache. He wore brown corduroy trousers and a loose calico pullover unbuttoned at his throat.

He resumed playing as she hovered inside the open doorway, unwillingly entranced by his music's furious rhythm and fascinated by the sure and rapid movements of his flashing fingers.

He did not look up from the guitar. "Arousing, is it not?"

"Disturbing would be more accurate."

He paused his strumming to look at her then. "Come, sit beside me. I will show you a few chords." His fingers resumed their lively dance across the strings.

Her eyes fixated on the battered guitar. She simply could not hold his gaze. It was so deceptive, full of warm amusement, but deadly dangerous nonetheless. "I was looking for my fianc—for Lord Paladín."

"Ahh, yes. Your fiancé rode off very early with your companion. Bound for Matamoros is me guess."

A frustrated groan escaped her. She had failed to keep her word to Fiona.

"So, apparently, there appears nothing much requiring your attention for a time. Nothing but my 'disturbing' music." His adroit fingers changed abruptly and the flamenco rhythm segued into a lighter, more frivolous tune.

She took several tentative steps into the room, welcoming its warmth. As she approached, an encouraging smile tipped the ends of his mustache.

One tentative step led to another as she followed a splash of wintry sunlight beyond the doorway. Gradually, her steps drew her closer and closer to her Pied Piper. Completely enchanted, she settled onto another cot near his. Beneath her spread skirts, a kid slipper tapped in time to the music's lively beat.

Without her being aware of when it began, he progressively shifted the music's tempo yet again, this time into a slower, more insistent rhythm—constantly swelling and building upon itself. It was a pure joy to her senses. Lost in his performance, her shoulders began to sway in time to the sensual music.

"Have ye never danced?"

Drawn back to the present, she stiffened a bit. "Danced? Not exactly. Most of my years were spent in boarding school. I never had a coming out season."

His watchful eyes fastened on her face, his fingers slowed their strumming imperceptibly. "But ye do know how to dance?"

She struggled to look away, but his stare held her fast. "Why… yes. At the boarding school, we were… taught steps."

"So ye danced only with other girls?"

His chuckle was infectious and she could not help smiling back. Something told her she would be wise to retreat right then, but she sat, as if she were… yes, spellbound. Had he not described himself as a spell castor?

He laid aside his guitar and, unfolding his legs with easy grace, rose and crossed to where she sat. When he stepped into the shaft of sunlight, the dust motes drifted about him like gold dust. His sun-beamed skin glowed magically like a pagan's. He held out his hand. "Then this is the time, lass, to learn what a man is for."

"Dancing?" *And that was about all.*

"Why not? To lead ye where someone of your own kind never could."

"I… I do think this would be imprudent."

"Why? Because ye share the common opinion that we Irish are of a race more savage than human?"

"That common opinion does not happen to be one I share."

"'Tis believing ye, I am. I see not a single thing common about ye."

He was so close, her merino skirts brushed across his stockinged toes. She glanced up from his feet. The lids of his laughing, daring blue eyes crinkled at their corners.

She was not so foolish, nor so passive, as to succumb to charm and head-turning flattery. At least, not anymore. Not after the very man to whom her own father had misguidedly trusted her well-being had abused it both financially and physically.

But this Irish Traveler possessed something more, something that she had never been aware that she hungered for so desperately. Life. Yes, that was it. Life itself. He vibrated with it.

Well, she was a bit older, a tad wiser, and with far stronger moral character. She rose to her feet and drew her shoulders erect. "When I said imprudent, I meant I am already affianced to Lord Paladín. I would feel it unseemly were I to dance with another man."

Niall's lips crimped in a maddeningly cool smile. "Do ye truly believe your fiancée gives a tinker's dam about your moral rectitude?"

In all honesty, she did not. Lord Paladín cared only about the four-thousand pounds she was bringing to their marriage. In truth, if her betrothed had a heart at all, she would say it might be more partial toward Fiona, which could not be better luck for herself, she believed.

Evading Niall's question, she asked him, "So what does a tinker such as yourself give a damn about?"

He grinned hugely. "Spirited horses. Stirring music." He nodded at the cat. "Sensitive kitties." Motionless, his gypsy-like eyes stared into Rafaela's. "'Tis a right sensitive soul ye possess, my lady." He held out his hand, palm up, inviting her to make up her mind.

His simple, kind words—surely, they were trustworthy. While she knew better, his proffered palm unfettered the reluctance she had been feeling. Now the option was hers.

Four years before, she had not been given an option. The constraining.... The skirts thrust up.... The careless, hasty entry.... She knew all she needed to about that brand of seduction.

Ignoring her own fears, she lay her hand lightly upon Niall's. Her hands were longer than most women's, her fingers tapered and refined. His hand was wider and thicker than hers—calloused and engulfing. At his touch, a quicksilver thrill coursed through her. At once, she gasped, staring up at him from beneath spiked lashes. Something like that did not happen but in fairy tales and story books. Impossible.

"I warned ye, did I not? We Irish Travelers do cast spells."

He was so broad and so brawny, reminding her of a fortress—secure and unbreachable. He drew her to her feet. One arm circled her waist, drawing her closer than propriety dictated.

With surprising gentleness, he began to guide her into the steps of the dubiously moral waltz, all the while humming softly near her ear, his breath gently stirring the tendrils of dark hair gathered there. He whirled her about the confined space of the cot-cramped barracks floor.

Soon, her head was spinning and she was smiling broadly. The feeling was altogether exhilarating.

"Why, 'tis shooting stars ye have for dimples my lady."

Then he whirled her even faster, and she laughed as he grinned. If that was all there was to his proximity—the dancing that melded them at breast, hip, and knee—she would have wished to go on forever, just so.

He stopped abruptly, as her skirts whiplashed about their legs. Turning over her wrist, his broad finger traced across the inky veins beneath her opalescent skin before slipping onto her palm.

Her breath double-timed and tiny hairs at her nape and along her arms rose briskly, as if lightning were striking nearby. Stupefied, she stared openly at him.

"I read palms, ye know."

"I do not believe in that foolishness."

His eyes relinquished hers, and he studied her palm intently. His blunt forefinger followed a line in her palm. "Unseen scars. Aye, ye have been scarred. Badly. By a man. But ye will find happiness with another man. But only if ye will bravely step past your fears."

She should have expected this, the glib payoff. Her voice sounded thin and cutting in her ears. "And what step exactly would that be?"

"Whatever step ye think the most foolish. In our gypsy lore, such a step can be represented by the Fool's card in our fortune deck. The fool is a spirit searching for experience. We call that the Leap of Faith."

Scoffing a harsh-sounding huff, she tugged on her palm, which he released instantly. "A child could have improvised better than you, Mr. Gorman. I would add, in my case, the quote would not apply as aptly to a 'Leap of Faith' but more like the warning, 'Look before you leap.'"

He shrugged, grinning. "But no mere child can ever see what I can."

"And just what do you see then? An easy mark, pray tell?"

His eyes roamed across her features, then settled at her mouth. "Why, my lady, I see a young woman ready to be loved. Nay, needing to be."

"Loved or bedded?" The question surprised herself, though she took perverse pleasure in the rise of his brows at her crudity. "Because I have already been bedded and that was most definitely not what I *needed*. Why do I have the distinct belief that is exactly what you have in mind, Mr. Gorman?"

He sighed. "My lady, ye have no idea what I have in mind."

"And I certainly have no need to find out, I assure you!"

"All right then, but me own warning—should I ever take ye to bed, do not expect to find me there when you awaken."

"As if I would want you in my bed."

"I believe ye do."

Oh! The man was the epitome of exasperation. Gathering her skirts, she stormed out the door.

Irish Travelers had a dual set of ethics—one for dealing with Travelers and the second for all others.

Palmistry and fortunetelling were practiced only outside the clans. Niall's mother taught him the crafts but rarely had he practiced them. But aye, palmistry did give him an excuse to hold Rafaela's hand—not that he needed one. He could have taken her right there in the barracks, even seduced her past her intense fear. She was that vulnerable, as someone had taken her against her will.

Oddly, what he wanted her to do was to come to him of her own free will. Aye, much better to tame a wild horse than to break one. That she might come to him freely was most unlikely ever to happen. Not in this lifetime at all. She was already betrothed. She herself was Spanish landed gentry. Not only was he Irish, viewed as little more than baboons by many of those living outside Eire, but he was an Irish Traveler. Worst of the Irish's baddest lot. Gypsy. Coarse. Disreputable.

During his adventures, Niall had tumbled with dozens of women. Fat, thin, rich, poor, old, young, comely, homely. None could detain him. None ever would. He would not be staying here much longer, so why would he want to tame the cool, disdainful Rafaela Carrera?

His instinct for danger was infallible. So were his instincts with women. His instincts reassured him she was neither so cool nor so disdainful toward him as she appeared to be.

Those same finely-honed instincts of his also warned him that to court her would be to court disaster.

6

IN THE *PRESIDIO* GARDEN, FIONA yanked at the vines that threatened to choke the tendril shoots of yarrow, dandelion, and chili peppers. Choke—just what she wanted to do to Paladín. The licentious Lord too easily bent others to his will.

The very thought of the man elicited a maddening sigh. He clearly possessed no moral compass whatsoever. Where was the rake? Certainly not with his betrothed. A clearly agitated Rafaela had retreated to her room immediately after receiving Paladín's message regarding Cavett Magnum's gala that evening—to hem a gown of hers for Fiona to wear, she had explained rather stiltedly.

Fiona feared that the younger woman was sequestering herself with her misery. And why should she not? What fool of a female would want to be married off to Paladín?

Sighing again, she abandoned her attempts at gardening and, carrying a reed basket of cilantro she had managed to salvage, set off for the kitchen.

Solid stones lined the kitchen floor, leading to its wide brick hearth. In the fireplace, a stout iron crane suspended a brass kettle of turnip tops. A single window, its shutters thrown open, let in midafternoon sunlight to slant across the vast worktable of dark, scarred wood.

Liam was stacking kindling in an alcove beside the fire pit, and Winnie was chopping what looked to be wild onions while weaving some fantastic story about rogue elephants and cobra snakes and Bengal tigers.

"… Remittance Man. You know, second sons of prominent families sent off to out-of-the-way locales because they have no place in the home scheme of things. I have been with the family, since he was but a boy…."

Sensing the subject was Paladín, Fiona paused just inside the kitchen doorway and listened.

"And he was made a… a raj?" Liam's eyes were alight with youthful and avid envy. "Like a king?"

"Aye, that he was. After he had seen military service in Canada, his family sent him to its East India Tea Company in India to head up its Punjab region. The Sikh ruler there became bosom friends with Master Alex. Created him a raj, the Sikh ruler did, in return for Master Alex's military and political advice—and, of course, for his strong British connections. Why, barely twenty-one, Master Alex had the power of life and death over those natives."

"Eavesdropping?" asked a male voice from behind Fiona.

She whirled to confront Paladín's hired hand. "Oh, Niall, ye scared—"

His eyes were more a stormy gray than blue. "Where is the lady Rafaela?"

"Why, in her room… at least, the last time we spoke. Did she—"

"Our best mare is missing."

"Perhaps Rafaela just went for a pleasure ride?"

"Pleasure ride? If she is beset by bandits or Indians, it will not be much of a pleasure ride." He spun away, ordering over his shoulder, "Tell Paladín I will bring back the lady Rafaela… or her carcass."

"Her carcass?" Paladín repeated. Fiona had caught up with him at the door of the *padre's* bedchamber.

The Baron dropped the frockcoat slung over his shoulder onto his bed and began stripping out of his cotton shirt, obviously unabashed about exposing his upper torso—bronzed by months, maybe years, spent under India's tropical sun. Where had he been? Back to one of Matamoros's gambling table or groggeries or brothels?

She waited uneasily, curious as to the libertine's response. He did not seem at all distressed by Gorman's news of Rafaela's disappearance.

Arched windows, sitting high in the vaulted bedchamber, provided an almost unholy illumination of Paladín. She stood there in the doorway, fascinated by his body—his wide shoulders, long ribs, graceful arms, and legs like stone columns. His unruly and overly long hair glistened at the temples with perspiration that also sheened the dark curls lightly matting his chest.

Surely he was not sweating from any prodigious day spent at a monte table. Maybe from one spent in a lover's bed? He was an enigma to her, so difficult to read or to anticipate.

She beamed a bright grin that displayed all her teeth. "Without a bride, ye would be without her dowry and without the resources to pay off the taxes on that league of land—nay, me league of land—that ye claim as yuir own."

"Niall will find my bride and return her alive, never you fear." He tossed his shirt onto an intricately carved pine armchair and crossed to her with that languid grace that belied his quick striking power. He pushed the door closed behind her.

She gulped as his free hand splayed its fingers beneath her jawline, gripping her chin.

"Speaking of alive or dead—has it not occurred to you, Fiona, that if you were dead, it would present me with one less problem regarding our mutual claim on that league of land? Right now, I could wring your scrawny neck with a mere twist of my hand, and there would be no witness to protest."

She swallowed the rotten egg of fear that nigh corked her breathing. His obsidian eyes reflected nothing, not even a soul, within. She knew it had not only crossed his mind to take her life, but his conscience would not stand in the way. Simply put, she knew the man had no conscience, no soul, no heart.

Truth be told, no one would miss her. Parents' and sibling's graves had been left behind in Kerry, victims of mass evictions, starvation, and disease of one sort or other… except for one sister, the eldest. Peggy had chosen the oldest profession. Fiona's fingers slipped onto her four-leaf-clover locket. It had little monetary value, but it was a gift to her from Peggy.

Bluster and bluff had gotten her this far. She forced another cheery smile. "Twill not change your circumstances, me Lord. Without Rafaela, ye be without a dowry to pay the taxes on—"

His gaze dropped to her lips. "For such a small, insignificant person, you have a mouth on you, Miss Flanigan, that—"

"While ye are at it, me Lord, ye might think about puttin' in a cash crop— and a water well, too—on me league of land, if there is not one there alr—"

He pressed his thumb gently against her larynx. Her breath stuck in her throat in mid-sentence. She stared up at her own beautiful Grim Reaper.

Oh, Mother of God. He is going to kill me after all.

"We short—" she gulped again when he released her throat and started over. "We wee people like meself are leprechauns, me Lord, and ye never wanna be harming us. Twill only bring ill fortune yuir way. Forever."

For an eternal moment, he looked to be considering his choices. "This may not be the most effective way to silence a leprechaun, but it is one that gives me almost as much pleasure." He bent over her, his eyes blazing with wicked intent.

Oh, crikey, he is going to kiss me! Her lips compressed, sealed as tightly as a coffin.

"Calm yourself, Fiona. You have yet to experience my kiss."

"I will not tolerate this. Ye are a blackguard, a mercenary, a man utterly and completely without—"

Nudging her backward a step until her back pressed against the door, she began to feel… not fear… but a confusing sense as his lips brushed hers with the lightest touch.

She froze—if one could freeze in the grasp of hell's emissary on earth. She had expected a ruthless, brutal punishing of her mouth, but this… this touch caused a thousand butterflies to take flight in her stomach. Her lungs remembered their duty, and she gasped into his kiss.

He raised his head, a slight frown creasing the bridge of his aristocratic nose. "Never been kissed, have you? And yet you sell your—"

"—me body to the highest bidder. At least I did until I got the French pox." To her despair and lifetime torment, that was exactly what had happened to her sister Peggy. That tortured soul had ended her life tidily with her woolen scarf looped from her neck to the timbered ceiling of their tiny shared room in Five Points.

At her cheeky remark, he threw back his head and laughed. "Sell your puny frame 'to the highest bidder?' Then why do I now entertain the suspicion there were neither bidders nor pox?"

A roaring noise in her ears—a fury that she could actually hear roiling throughout her body—infused her with superhuman strength. She shoved away from him. A twisted smile curled her lips. "But dare ye risk that chance?"

"I have bedded my way across England, Canada, India, and back, judiciously selecting partners. And sheaths have been my choice. But some would claim I am, indeed, demented, most likely by the pox. So, should I decide to bed you or not, fear of the pox will not deter my ardor."

"Well, should I have the choice, ye willna ever bed me." Prompted by his raised eyebrow, she added, "Me Lord!"

Gently, his forefinger traced the bow of her collar bone until she thought her heart would explode if he continued. "I assure you, I am quite capable of changing your mind, wee one. Now go prepare for tonight. We cannot let my intended's disposition, absent as she presently is, prevent us from enjoying Magnum's hospitality, now can we?"

FEW WOMEN POSSESSED RAFAELA'S RIDING skills, and time gave her an edge. Surely, she would not be missed at the *presidio* for several hours. She hoped the Baron would assume she was only out for a leisurely ride.

Galloping her mount furiously, she followed the River Road that was indeed a river of dead leaves, the last to succumb to autumn's scythe. Chilly wind stung her cheeks and shoved back her cape's hood to yank at her up-swept hair.

At the scattering of *jacales* and adobe homes that signified Matamoros outskirts, she reined in the mare. Paladín would be expecting her to make for Matamoros and await a vessel bound for New Orleans. By the time he searched out the various inns and lodging houses, she would be too far away for pursuit.

Her recollection of the map of the Department of Tejas that had accompanied her marriage contract indicated a port somewhere between Matamoros and New Orleans, a port where she could purchase passage to Savannah—and seek the refuge of her aunt's home.

Copano Bay, that was the port's name. She was not certain she had enough pounds left or even if the port of Copano Bay accepted pounds, rather than bank notes or Mexican doubloons, in payment for passage.

Between Matamoros and Copano Bay, nothing existed that she could recall from the map—just an ox-cart road paralleling the Gulf shore on one side and skirting the Wild Horse Desert on the other.

She had already heard frightening tales of the desolate Wild Horse Desert, as well as tales of the cannibalistic Karankawa Indians along the coast.

The mare jigged impatiently, yet still Rafaela wavered in her flight. She had taken time only to hem quickly, and rather poorly, the green gown—it was the least she could do for Fiona, given that she was abandoning her new-found friend. Then Rafaela had packed as little as she would absolutely need to take with her.

Unbidden came the memory of Niall's accusation that she was not a participator but only an observer in life. Well, she could no longer afford to act as the passive Rafaela Carrera.

One man not only had finagled from her the mounded pocket money she had so heavily invested but had then also robbed her of her maidenhood—and had gotten away with the injustice.

There was nothing she could do about that, but, by all that was holy, no other man would have control of her again, financially or otherwise—not if she had her way about it. From now on, she would chart her own course.

Drawing a resolute breath, she kneed her mount toward the wagon wheel-grooved dirt road that skirted Matamoros Bay and headed northeast toward Copano Bay.

A blustery wind was blowing ashore from the Gulf of Mexico. The strong scent of salt in the air informed her she could not be very far from the ocean. She turned up the fur collar of her capote, hunger pangs already grumbling in her stomach.

She knew not how far she rode that day, but toward sundown, she began to search for a safe and warm place to pass the night. Off to her right, a proliferation of wind-tossed cypress branches and palm fronds alerted her to a bulwark against the night's cold—as well as the possibility of some berries, edible plants, and, most likely, a creek for drinking water.

Yes, she knew she had made the right decision to escape to Savannah, whether the aunt wanted her or not. Nevertheless, Rafaela felt uneasy.

The roar of the waves beyond her sight was deafening, so she only heard the shouts of the blue-coated Mexican soldiers, crashing through the brush and surrounding her, after it was too late.

WITH SPRITELY OLD FREDERICK AT the reins, the hair-raising ride in the coach from the *presidio* to Matamoros was bad enough. Rigidly, Fiona sat opposite the satyr Paladín and refused to speak to him. She even drew aside Rafaela's silk-lined cape and the skirts of her altered gown, all green *peau de soie* and lace, so they would not intermingle with the long legs Paladín was stretching out.

For his part, he looked moody—no doubt irate at the departure of his intended. At one point during the ride, he commented in a bored manner, "If you expect me to take advantage of you, Fiona, please rest assured. I have no plans to take you by force."

"Well, not me body, maybe, but me land grant, aye. Me Lord."

His eyes narrowed. "Careful you do not push me too far, wench."

She was not foolish. She and Liam had a safe roof over their heads and food for the moment. Wisely, she shut her mouth for the remainder of the journey. If only she was not attracted to him.

The Land Commissioner's house, encircled by an iron-picket fence, was a sharp contrast to the predominately stucco homes of Matamoros. The stylish two story was built from timber with verandas around both upper and lower stories. Inside, Spanish *hidalgos* and French *chevaliers* mixed and mingled with emissaries from other countries, as well as with American diplomats.

The genteel female she hoped to pass herself off as was as unlikely to pass muster as her being crowned Queen of England. For all her voracious reading, she was still an indigent castoff.

The Baron's grip at her elbow held her fast, so she could not bolt. Bending close to her ear, Paladín whispered, "Smile."

Displaying his own smile, Cavett Magnum bowed low over her hand, his mass of chestnut brown curls almost brushing her fingers. "Your attendance will charm all our guests, Miss Flanigan."

Charm the guests? More likely nonplus them. Aye, the gown's blatant, bright emerald green did wash-out her freckles, but it also enflamed her hair color into an eye-blinking red. Her rebellious curls strained mightily to escape their loops at either side of her face.

"And your fiancée, Lord Paladín?" Cavett inquired of the Baron.

"My fiancée sends her regrets," Paladín replied easily, all the while his eyes scanning over Magnum's head to inventory the guests. He returned his attention to his host with a perfunctory smile. "Unfortunately, she is not feeling quite herself."

Fiona wanted to roll her eyes. Sooner or later, Matamoros would realize Paladín's intended had fled. God speed Rafaela, safely to the haven of her aunt's home.

With a display of pride and devotion, Cavett turned to introduce his wife *Doña* Margarita, chatting with another guest, and politely relayed to her disappointment at the absence of Paladín's fiancée.

Not the social creature her husband was, Margarita appeared more reserved. A homely woman with bountiful hair, she possessed only the slightest accent, more British than American.

"Then it is most felicitous that you have brought Miss Flanigan to our soiree." She spared Fiona a kindly glance. "With the dearth of females, your presence will enliven our many bachelors' prospects of dancing tonight."

"I fear I am not up to date on the latest dance figures." She had never danced with anyone in her life and was not about to make a fool of herself in the presence of the Matamoros elite.

"That presents no difficulty. We don't hold to the highest social etiquette in Matamoros."

Margarita linked her arm with Fiona's. "Come, my dear."

Fiona glanced back at Paladín, but he and Cavett were already engaged in tense conversation with another guest, a distinguished man as tall as Paladín but older.

"You must be parched after your journey. After we visit the punch table, I'll introduce you around."

This was the last thing Fiona wanted. She had expected, hoped, to be a wallflower. When everyone was preoccupied with the festivities, surely she could fade into the background for half an hour or so and not be missed.

She had counted on having Liam as an accomplice, but Paladín had tasked him with boot-blacking his Wellingtons that evening. She only needed time enough to find the stamp Cavett had said was necessary to validate her land claim.

After that, she and Liam would not be far behind Rafaela in flight—but their destination would not be Savannah but San Patricio. They would be there one step ahead of the devil himself, Lord Paladín, who held the dubious distinction of being, in her inexpert opinion, both highly detestable *and* most desirable.

In arm with Cavett's wife, she got no farther than the double-door entrance to the parlor, where laughter and loud conversations were accompanied by the music of a violin, harp, and melodeon. Perhaps a dozen couples or more were either dancing or watching others.

"Moses," Margarita was saying to a small, olive-skinned man with thumbs hooked in his vest pockets, "this is Miss Flanigan, a companion of Lord Paladín's fiancée—and their house guest."

She turned to Fiona. "Moses Solomon is owner of the Emporium, and I might boast it is the largest commission-merchant firm in Tejas."

The man sketched a bow. "Forgive *Doña* Margarita's bias. We Texicans do tend toward the grandiose." He had a flattened nose and kind raisin-colored eyes. His Mediterranean-smooth voice contrasted to Paladín's rough textured tone. "May I have the honor of leading you in the contradance?"

"I really do not know how—"

"Oh, do go along with Moses." Margarita gave her a soft nudge toward the gentleman.

Fiona accepted his hand and proceeded to stumble embarrassingly through the steps. Her eyes darted about, looking for an excuse to escape.

The only viable one—Paladín—stood among guests who had drawn around him, most likely curious about the good-looking nobleman with the scandalous reputation. Debonair he might be in his black tailcoat and layers of ruffles at the throat and wrists, his bored expression said that he was not in the least tempted to gratify their curiosity, nor rescue her.

Mortified, she looked up at Moses. "I beg your pardon, sir, but I tried to tell ye I do not dance."

He beamed. "No worries there, Miss Flanigan. With a little practice, we can—"

A lanky man looking to be in his late forties with thinning hair and large ears intervened. "I'll claim the lady's hand, if I may have that honor." A tomahawk hung from his waist. His leather breeches and fringe deerskin shirt had seen better days, as had his moccasins.

Introducing himself as Deaf Smith, a scout for Major General Houston, he preceded to prod and pump her around the parlor, bumping into other pairs. Obviously, he was not only partially deaf, but he didn't have any ear for music. What he did have was a Mexican wife in San Antonio.

At last, Fiona escaped and headed straight for the punch bowl. One taste from her crystal cup and she realized the punch was spiked. All the better. Perhaps, that would help her get through the evening.

A second swig and the candelabra's heat seemed oppressive. She scanned the room again, her gaze tripping once more over Paladín. He did not appear bored now. Only a short distance away, he was listening intently to a beautiful and vivacious young woman gowned all in black, her auburn hair tiered in ringlets at the top of her regally postured head.

"*Señora* Therese del Valle," claimed a male voice at her side.

Fiona's gaze swiveled to find Cavett Magnum. "What?"

"The young woman Lord Paladín has engaged in conversation is *Señora* Therese del Valle. She is the widow of a *capitán* posted with the Mexican troops here in Matamoros. Gossip says she was expelled from a convent school in New Orleans because of her escapades—which makes her all the more dazzling, don't you think?"

Fiona glanced again at the young woman with more than ample skin and cleavage showing. Obviously, Cavett was waiting for a response, so Fiona turned back to him and smiled serenely. "Me fears I lack words enough to do her justice."

At that, Cavett laughed. "Yes, I see you will provide a worthy opponent for Paladín in the face-off for the land grant."

"Ahhh, but we are on the same side." Paladín surprised her from behind, his hand spread proprietarily at the low of her back.

The remaining punch in her cup sloshed precariously. Aye, Paladín was dangerous, intent as he was on separating her from both her maidenhead and her land grant.

"And which side is that?" Cavett inquired with a mischievous grin.

"Why, the side of might makes right, of course." Paladín looked down at Fiona and held out his arm. "You have yet to meet everyone."

If she hoped to be about her main purpose for attending the party that night, she was to be disappointed. Sighing, she let him escort her back to the hostess's circle, introduced her to even more guests, including the beauty Therese del Valle, then promptly vanished once more.

That close to the young Spanish belle, Fiona could see hers was not a perfect beauty. The nose was perhaps a wee too long, the chin a mite too jutting, but, regardless of slight imperfections, Therese's confidence, poise, and energy bestowed her with undeniable appeal. Furthermore, her eyes evidenced considerable intelligence.

"I understand you are companion to the Baron's intended. She is not feeling well tonight, he tells me. Alas."

"Alas." Had Paladín bedded the widow?

Therese's dark brown eyes swept over the guests to alight on Paladín. "Perhaps he has chosen the wrong woman for his future bride."

"And the right one would be you?"

She blinked, then chuckled. "We do enjoy ourselves together, but my coffers are not adequate for Lord Paladín's expensive tastes."

Unlikley. Fiona could not imagine anyone enjoying being around Paladín for too long.

"Non," the young widow continued, "I was thinking more along the lines of yourself as his bride."

At that, Fiona laughed aloud. Too loudly. Had she, also, imbibed too heartily? "I'd rather be boiled alive. Besides, as ye pointed out, Lord Paladín has expensive tastes."

With time passing too quickly, Fiona escaped, at last, by pleading the need to refill her cup. But she bypassed the refreshment table, staying to the room's perimeter and easily losing herself behind the taller guests watching the dancers.

Surely, there must be a back way out of the house. It was around the corner from the Land Commissioner's office, Cavett had said. She had only to pick the office door lock. Had she not learned that shameful art from some of the best Five Points had to offer?

———————————

CAVETT MAGNUM'S STUDY REVEALED HIM to be a man of broad and eclectic education. One entire wall was shelved with books covering subjects from cartography to finance and economics.

From a cedar-lined pewter humidor, Magnum offered Havana cigars to the other five men present. In the midst of the ongoing soiree, he was hosting a clandestine meeting of the newly formed Committee of Correspondence and Safety, one of many organizing across Tejas on behalf of its Mexican colonial citizens.

The six had gathered in a privy council to discuss what military and financial aid the central Committee of the Texican Provisional Government out of San Felipe de Austin could expect from Matamoros in their opposition to the despot, Santa Anna.

Paladín contemplated the five—Cavett Magnum, Moses Solomon, Captain Brown, and Sam Houston—and Houston's guide, spy, and scout, Deaf Smith.

Known as *El Sordo*, Smith was a fearless fighter Paladín had met several times during the past several months. Married to a Tejana widow, Smith moved freely among Anglo and Hispanic Tejano societies and was known to be a man of few words. He could read the Tejas terrain flawlessly.

The year before, Stephen Austin had appointed him to lead a company of ranging riflemen known as Rangers. At this stage of the probable revolt against Mexico, to which culture would Smith vow his allegiance?

Paladín was acquainted with Moses Solomon through several social functions in Matamoros they had both attended. The Jew, who had immigrated to Matamoros to escape prejudice and prosecution, owned the Emporium, which controlled much of the cotton trade out of Matamoros. He held interests in land and banking and had pledged to provide vessels for a navy of the newly formed Provisional Government.

Famed for his skill with the Bowie knife, Solomon seemed a solid individual, good for his word. Of course, pledging was a far cry from committing. He voiced a goal of Texas as a Mexican state, separate from the state of Tejas y Coahuila. Many saw his approach not as one of moderation but as suggestive of shiftily keeping one foot in each camp.

Then there was Magnum. Paladín had first met him when the man had served as American consul in London. Polished, intelligent, and persuasive, he nevertheless impressed Paladín more as a glib speculator.

Just behind the seated Houston, Captain Jeremiah Brown, a lively young soldier, stood at ease, hands clasped behind his back. Brown had just been appointed commander of the *Invincible.* Originally a slave trader, the schooner was now the only war ship of the incipient Texas Navy. The funds for purchasing the *Invincible* were to be donated by Solomon. Nothing about Captain Brown suggested anything untoward. Nothing that could finger him as a Tejas Tory—possibly the most important reason to keep an eye on him.

Of the five, Paladín had known Houston, the former Tennessee governor, the longest—since 1828, when Paladín was invited to President Jackson's inaugural ball as one of the British ambassador's attachés. Houston, the President's protégée, had taken a liking to Paladín and the feeling was mutual. Both Jackson and Houston had seen military service. They favored a limited government… and harbored bitter memories about their respective disastrous marriages.

When Houston's marriage failed after only eleven weeks, he had gone off to live with the Cherokee. They referred to him as both The Raven and Big Drunk. At the moment, Paladín imagined Houston had to be questioning his wisdom in agreeing to lead the rabble-rousing army, raised from scratch, to fight for independence from Mexico's omnipotent central government.

Reclaiming his seat at the massive desk, Magnum leaned back. "I can assure you, the rebel resistance to Santa Anna's aggression would receive enormous support here in Matamoros."

Moses spit out the cigar tip he'd bitten off, then growled. "It's true that the growing size of the Mexican army garrisoned over at the fort has pissed off the people of Matamoros. However, there are dire warnings against us Matamoros folks aiding the rebels in any way."

Houston leaned over the desk lamp and lit his cigar. He turned to Magnum.

"What makes you so certain of that support?" Houston had told Paladín he'd purchased a general's uniform in New Orleans after being named Commander-in-Chief by Tejas' Nacogdoches Committee of Vigilance, but he had yet to wear it.

Magnum settled back in his chair. "The political rift between our city and Santa Anna's central government is growing. Tensions and complaints have escalated. There have been a number of confrontations between residents and soldiers posted here, bar fights, stolen property, and unpaid rent. The invading army is demanding we provide provisions, livestock, money, housing, transportation—even recruits."

"While all we Texicans and *Tejanos* have for war materiel," Moses mused, "is two wagons, two yoke of oxen, and a few spavined horses."

"And a navy." Houston glanced over his shoulder at Captain Brown. Houston's scrutinizing gaze shifted now to his scout. "What have you learned from the local tribes—who will the Indians side with?"

Deaf Smith shrugged. "Whoever offers them the most wampum. Right now, it would seem to be the Chaparral Fox."

Houston drew on his cigar, blew a helix of smoke, and, without glancing at Paladín, felt out the others. "Who is this Chaparral Fox?"

Moses spoke up. "Someone among us who feeds information to Santa Anna himself. That is all we know."

Paladín could have told the men that Niall, who had lost his sister to an Indian raid, also wanted to know the man's identity. As though thinking along the same lines, Houston asked, "Where *is* Gorman?"

"Regrettably, duty has called him elsewhere." *Duty or desire.*

Magnum leaned forward, his arms braced on his desk. "I recommend the Provisional Government mount an expedition to take Matamoros from Santa Anna's Centralist forces stationed here."

"And we should do this because…?"

"I think it is urgent to meet the enemy on the frontier." Magnum looked around the room. "Keep Santa Anna's soldiers out of the populated part of Tejas. Protect the cabins, farms, and towns—and families—from destruction. Even better, to lay claim to the vital revenues at the Port of Matamoros. Such an expedition might draw support from federalists within other Mexican states, perhaps inspiring even more armed uprisings throughout Mexico against Santa Anna."

While the other men digested the magnitude of Magnum's impressive proposition, silence reigned in the study. Houston, keeping his own council, shifted his uncompromising gaze to Paladín. "What say you?"

Paladín exhaled an eddy of smoky whorls. "Solomon's assertions that the rift between Matamoros and the army posted here are true. But as to staging an expedition of our ragtag army to take possession of Matamoros and its fort… I have serious doubts."

Houston frowned, taking another puff from his cigar. "Why?"

"Because there is a shortage of reality when you rely on rumors—whether those are of great numbers of volunteers arriving from the United States to join your ragtag army or those of massive support by the Mexican Federalists here in Matamoros."

He refrained from saying that he suspected Magnum's suggestion as a way to safeguard his possible land speculation enterprise.

"There is also the problematic position we may be put in by siphoning our forces from San Antonio de Bexar, such as they are. Not to mention that the *rancheros* around here are disaffected with the Texicans."

"Then, too, there is the factor of Santa Anna," Houston finished with a grim smile. "Aptly called the 'Napoleon of the West.' I am neither Napoleon nor Alexander the Great."

"But you might well borrow some tactics from another general—a general who fought a war against a professional army with nothing more than volunteer civilians. General George Washington."

Houston ignored the flattery. "I tend to think, gentlemen, that an expedition to take Matamoros would be a recipe for disaster."

With that comment, the discussion and cigars were left behind in favor of rejoining the party… with the exception of Paladín.

A quick survey of the guests prompted him to turn his attention from the critical meeting with Houston to the critical absences of Rafaela and Fiona.

He was more than a little concerned for his betrothed. The young woman had no idea how much danger she was placing herself in. Nevertheless, he had faith that Niall could track her down.

As for Fiona's absence, he would resolve that untidy problem himself. A brisk stroll to the plaza found him leaning with folded arms against the plaza's gazebo, watching Fiona across the cobbled street. In the dark, she furiously jimmied the lock of the Land Commissioner's office.

Whore, pickpocket, burglar…. Was there anything of which the woman was not capable? Clearly, she came from the dregs of humanity, as he should know, because he was of even worse ilk. He was a murderer. Not even Fiona Flanigan was capable of that.

Obviously, she was not giving up her claim to his land. There had already been moments when he wanted to eliminate his competition by placing his hands around her skinny neck and pressing his thumbs just hard enough.

Why did she possess that ability to arouse him when even the most gifted European courtesans and sexually liberated Hindu *asparas,* wise in the matters of pleasuring the *lingam* and *yoni,* could stir no more than some passing interest from him?

Her recklessly plucky spirit at war with the soft, vulnerable look in her eyes had totally disrupted his lifelong ennui. That was all there was to it—the amusing, resilient, and sassy Fiona Flanigan served only to relieve his innate boredom.

Whom he should really murder was Cavett Magnum. Paladín suspected Magnum, the leading legal expert on land titles, was the architect of an enormous and audacious scale of operation—buying and selling titles under the table.

The Spanish land deed, located between the Irish colony of San Patricio and the Gulf coast to its south, had been bestowed upon Alex's grandfather, Fifth Baron Paladín, for meritorious service in the Seven Years War of 1767. The massive acreage was one of the most desirable and valuable land holdings in all *Tejas.*

However, murdering Magnum would still not secure Paladín's family's deed. There was always someone ready to step in to take Magnum's place. Perhaps that was why he had accepted Houston's request that he serve on the advisory war council on behalf of the southern colonies of *Tejas*—it was self-serving opportunity to keep a close eye on another council member, Cavett Magnum.

Oddly enough, after a bloody and ferocious life abroad, Paladín had sworn to himself that he had had enough of war and death.

He felt like he had lived in the face of death for so long that death had lost its terror. With that thought, he abandoned his post at the gazebo and started across the street.

One foe at a time.

LACKING ONE OF ITS PINS, a loose swath of Fiona's hair tumbled across her face, obscuring her vision. Lips pursed to blow aside the errant strands, she tried yet again with her pick. Her bent and twisted hair pin was not strong enough to turn the lock's lever. She had not counted on the lock's being old and rusted by the salt-laden air. "Ye bloody bastard!"

"Bloodthirsty I may be, but my parents would have objected to your slur on my heritage."

She whirled. There, of course, stood Evil Incarnate. Naturally, he was too near for her to make a dash for it. Retreat was also impossible with her back to the timbered door. May as well brazen it out.

Hands at her back, she attempted to conceal the hair pin. "I forgot something I left inside on our visit to the Land Commissioner's office." She knew she was whistling through the graveyard.

Paladín lifted a dubious black eyebrow. Propping one hand against the door within an inch of her head, he leaned over her. "I am sure you did. That something would be a land deed, I suppose? Did you ever consider duplicates may have been made? That in an absence of a deed, affidavits are taken, and old maps studied to reconstruct titles of ownership?"

Before she could improvise a reply, the emotional derelict leaned his head very close to hers. "And did you ever consider that breaking and entering carries some harsh penalties?"

"Ye have no proof."

His elegant fingers twined through a recalcitrant swag of her hair. "A hair pin crooked in a shape to turn a lock's lever might constitute proof in some courts."

"Ye'd be laughed out of any and all such courts."

"Possibly, but, as you earlier challenged me, dare you risk that? On the other hand, we can return to the party as though we had merely stepped outside for fresh air... provided I feel in a forgiving mood."

Her eyes narrowed. "And whatever would put ye in such a mood?"

"My Lord, if you please."

Of course, it did not please her. Her lips tightened. "Me Lord."

When he tucked her tress behind her ear, she barely managed to control the shiver. "I realize asking you to give up your claim to my land—"

"*Me* land!"

"—would be over your dead body, and I am not inclined to kill you… at least not yet. So, I would propose as a temporary truce an offer of conciliation on your part—that you will indulge my whimsy. Let's say, by allowing my seduction of you."

"Are ye daft? I would never go to bed with—"

"I did not say I required that. The choice is yours. If at any time my touch displeasures you, you need only say so."

Obviously, he took perverse pleasure in toying with her. She was silent, rapidly turning over the offer in her mind. Easy enough. She had nothing to lose. Still….

"Yuir word is good?"

"Rarely."

Her eyes flashed up at him. "Then why should I agree?"

He offered her that easy, sensual half-smile that was his alone. If she had not been looking into his empty eyes, her heart would have fluttered like a young maid's at pagan Maypole time. "Because you have no other choice."

She tried to draw a reflective breath, but that was a wasted effort. How could she think clearly or at all with him dominating her space? She shrugged. "Aye, I can tolerate yuir seduction attempts."

Because, if a simple 'no' did not halt him, then there was always a well-aimed kick at his privates. The sisters-in-trade had taught her how to thwart unwelcomed attentions most effectively.

"Tolerate?" His grin broadened and was startling genuine.

"Aye."

"*Tolerate* will turn to pleading for more, on that you can depend, *mi querida.*"

His lips lowered over hers in the kiss she had fretfully anticipated.

"No. Ye said ye would stop when I said no."

"That's not what I said. I said if my touch displeasures you, you need say only no. I have not touched you… yet." With that, his lips did brush over hers as lightly as goose down drifting onto her open palm.

She had been tempted to say no outright. But this, this she could tolerate. Had she not lived through just such a kiss from him once before? Her lids glided closed.

Yet this kiss did not end with the brushing of his lips. Nay, next she felt his long, narrow hands cradling her face, his tongue nudging teasingly at the center of her lips. She opened them to say the magic incantation of 'no' and his tongue took the advantage.

At the same moment, hands dropped to clasp her waist at either side, drawing her against him. She made a noise of outraged protest. Which, to her ears, sounded more like a moan of pleasure.

Her fingers grabbed each of his lace-draped wrists, yet she did not push them away. She was clutching a trapeze with no net to catch her… and so she clung to his wrists even as her stomach clenched in a spasm of sudden heat.

And then… then she was free.

He had released her and stepped back. Her lids snapped open to behold that sinful, all-knowing smile. "Not here. Later."

"Never."

"Never *never* comes. Now, perhaps we'd best return before we start tongues to gossiping."

7

SAN ANTONIO DE BEXAR
STATE OF TEJAS Y COAHUILA, MEXICO

A tumbling line of dark clouds rumbled ominously toward the roving company of Mexican dragoons and their captive, although Colonel Santiago Calaveras referred to *Señorita* Rafaela Carrera as "his guest."

Her regal bearing indicated a highborn lady. She may be Spanish, but one could never be sure on which side sympathies in Tejas lay—that of its patriots or that of the rioters.

He rode up alongside her. A sprinkle of rain that promised to turn into a drizzle had begun, and she shivered beneath her woolen cape.

"We shall reach Bexar shortly. You will find Veramendi Palace quite comfortable." Truth was, the rambling, one-story Spanish Colonial building fell far short of being a palace. At least its enormous double-door entrance could withstand attacks... which could well be imminent.

She turned those marvelous caramel-colored eyes on him, her polite smile feigned, as was her interest. "Veramendi Palace?"

"The official residence of the Governor of Tejas. It has been evacuated and is now garrisoned by the staff of General Cos, commander of the military forces in Tejas." In fact, Bexar was home to the largest Mexican garrison in the province of Tejas.

"And how long am I to be a *guest* there?"

Santiago shifted in his saddle and, swiveling his gaze toward the cloud-shrouded horizon, chose his words carefully. "Once the rebels decamp from the Mission Concepción outside Bexar, it should be safe enough to resume your journey."

A lady traveling on horseback, unaccompanied, along the old Camino Real—now the Matamoros-to-San Antonio de Bexar Road—certainly aroused one's suspicions.

Aided by the overcast weather, his cavalry managed to circumvent the rag-tag rebels, who had been laying siege to the town for more than seven weeks. After that, there was only the formality of being admitted through the breast-works and batteries Cos had ordered erected on Soledad and Main Streets.

Installing the lady Rafaela into one of the Veramendi bedrooms proved to be more challenging. The troops garrisoned there, most of them ex-convicts, were stumbling over each other in their efforts to accommodate her.

Nevertheless, he posted a guard at her door, more to protect her from the soldiers' approaches than to keep watch on her movements. "When you have rested, I would count it a boon if you would join the officers and myself for dinner."

Her eyes flickered uncertainly. "Is that a command or a request?"

"As I said, my lady, you are our esteemed guest." Santiago bowed low, as if he were at the Spanish court of King Philip.

"But, of course." She dipped into a curtsey before closing the bedroom door on the guard and on him.

He spent the next two hours closeted with Cos, who had ridden over from his command position at another mission, the Alamo, just outside the town. They pored over a hastily sketched map of the area, indicating positions of the enemy, fortified on the town's east side.

The news was not encouraging. In Santiago's absence, a cavalry troop had fought a skirmish with the rebels. They and their leader, James Bowie, had captured supply mules with fodder. A mere grass fight, but now Cos was forced to keep the soldiers divided between the town and the Alamo.

"Worse, our troops' morale is declining," the general frowned. Cos was married to Santa Anna's sister and was thirty-five, the same age as Santiago himself.

"The good news," Cos continued, "is our dispatches indicate Col. Ugartechea should arrive soon with six hundred veteran troops from Laredo."

Pues, that should help rout the rebels."

Cos winked at him. "And I take it your good news concerns the pretty captive you have taken? Do you plan to keep her for yourself or to share her?"

"I am not the tactician Santa Anna is." He alluded to the president's penchant for wedding a young girl from a conquered town through a sham marriage performed by one of his soldiers dressed as a priest—this, despite the fact that Santa Anna was already married.

"But you will bed her?"

"I am engaged, general."

"Ahhh, that has not stopped you before."

No, but Rafaela Carrera is different.

When later she appeared at dinner, she had washed away the dust and tidied up. Along with two lieutenant colonels, a major, and a first captain, they gathered at a table set up in the overly large reception room and partook of roasted venison and local wine. If she was at all flustered by his men's distracting attentions, she gave no indication of it. Her replies were brief but courteous.

Though reserved, when questioned, she spoke eloquently of her life in England and was knowledgeable of literature and politics. "Yes, it is gossiped that the Heiress Apparent Victoria is controlled by Sir John Conroy, but I suspect she has more mettle than yet evidenced."

When he asked what she knew of Urrea's troops garrisoned at Fort Guerrero in Matamoros, she shrugged. "I have never been in the city itself, Colonel Calaveras, and devoutly hope I never shall be. Since disembarking at its port, I—and my lady companion—have stayed at the residence of… of a family friend who lives outside that city."

He wondered whether she had lost her way while out riding, as she had claimed when he and his lancers had chanced upon her—or if she was perhaps a spy for the rioters. She was a study in ice, and something in him—some vestige of the savage beast that lurked in a man's breast—wanted to melt that ice.

As the general had pointed out, there had been women in various Tejas pueblos he had bedded. Never had he the need to resort to rape, as had some of his soldiers. He liked to think it was his good looks that enticed the young women, but suspected it was more likely their prospects of escaping the pigsty that was Tejas in hopes of moving elsewhere.

He took another drink. Perhaps it was the wine, or rather too much of it—that, and his lengthy time without a woman—that prompted him to dismiss the guard posted outside her door when dinner was over.

The hour was well past midnight, but that did not prevent him from entering her room ahead of her with his oil lamp, which he set on the commode. She stood just inside the doorway, waiting for him to leave. So maybe she was not attracted to him. He crossed to her. "I find I am desirous of your company tonight, *Señorita* Carrera."

Her eyes were twin pools of melancholy. "I had thought you a gentleman."

He flung off his scabbard belt and rapier, shaking his head, perhaps to shake off the spirits' affects. "No. Only a lonely officer in need of a woman's touch."

Her face froze. She retreated a step toward the door, ajar. "You had said I was to be your guest."

His crossed the intervening space and grasped her wrist with one hand, the other shoving the door closed. Her free hand slapped at his jaw. He ducked his head, avoiding her palm, and pulled her to him. "Is that so difficult? To be held by me?"

She tried to tug away. "To be held—or to be defiled?"

"No." He shook his head again. "No, I have no intention of—"

She spun from him, stumbling over a footstool and taking both of them down, crashing against the bedstead's footboard.

Angry at her accusation, angry at himself, he hauled her onto the mattress. She fought him, fists pummeling his brass buttons and epaulets. She rolled free and sprang for the door, jerking it open. He caught her by the waist and whirled her around.

The sight of the tears welling in her eyes stopped him cold. That and the heavy gunfire that rang out—both in the street outside and on the roof directly overhead. Axes were splintering the ceiling. In the room beyond, his officers rushed with weapons drawn. His sergeant wore only his sleeping shirt. Somewhere, a bugle sounded the alarm.

At the wrenching of wood at the window, he spun around and groped for his rapier. Behind him, the window's shutters burst asunder. The young woman screamed as he whirled to face the assailant.

Wielding a crowbar, a mustached man in a sheepskin coat shoved through. Santiago lunged with his rapier. The man dodged and landed on his feet, catlike. Knees bent, they circled one another. Behind him, Santiago could hear the other officers engaged in their own combat.

He feinted left, dodging a blow and slipping in. The man was quick as a cat. His crowbar sent Santiago's rapier sailing. At that, Santiago flung himself at the attacker. The crowbar swung toward his head. A crushing blast of light and incredible pain exploded through Santiago. The last thing he was ever to hear was the young woman's outcry.

"*Niall!*

DESPITE THE COLD, GUSTY WIND, sweat beaded underneath Paladín's leather jacket—in the dark hair matting his chest, underarm tufts, and narrow line of hair that arrowed past his navel.

As he swung the pickax into the charred oak slab that had once served as a fireplace mantle, muscles roping his stomach, back, and arms stretched tight beneath his jacket. His filthy leather breeches barely clung to his hipbones.

He was thankful for the message, coming the day after Cavett's gala, that called him away from all the ongoing drama in Matamoros—and from Fiona Flanagan.

His twenty-five-plus years had seen more than enough drama. He might blame his coming to Tejas to restore his brother Enrique's property to functionality as a means to find peace.

Instead, he had found wholesale murdering, unscrupulous dealings, and a firecracker of an Irish lass that rivaled the fireworks so prevalent in India.

Of course, Rafaela's monumental inheritance upon her father's death was not to be dismissed so cavalierly, but after his sojourn in India, all else had lost its value and powerful appeal, even wealth. Even love. Even sex.

Until Fiona tripped up his life.

The Mexicans deemed coyotes the tricksters, though Hindu mythology likened Hanuman and even the infant Krishna. But the scamp Fiona Flanigan was amongst a class of tricksters all her own, with that resolute will and innocent face, complete with its cinnamon dusting of freckles.

What a sinfully sensuous delight it would be to have her beneath him and to play connect the dots with all those freckles of hers.

The need to restore the ruins of Enrique's property was a welcome excuse to put distance between himself and the Irish lass.

He left off dismantling the fireplace of the burnt-out hacienda and strode, ax in hand, up the bluff that overlooked the Nueces River. Downstream another sixty or so miles, the river emptied into the Gulf of Mexico.

The river provided the land grant with rich river bottoms, alluvial soil to fertilize its luxuriant wither-high prairie grass, and timberland that supported elm, cottonwood, pecan, and mesquite—and would comfortably support the herds of Brahman cattle he planned to import from India.

At the apex of the bluff, a huge, one-hundred-foot tall live oak tree spread a seventy-five-foot canopy of branches beset by mistletoe. Beneath the tree, three tombstones commemorated lives that had come and gone—his older brother, Enrique's adoring and frivolous wife Graciela, and their three-year-old daughter Lucera.

The entire family scalped and murdered by the Comanche—all for the sake of payment in the form of firearms, liquor, and gewgaws.

But who paid the Comanche raiders?

The lives of Enrique and his family had been for naught. As had the life of Paladín's mother... and his sister... and Annapoorna, his lovely, dusk-skinned Punjabi wife.

His memory of her—her soft laughter, her exotic brown eyes, her sparkling teeth that contrasted with the caramelized color of her skin, her sensually tapered hennaed hands—was blurred by a sometimes unbearable and tormented guilt.

Aye, he had extinguished her life—one shot aimed directly at the bright red bindi between her eyebrows, the exit for her Kundalini energy.

More the sense of something behind him than an actual sound prompted him to pivot, axe raised for the throw.

Deaf Smith was approaching through the grass, palm upraised. "Whoa!"

Alex faced Smith squarely and spaced his words for the partially deaf man, who read lips for the most part. "You have lost your skill, Smith. An armadillo would rumble through the grass quieter."

Smith shot him a crooked grin. "You'd be dead two minutes ago had I had a hankering. But the general wants your carcass alive."

"And why is that?"

"He thinks some chicanery is going on over at San Felipe. Word got to him that a secret meeting is being held tomorrow. He wants you there."

They hunkered down against the live oak's broad trunk, shielding them against the wind. Paladín scoured his knapsack and offered Smith a hunk of deer jerky. "You do not give me much time."

The man's yellowed teeth yanked at the plug of dried meat. "Let's say I got delayed in a little skirmish. We took Bexar from Cos yesterday. 'Cept old Ben

Milam was struck in his temple during the house-to-house combat. Dead in front of Veramendi Palace 'fore we dragged him outta the line of fire."

"Sorry to hear that. Houston said Milam was invaluable treating with the Comanche."

Smith bit off another piece of jerky. "Don't guess you'll be sorry to learn Niall tracked down your fiancée. She was detained by one of Cos's dragoon officers. Holed up there in Veramendi Palace."

Then both were all right. He was mildly surprised to find the two this far north, but, at least, that was two fewer to worry over. Although, this trip to San Felipe Houston was asking him to make would mean he wouldn't be there when Niall delivered his fiancée back into his keeping.

Paladín knew if he were an honorable man, he would send Rafaela back to her father, along with her bridal dowry. If he were an honorable man, he would give Enrique's land to Fiona, for there was really nothing to hold him here—nothing to hold him anywhere.

But he was not an honorable man.

8

Rafaela Carrera was the height of Niall's folly.

She had been shattered. He had seen it in her vacant gaze. He had stepped around the accumulation of soldiers' bodies and approached her softly, gently, one step at a time as he would a mistreated horse. "Easy, girl," he had whispered.

She had stood in the midst of mind-stultifying carnage and blinked, staring blankly up at him.

He had held out his gloved palm. "Let us go home."

"Home?"

"Home." Whatever that word meant for her. Surely, it had stirred some resonance of safety, at least, more than the present circumstances had offered, with bloody bodies strewn around her.

For him the word "home" held no meaning whatever—or, at least, not the significance people outside the clan attached to that word.

Patiently, he had waited. Still, she had yet to offer her hand. As he had leaned near her ear, he had kept his features expressionless. "'Tis all right. Everything is going to be all right. Get your cloak and come with me."

She had.

He was taking her home… home to *Presidio* La Espada. It would take two more days of all-out riding southwest, two days if weather cooperated.

It did not.

———

THROUGHOUT THAT COLD, DRIZZLY DAY, she sat like a stone statue in the saddle of the bay he had commandeered. He had hoped to cross the Nueces and a goodly portion of the Wild Horse Desert before nightfall, but the lightning, rare for that time of year, prompted him to halt at an escarpment that offered shallow shelter.

He dismounted and held up his hands to help her dismount. She did not move—just sat there with the rain making a soggy mess of her hooded cloak.

He sighed and, clasping her waist, pulled her out of the saddle. Docilely, she let him draw her into a lee offered by a five-foot bluff. Staking the horses, he unsaddled them and made a bulwark of the saddles in front of this make-shift shelter to offer protection, slight though it was, from the light but frigid rain.

By the time he ducked under the ledge, the stormy sky was a ghoulish blend of purple and ebony hues. With her arms wrapped around legs, drawn up against her chest, she sat with her forehead propped on her knees.

Out of a saddlebag, he fished a threadbare blanket, as rank smelling as he no doubt was, but it was about as good as he could provide against the cold. A stick of wood, much less dry wood, would be difficult to scrounge between there and Matamoros.

He draped the blanket around her shoulders.

Neither a word from her or the flicker of a glance at him.

He shrugged. All the better. She was Paladín's fiancée, and it was better for her and him that he keep his distance. He withdrew a tin of hardtack and jerky from another saddlebag, along with a wooden canteen. "You need to eat."

She said nothing. Did not stir.

Well, he would not force-feed her. He wolfed down a biscuit with a couple of plugs of jerky, drank the last of water from the canteen, and, holding it arm's length, refilled it with the steady-dripping rain. He turned on his side for some shuteye, with his crooked arm serving as a pillow.

Sometime during the night, he was aware of her body scrunched against his back, her teeth chattering like castanets. He rolled over and gathered her into the warmth of his concaved body, spoon-fashion. His arms overlapped hers, and they lay like that while the rain plip-plopped inches away. After a few minutes, her teeth stopped chattering, but she was feverish.

A lightning bolt zig-zagged across the black firmaments, leaving the smell of scorched hide and sulfur. Gradually, he became aware of only her. Her unique smell. Her hair, her skin, her sweat. He had discovered that however attracted he might be to a woman, if her particular scent did not please him, he was not meant to be with her.

His nose, broken though it might be, was reliable in the matter of scents. Rafaela's scent was powerfully arousing.

Lean though she might be, with only a slight swelling of breasts, she looked to possess stamina and would be a woman who would weather the years well.

Strange. Usually when with women, it was all about charm and seduction, giving and leaving. If he took a little pleasure also, then he considered his efforts well paid.

But this young woman who could read and write and spoke half a dozen languages elicited a gentleness in him that he normally reserved only for animals, for he believed they were far more civilized than humans.

She began to cough—a deep, wracking cough. Instinctively, he settled his hand on her flank, as if gentling a spirited filly, and sought sleep. With the dawn's scanty light, he would have to scour the area for rabbit tobacco.

With luck, the plant's silvery leaves, mashed to a pulp, would sooth her throat and reduce the mucous build-up in the lungs. Without it, he would be bringing back her carcass to La Espada after all.

SAN FELIPE DE AUSTIN

The provisional government of Tejas convened in the unfinished one-room house serving as San Felipe de Austin's town hall—now temporarily housing the printing press for the *Telegraph and Texas Register,* the unofficial voice of the Texas revolution movement.

In lieu of glass, cotton cloth stretched across the structure's windows, in-sulating only partly the crude building from a bitterly cold and damp after-noon. A single brass lamp hung suspended from the ceiling by a chain that creaked each time the door opened and let in the wind.

Outside the hall, occasional rumbles of thunder interrupted a steady drizzle. The dozen or so thoroughly soaked council members shuffled inside, seeking chairs around the table close to the hearth's small, but crackling fire.

Although there were enough benches and chairs to seat the entire secret meeting of the General Council, the Chaparral Fox stood at the back and off to one side.

The General Council sought to create a separate state out of Tejas. He sought to create his own empire.

He had been creating that empire since he was nine years old, when his doting mother parted the blanketed bundle cuddled with her in bed to reveal the baby. His sister, his mother told him. His rival in a household that had been wholly dedicated to his welfare. After his sister's arrival, he was either overlooked, forgotten, or dismissed. As if he did not exist.

The pain of being consigned to oblivion had tortured him every breathing second, soon becoming unendurable. Awake or asleep, his mind bled.

A pillow silenced the baby's squalls and his pain.

It was not the first time. There had been his mother's pampered lap dog and his father's cherished Bible that he had been forever, monotonously reading. And other rivals that blurred with time. Others of which he had disposed. Through the years, with repetition, he had become more skilled, admirably inventive, and deceptively adept at ridding himself of rivals.

These latest rivals—this swarm of settlers, thinking to come and take whatever they wanted —well, it was easy enough to cover one's tracks when dealing with oafs and idiots who understood nothing about the complexity and problems of overseeing something as large as what he envisioned.

Observing the noble council members, he was barely able to keep from sneering. If anyone ever thought a revolution was solely about patriotism, he was a fool. Most revolutionaries were in it for power and profit.

Next to him paced the wealthy Scotsman, Dr. James Grant. Fretting over large properties he owned in Parras, Mexico—which he wanted back—he was only posing as a Tejas patriot when self-interest motivated him. However, Dr. Grant was a small-time schemer. His values and principles were so liquid, they were easily molded to the Chaparral Fox's own purposes.

Because of some amount of subterfuge on the part of the Fox's, two council members were noticeably absent from the secret consultation. One being the Texican's provisional governor, Henry Smith. The American did not believe in compromise and did not exercise the language of diplomacy. The General Council had recently felt compelled to impeach him in office.

The other absentee was Smith's colleague, Sam Houston. Fox had managed both directly and indirectly to influence the General Council to order the Texican general to the eastern part of Tejas to broker a treaty with the Cherokee.

A weary James Fannin slouched in a chair alongside San Felipe's attorney, William Travis. Both had returned from the siege of San Antonio, and Fannin was reporting.

"After four days of house-to-house fighting, we forced General Cos to surrender and to sign a pledge never to return to Tejas." The slave trader waited until the congratulations of the dozen or so men died down, then continued. "Our casualties numbered thirty to thirty-five, while Mexican losses totaled about one fifty."

"The difference reflects the greater accuracy of our Texicans' long rifles," an equally worn-out Travis said. His features fatigued, his hand was braced on his own rifle, upright and supporting him. "Our men were as brave as ever shouldered a rifle. All the Mexican soldiers have been driven from Tejas, which puts all of Tejas under our control now."

The favorable moment had arrived. The Chaparral Fox nodded at James Robinson. As lieutenant governor, Robinson had acting authority to set in motion the impeachment of Governor Smith.

But, first things first.

The portly, balding man spoke up. "Then I believe now would be the opportune time to take Matamoros, gentlemen. It is Santa Anna's most strategic point from which to supervise the political and military affairs of northern Mexico. You would have command of its port's $100,000-month revenue and command of the Gulf of Mexico from there to New Orleans. What is more, you would prevent Santa Anna using it as a staging ground to invade Texas."

The Chaparral Fox had coached him well. Robinson capitalized on the prospect such a cause offered his fragmented provisional government. "Think of it! You would only need to gather whatever provisions you can from San Antonio de Bexar, and the three or four hundred men left garrisoned there, and march on Matamoros."

"I would think that decision would fall under General Houston's directive," came a harsh voice from the doorway behind the Chaparral Fox. All eyes turned upon Paladín, who had just entered the town hall, shedding his rain-drenched coat and floppy, wide-brimmed black hat.

What a damned shame, the Chaparral Fox thought, that Lazarus had failed to take him down. He raised a brow at the lieutenant governor, who took his cue. "We have no time to await the Commander in Chief's return. I put forth that Dr. Grant be appointed acting commander in chief."

Grant stepped forward, a humble smile plastered on his lantern-jawed face. "I am honored to accept. I can think of no better associate to help me lead the expedition than Fannin here."

The suggestion of the slave trader Fannin as an agent for the expedition came at the Chaparral Fox's prompting. The West Pointer had seen action and had experience leading others. The Chaparral Fox knew that would mollify men like Travis and the others, who were uncertain about the wisdom of such an expedition.

Wet coat draped over his arm, hat in hand, Paladín strode toward the table to confront Robinson. "I do not believe you have a sufficient quorum present to authorize such an action."

Robinson's faced reddened, and he blustered, "I say we take a vote. All in favor of the Matamoros Expedition?"

With the barest of smiles, the Chaparral Fox watched as, one by one, the hands raised, albeit more than a few hesitantly.

Smugly, Robinson struck his gavel. He rose, hands planted on the table, to face the much taller Paladín. "Motion passed."

The Chaparral Fox had won the battle with Paladín, but he also intended to win this war, giving no quarter.

SLOWLY COMING OUT OF A deep sleep, the first thing Rafaela was aware of was the rank smell of wet leather. Then the sound of light rain dripping near and the cold feeling of her nose, toes, and fingers.

She lay on her side. When she opened her eyes, she made out saddles in front of her... and then felt the solidity of something behind her. With the horror at Veramendi Palace prowling in the back of her mind, she peered over her blanket-draped shoulder warily.

Niall hunkered down next to her. Patiently, he was watching her, which clued her that he had been waiting for her to awake.

Her thoughts as hazy as the fog beyond, she knew he had been tending to her, but she knew not for how long. It was all a blur. "Where are we?"

"Ye've been sick for nigh on two days now." He held out a canteen and biscuit. His face was smooth of expression. "Fresh rainwater."

She made no move to accept either. As much as she was attracted to him, he was the enemy. He was hauling her back to *Presidio* La Espada. Her flight had been for naught... except for more misery.

Lord Paladín's polite but command performance to attend a soiree at the home of Cavett Magnum had inspired her practically headlong flight.

It had been a shock to learn that her father's legal representative in London had settled in the Mexican province of Tejas. She could not fathom why Cavett, who had taken from her all she held dear, had now decamped to such a Godforsaken outpost. What could possibly have motivated that swine's presence there? More than likely, his deep-seated greed sensed some extraordinary opportunity to expand her purloined fortune.

"I think ye should drink, me lady. 'Tis the smart thing to do."

She looked deep into those eloquent blue eyes that sloped at the outer corners. They warmed her as the blanket could never. "You think I am smart?" It was a caustic comment.

With his mustache hitched at one end, she mused that his skewed grin likely caused the hearts of women, young and old, to do somersaults. "Why would I think not? Ye read and ye write and handle your own finances, so Paladín says."

With care for her pounding head, she sat upright and took the canteen, feeling his fingertips touch hers momentarily. She was reluctant to lose contact, but she gulped the water. The biscuit was like biting into brick. She made a face.

Chuckling, he withdrew a knife from his boot and cut the biscuit into small pieces.

Between hungry bites, she managed, "You might think not if you knew I had lost all my carefully horded savings."

His bloodhound-like brows that followed the outer slope of his eyes furrowed in puzzlement. "An unwise investment does not make ye a donkey, does it?"

Unable to meet his gaze, she finished the biscuit in shamed silence.

"Come along now. We have a long ride ahead of us. This weather tisn't cooperating." His words fell lightly, as if he were Hansel dropping white pebbles for her to follow. He grasped her hand gently and lifted her upright.

She faced him squarely, eyes on level with his. Anger simmered within her. Anger at herself—how she so easily accepted the dictates of others. Anger at him—that he was forcing her to return to a life she did not want.

That anger was compounded by the wholly illogical anger at the unconscionable, despicable act that had held such horrendous consequences for her. "I did *not* unwisely invest. My money was stolen from me by a man trading on my adulation!"

His eyes searched hers, looking for what she knew not. Could he read minds, as well as palms? At last, he said in that musical voice that could soothe the soul, "I truly am sorry for your pain, my lady."

Her battlements of anger had been breached. She felt herself blinking faster and faster... felt her lower lip quiver.

He took her by surprise. Gently pushing back her cloak's hood, he brushed with his gloved fingertips one cheek, where wetness had spilt over the lid's dyke. That was all. She saw compassion in his eyes. That was more than she could endure.

She spun away and ran to the staked horses. Her only thought was to mount the bay and ride like the hounds of hell were hot on her heels. She stopped short, standing in the cold drizzle and feeling very foolish. The horses were still unsaddled.

Niall bypassed her, saddle slung on one arm, and began to saddle and bridle his roan. His back was to her. "How did it happen, me lady?" He jerked the cinch tight.

"How does not matter. The deed is done."

Finished checking the strap, he circled around her to retrieve the remaining saddle and set about saddling and bridling her bay. "It matters to you, so tell me."

Her lips compressed into an unstable conjuncture. Her lids squeezed shut. "He was an American in London." Bile, as foul tasting as the Cavett's kiss had turned out to be, burned her throat.

"Go on now." Niall was close enough that she could feel his breath on her cheeks.

Eyes closed, she tilted her head back, her face heavenward, as if expecting redemption from the Almighty. Rain drops splashed her eyelids.

"A business associate of my father's." Her voice seemed more rasp than whisper. "He had agreed to check in on me occasionally at the boarding school. Formality... at the beginning. At least, that was what I presumed."

She hesitated, hands clenching and unclenching, afraid she would give away the man's identity. She could not risk involving Niall.

"I was scarcely fourteen that Christmas, when most of the teachers and students were away. I was so lonely... and he came bearing gifts—chocolate from the Sweet Shoppe Confectioners and a lace handkerchief embroidered with my initials—as well as kind, understanding words for me.

"He even took the time to help me invest money forwarded by my father for daily necessities. I had horded the monthly cheques against... against just such circumstances as I now find myself. A forced marriage." She choked, unable to force any more words past her lips.

"Do not stop until your story is told."

She bowed her head, drawing a shaky breath, and the rain droplets slipped down her face. "I... he was my father's loyal surrogate, in a sense. Someone who loved me. When he bestowed a chaste kiss, I had liked it. He cared for me. I trusted him. Felt safe with him. And I did not protest when he went further with his... his affections."

Still, not an interruptive word from Niall.

Shame warred with bitterness. "And I... I welcomed any attention.

Even later, I penned him a note about my… strong feeling for him. So, one fateful day, I signed without even looking at the paper he put before me."

She shuddered, then finished with an expenditure of energy that left her depleted. "I do not imagine the Crown would deem it embezzlement. And how could I tell my father of his friend's betrayal without divulging my own deception, my own complicity?"

Once again, Niall lifted her chin to brush away the tears she had thought raindrops sliding down each cheek. His square, gauntleted palms cupped her face. "Me lady, let us go home."

She looked into those blue eyes. Such translucent depths. How had she ever thought him a simpleton? Drained, she sagged into his arms. Scooping her depleted body against his chest, he carried her to the bay and set her astride it. Wearily, she looked down at him. "Thank you, Niall." She used his given name for the first time.

"For what?"

She did not know what to say and ended up with, "For taking care of me."

"'Tis my duty." With that, he mounted his own horse and headed out into the drizzling mist.

"For how long?" she called after him, wondering if that duty could ever evolve into more.

"Until my gut says giddy-up and go."

Falling in behind, she nevertheless thought it strange he had used the word "home" more than once that morning, when he was a man repelled by that concept. He treated her with a formal gentility that seemed as much a part of him as his spontaneous violence.

As the morning passed, the rain stopped, and the air became chillier. Frost winked on the ground, and vapor steamed from the horses' nostrils like dragon breath. Her thoughts continued to dwell on Niall.

God help her, she had gone and started to fall in love with the worst of the lot. A paddy. A gypsy. A wandering minstrel. A *Traveler*. Here today and gone tomorrow. But then, he had gone and turned her world into one of those wondrous songs he played. He had traveled a hundred miles to find her, had killed three soldiers, storming the Veramendi bedroom in order to keep her safe.

And all that was only in the name of "duty?"

"Those three soldiers you shot at Veramendi Palace, you were one against three. What if you had missed?

"I do not miss."

"And if there'd been more soldiers who poured through the bedroom door?"

"I still had one bullet left."

She rode up abreast of him. "But not enough to kill them all," she stated, feeling somehow self-satisfied.

"No. The one left would have killed you."

Her breath wheezed, as if she had taken a blow to her stomach. "So, you are my Angel of Death?"

"If need be. And if one of them had plugged my brain with a bullet, I still would have killed them all before dying."

She shivered, and it was not from the bone-penetrating cold alone. The rain eventually stopped, but a cloudy haze accompanied them on their ride southwest... and the shadow of her love for—aye, a killer—accompanied them. Without halting, he offered a midday repast of still tart blueberries dug from his saddlebag. He was in a haste to reach the mission before nightfall.

"How did you come to know my fia–Lord Paladín?

She could almost feel Niall grinning. "You might say he saved me body from becoming a pin cushion for bullets."

Wiping the blueberry juice from her lips with the back of her hand, she twisted in her saddle toward him. "He what?"

His eyes darted to her blueberry-tinted lips, doubtlessly blue from the cold as well, before settling his sights on the mist-shrouded horizon. "When I learned of my sister's death, I traveled all the way from Kentucky to Tejas."

"I'm sorry to hear that. You two must have been very close."

"We were twins. Looked so much alike that as children, we fooled others."

He chuckled. "Got out of lots of scrapes that way. When Bridget would start to say something, I would know her thoughts and finish her sentence before her first few words could tumble out. When she died, I knew of her death before any message ever reached me. I awoke that morning to attend a horse auction but never went. I sat drinking coffee, while aching hurt coursed clear through all me bones. I knew something fierce was about to happen to one of us—or had already."

"Of what did she die?"

"Indian marauders scalped her and the man who had brought her to Tejas. Mexican authorities pay bounties for Indian scalps. Bloodthirsty scalp hunters—Indians, Americans, Mexicans—they all take scalps, doesn't matter whose. They sell the scalps of men, women, and children to the government of Chihuahua in northern Mexico. The pay rate of $200 per scalp exceeds a soldier's wages for a year."

She shivered again, but he went on tonelessly. "Through discreet, or indiscreet, inquiries of the underworld at Baja Matamoros, the Port of Matamoros—these days it abounds with such ilk as adventurers, smugglers, and pirates—I learned the attack was no unplanned spate of violence. Those marauders were on someone's payroll. Someone with money and influence. Someone called the Chaparral Fox."

Against the mist's cold fingers, she pulled her sodden cloak more tightly around her. "But how then did Lord Paladín play a part in saving you?"

"When I look back, I had been drinking and was spoiling for a fight that first week. I shouldered through the Caballo Negro cantina in Baja Matamoros with the intent of tracking down a man named Camargo. Word was that he and his *vaqueros* rustled cattle and was not above carrying out other illegal activities, for the right money. Activities like murder and mutilation."

He paused, seemingly for the purpose of merely stroking the mane of his mount. "So, it happened that Camargo and his crew were there that night. He was playing monte at a table where Paladín also sat. He had seen me coming and must have deduced my intention. He rose and coaxed me to accompany him to the bar. Reminded me over several Irish whiskeys—a man after me own heart—that I would reap me revenge more thoroughly if I would but just cut off the snake's head, then the body would die on its own. 'Tis the Chaparral Fox we're after."

Once Niall found the viper's head and cut it off, he would be on his way again. But not her. She was going back. Returning to marry Lord Paladín, when she had felt drawn to Niall Gorman from that first moment of their meeting at the Port of Matamoros landing.

His sense of wonderment delighted her. The far-away look in his eye beckoned her to look again. Yes, this gentle minstrel and fierce gunman had enchanted her heart.

The swirling cold mist was thicker now, making it nigh impossible to see each other clearly, even from the half-dozen feet that separated their two mounts. For that she was glad. "You know I cannot go back to Lord Paladín."

"Why not?"

"Because I am in love with you."

A silence followed that revealed everything. "What you are feeling... 'tis only gratitude."

She felt as if he had slapped her. "Do you think you have put me in my place? Making it clear to me that you are a man not to be restrained by such foolish ties as love?"

"I warned you." His usually musical voice was hard, flat, and toneless.

"You might not love me, but I know you desire me." She could hardly believe she was saying this.

"You are to marry Paladín, and that is all there is to it—to *us.*"

9

MATAMOROS
STATE OF TAMAULIPAS, MEXICO

With a paring knife, Fiona scraped vanilla beans from their long mahogany pods. The faint fragrance of the beans she had harvested the day before from a straggly vine in one of the garden's far corners was heavenly.

Since childhood, she had loved playing in the dirt, digging in the soil and fingering plants, cupping her hands to her nose to inhale deeply their various scents. Today, with a winter storm threatening, there would be no working with the earth. So much for Matamoros's famed semi-arid climate, with mild winters and hot summers cooled by Gulf breezes.

Since returning from Cavett's party nearly a week ago, she breathed a little easier. Paladín appeared to have shrugged off the episode with her in front of the Land Commissioner's office. Indeed, he had absented himself from the *presidio* shortly thereafter, more than likely occupying his time at one of Matamoros's bordellos or gaming palaces.

But where now was Rafaela? Had she safely escaped Paladín's long-armed reach in the form of the Irish Traveler?

Fiona meant to do so as well, as soon as the deed to her land grant was confirmed. Suppose it was not? She jabbed the knife blade at the pod. By God, she would go all the way to Mexico City to appeal if she had to.

Across the kitchen table, Winnie chopped garlic. "The Mexicans say the vanilla alleviates toothaches. That remedy might be of use to my old goat."

"Your old goat?"

Winnie's smile creased her face into a fan of wrinkles. "Frederick. He's suffering something fierce."

"How long have you two been married?"

"Forty-one years, but we have known each other forever. He was a chimney sweep. A wee pint-size lad. The Master Sweep brought him often to clean the chimney of the Paladín home. A veritable mansion it was. Back then, I was the laundry girl. Only at first. Then I graduated to cook's help. More to my liking. That was how I met Fredrick. Caught him stealing a treacle tart, I did."

"Then you knew Lord Paladín when he was a boy?"

"And not any bit better mannered than me Frederick." She chortled. "Master Alex thought I never noticed when he stole me tarts. I would set them out on the windowsill to cool. The few times I was mad enough to reprimand the laddie, he would wrap his arm around me shoulders. Kiss me cheek until I got over me fit. I couldn't help forgive his knavish ways."

Ahhh, she felt some satisfaction that her assessment of the rake was justified. "Then he was a troublesome child."

"Oh my, no. There was a daughter, and he was the younger of two sons, but the most responsible of the three."

She made a scoffing noise. "Paladín? Responsible?"

Winnie cast the garlic bits into the kettle suspended from the fireplace crane. "Went off to King Edward's School in Birmingham and graduated with flying colors. From there he joined the East India Tea Company—while his older brother Enrique was dismissed from Winchester College and went on to squander the family inheritance."

Fiona's paring knife paused. She looked askance at the old woman. "But rumor has it that it was Paladín who squandered his inheritance."

"That's blather. Master Alex had none to squander. The Law of Entail prohibited him from inheriting. No, Enrique was too proud to counter that gossip. Ended up here in Tejas with the last of the family land. Frederick and I had already come with Enrique and his family to help them make this new start."

Winnie's perturbed expression caused Fiona to ask, "Did Enrique fail here as well?"

"No, no, he really tried. Me thinks he realized it was his last chance, but the Comanche murdered him and all his family. Frederick and meself were spared, because we had gone into San—"

"Hhmph," Frederick muttered from behind them. The cherub-looking older man wearing a woolen cap shoved Liam forward. "The laddie has something for ye, Miss Fiona."

The street urchin's mouth crimped into an inverted "u." He stuck out a grimy fist and unfolded it to display a gold watch and fob.

She glanced back at Frederick for an explanation. His ruddy cheeks became even redder, if that were possible. "Found him coming out of the master's bedchamber."

"I was bringing it for you to polish, Fio–er, Mam."

She bit back a bloody oath, though she could not blame Liam. The gold watch would have gone a long way toward making life easier. The boy had a quick mind, and she had taken to tutoring him at night in reading from books still unpacked in Paladín's office.

"I will see that it is polished, son. Meanwhile you can take a spell turning the quail on the spit."

A short time later, easing open the double doors to what had been the padre's quarters and was now the devil's playroom, she stepped tentatively inside, closing the doors quietly behind her. The four-poster's bedcovers were untouched. Not surprising. Like a vampire, Paladín stayed out until the wee hours of the morning most nights. She doubted that his misbegotten soul slept much at all.

Bleak sunlight falling through the high window illuminated the holy altar of stone, serving as Paladín's commode. On it stood a wooden statue of Saint Francis. With a sigh at what might have been, she returned the gold watch and fob, draping it from Saint Francis's neck.

She caught the statue's accusing wooden stare. Her eyes darted to Paladín's fine linen handkerchief carelessly tossed atop the altar. Perversity caused her to pick up the handkerchief and, with a few deft folds and knots, blindfold St. Francis.

"There." The patron saint should not be watching the orgies that doubtlessly went on in the bedchamber when Paladín was in residence.

Satisfied, she bypassed the huge bed again. As tall as Paladín was, he would need a bed so massive. Her fingers trailed across the heavy down-filled coverlets. What kind of pleasuring did go on in his bed?

Crikey, why was it Paladín ignited a rush of fire in her veins, a quivering in her belly? When with him, she felt woefully hampered by the straitjacket of language. Despite the norther bearing down and the dramatically dropping temperature outside, her skin flushed warmly.

She moved beyond the bed to one of the two arched doorways tucked at the back of the quarters. One led, of course, to the chapel. As she suspected, the other doorway opened to a narrow stone staircase that housed a frayed bell rope. Faint afternoon light from above barely illuminated the spiraling steps. She picked her way among the occasional loose stones as she ascended.

The view was breathtaking. In the distance snaked the chocolate ribbon of the Rio Bravo. Its cottonwoods held pieces of a tumultuous sky in their branches. The frigid wind yanked non-compliant strands loose from the haphazard knot at her nape and sent her lawn cap sailing over the parapet's edge.

Briskly rubbing her goose-bumped arms, she cautiously approached the parapet. Hands braced gingerly on its crumbling stone ledge, she looked over the dizzying height to the scene below—Frederick leading Raj to the stables. Which meant....

———————————

A STONE GAVE WAY AND Fiona teetered, arms flung wide. From behind her, Paladín's hands bracketed her shoulders. Should she fall, it would be one less claimant for his land.

He was in a foul mood. After the fiasco at San Felipe, he wanted to take his frustration out on the nearest thing at hand... and here it—or she—was.

The vote at the San Felipe meeting of the Provisional Government of Tejas had gone down disastrously. He wasn't surprised to see Magnum vote in favor of the Matamoros Expedition. After all, it had been his suggestion to begin with. Somehow, someway, the opportunist would find a way to profit from the Expedition.

Nevertheless, Alex had still held out hope the other members could be swayed to vote against the Expedition.

"Careful." His grip steadied her. Her zest and intelligence aroused him from his dark underworld of torment. Her wit and passion took him by surprise. Her latest caper, blindfolding the statue of Saint Francis....

She spun around, her eyes accusatory. "I almost fell to me death!"

One hand still anchoring her shoulder and his body pressing hers against the parapet, the fingers of his other captured a swath of spiraling hair the wind lashed across her face. "This tower is cursed. La Espada—the Sword. Death. You must have known."

"I do not believe in curses and spells." Her voice amplified to defeat the wind.

His thumb and forefinger twined the swath of curls he held. In the storm's eerie light, they were the color of cinnamon and copper. He raised his voice against the pummeling wind. "Ahhh, then you do not believe that a lock of someone's hair can be used to cast a spell on them?"

She glanced over her shoulder at the yawning space below and tried to sidle away, but he gripped her shoulders, holding her fast. "If ye believe in such nonsense, then ye are truly daft."

With thunder booming overhead and the wind wailing around them, he lowered his head beside hers to make himself better heard. "In feudal times, a chivalrous knight wore a lock of his lady's pubic hair into battle."

As he perversely hoped, her lively eyes widened in shock, then they shot sparks. "That ye will never have from me."

"You do see, my love, your hair symbolizes your life force that I would be carrying with me. That hair would serve as my connecting cables to heaven."

With a splattering of cold rain drops starting to fall, her eyes closed, and her heated response came as more a disgusted exhalation. "Ye do not believe in heaven."

"My Lord," he reminded her, "or else I shall release you—and a long fall it is, too."

Her lids snapped open. Their expression hinted that she was tempted to flout him. As if she had considered the possibility he might, indeed, mean what he said, she muttered, "Me Lord."

At that, he chuckled. "Maybe you don't believe in curses and spells," his hand drifted down from her wind-whipped hair to finger her shoddy four-leaf-clover locket, "but you do believe in good luck charms."

Only peripherally during the fortnight had he become aware of how appealing she was. He was truly surprised by his intense desire for the scurvy doxy. Moreover, he enjoyed her ready banter and her easygoing ways that contrasted so with her high energy.

"You know, Fiona, virgins were once sacrificed to appease the gods. But then, you are no virgin."

"Ye foul-hearted swine, I am!" Immediately, she looked stunned by her inadvertent admission. Then her eyes blazed in defiance.

Instantly, he halted his seduction of her. One of his hands caught her chin with its damnably enticing dent, jerking her face up so that he could see the truth in her eyes. Their thick lashes glistened with droplets of rain—or were they tears? Anger beat at him and he could not pinpoint its cause.

Both his hands gripped her shoulders, this time shaking her. "Why the hell did you not tell me you were a virgin?"

Her eyes blazed. "'Tis none of your bloody business, ye pile of dung."

"Even more important, I want to know why you led me to believe you were a common prostitute?"

Her eyes narrowed, so that her damp lashes all but hid the emerald specks of her pupils. A querulous smile tipped her lips. "Seems to me your willingness to jump to conclusions speaks volumes about your narrow mindset."

With that, she twisted free of him and, her skirts tight in hand, fled down the turret staircase.

Furious, he started after her, then abruptly halted as if smacked in the forehead. Smacked with the awful realization… he was right and truly obsessed and in lust with her. He had reveled in his infamy as the seducer and had most ironically become the seduced.

He should be vexed as to why Niall had not yet returned with Rafaela.

Instead, he was vexed with this tongue-lashing leprechaun—whom he now had to add to his protective concerns after inadvertently bringing about the death of every female he had ever loved.

In a silent, fossil-like collapse, he dropped to his knees on the stones. Rain pelted him, soaking him, and he did not care.

Damn the gods! How they must be laughing.

10

IGNORING FIONA WAS ABOUT AS easy for Paladín as ignoring the warnings of one of the chaparral's diamondback rattlesnakes. That scorpion of a doxy was so stubborn she would test the patience of a saint. And, so much like himself, she gave no quarter. To maintain his influence over her was a given. But there were other unknown quantities with which to deal.

Namely, she had to go. She and her urchin.

He knew he already possessed a well-developed ability to interpret what might appear to be insignificant openings and then convert them into major opportunities. The safe return of his fiancée held considerably more potential advantage than one of those insignificant openings.

Looking toward the mission's impressive double doorway, he saw Rafaela standing there as if framed for her wedding portrait—except her arms were wrapped tightly about her, and she was shivering, sopping wet, bedraggled, and… changed.

Behind her, Niall loomed. Paladín scanned his lieutenant's features. The grim set of the pistoleer's mouth might have indicated a multitude of emotions, but his bleak blue-gray eyes revealed to Paladín all he needed to learn.

Amid the legion of dangerous pitfalls and overwhelming perils that the Traveler must have had to overcome, he had lost his bearings, quite apparently, and succumbed to the pitfalls of lust.

But perhaps not, Alex thought. Instead, did he recognize the less obvious but tell-tale signs of that more mysterious human element—love?

Paladín's discerning gaze flicked back to Rafaela's face, sculpted raw by deprivation, the elements, and the hardship of the previous week. Yes, he thought, there it was—that same damnable lost-in-love look Niall was vainly trying to conceal.

From behind him, he could hear Frederick, Winnie, Fiona, and Liam coming noisily into the forecourt.

"Welcome home, my dear. You have returned just in time." Alex lifted Rafaela's hands—blue from the cold—in his and chaffed some warmth into them. For the first time since he had met her, her face had color. The recent, terrible weather had burnished her cheeks cherry pink.

This was another of those seemingly insignificant openings that he meant to convert immediately and callously into a major opportunity. While his fiancée was physically and emotionally exhausted, he would give her no quarter.

"Barring a winter storm, your father's ship is due to arrive at the Port of Matamoros this week—or the next at the latest. I have engaged the Rev. Engler to perform our ceremony."

In truth, Alex had never said one word to Rev. Engler about officiating, yet that could be arranged expeditiously after a generous donation to his First Presbyterian Church of Matamoros.

Glaring sternly at Paladín, Fiona stepped past him and put her arm around Rafaela's waist. "'Tis right worn out, ye are. So, my lady, let us get you into a hot bath and to bed."

Releasing Rafaela's hands, Alex stared down at Fiona. "Once the Lady Rafaela and I have wed, your services as her companion can be dispensed with. I am arranging for the parson's sister, Charlotte Madison, to provide temporary shelter for you and Liam until the next vessel sails for New York."

One contender out of the way, which left only the Texican's annoyingly fractious provisional council, the deviously elusive Chaparral Fox—and, of course, Santa Anna's six thousand or so soldiers.

Fiona's cheeks blanched so quickly her freckles disappeared. He spotted Liam shooting her a harried glance and saw, as well, the reassuring wink she offered the kid.

She jutted her clefted chin at Paladín. "That will not be necessary. Me son and I can make our way on our—"

With his usual creaking chorus of shoes and bones, Frederick stepped forward. "I could use the laddies help here, sire. Me old body ain't what it once was, for certain."

Winnie also piped up. "Fiona's help in the kitchen would be most welcome, to be sure."

"Regrettably, Winnie, those arrangements have already been made." Sometimes, it amazed even himself at his deft facility for lying.

Aristocratic Rafaela almost sagged against the smaller Fiona's supporting arm. Watching the two women leave, Paladín had the uneasy feeling he was miscalculating the force of Fiona Flanigan's determination. She would never give up her quest for land, nor would she depart Matamoros placidly.

Too bad. Whether she went placidly or digging in her heels, he would rid himself of her thwarting presence.

Without a functioning conscience, it bothered Paladín neither that his fiancée might love his closest friend nor that he himself was lusting after a different woman. Obviously, however, that indifference of his did bother others.

Winnie was the first person to disrupt his thoughts. Without knocking, she stormed through the commandant's doorway. He looked up from the intelligence-gathering report Deaf Smith had intercepted from a Mexican spy to find her glowering at him, arms crossed. She and Frederick had served his family forever, and it was his own keenly felt lack of family that allowed the old biddy to boss him so.

"I know ye might not open your mind and heart any longer to love or compassion or any of the softer emotions, but by Jove, surely that rational part of yourself shrieks that no good can come of forcing an issue!"

His brows raised. "And precisely what issue would that be?"

"Ye well know whereof I speak. Forcing Lady Rafaela to wed yourself."

Shaking his head ruefully, he rested his forehead on clasped hands, then glared ferociously at the old harpy.

"Your observation is altogether faulty, Winnie. First, it was never I who 'forced' marriage upon Lady Rafaela Carrera. Her father sought out and made me that magnanimous offer. Second, if I do not conclude the marriage, you may well find Frederick and yourself begging on the church doorstep and myself flung into debtor's prison. So, do dispense with any further of your erroneous lectures."

He glowered his best glower and thrust an imperious finger toward the doorway. "And next time, you had better knock first."

The door slamming behind Winnie was followed a half hour later by the wraith-like appearance of Niall. "Surely, Alex, ye canna be serious about forcing this marriage upon Lady Rafaela."

Once more, Paladín's brows slid upward. "Am I to suppose you can offer her better? And precisely what might that state of affairs consist of?"

Seeing Niall's taciturn expression, Paladín went on. "Marriage and home and security?"

The Traveler's eyes narrowed. His words sounded as if gritted through sand. "None of those. None a'tall. I *can* guarantee her safe passage to her aunt's home in Savannah."

Paladín sighed, all too weary of having to explain himself. For certain, he owed no one an explanation. The mustachioed young man before him was all too obviously intense... as well as befogged by his newly experienced runaway emotions. "First, Niall, you do not even know if her aunt will take in Rafaela."

"The letter my lady Rafaela sent should—"

"I never posted her letter. Besides, I need you to serve as my best man at our wedding."

Niall's palm moved ever so slightly and rested on his pistol butt.

Paladín pyramided his fingertips, lazily perusing the formidable young man standing before him. Without ever saying so, or in any way overtly acknowledging their reality, he had come to value the Irish Traveler.

In fact, Alex did and had trusted the man with his life.

Until now, Niall had lived wholeheartedly by his own personal code, and that alone was more than he himself could claim. *Whatever Proved Most Expedient* would be a fitting epitaph for himself.

"By all means, do feel free to offer Rafaela your escort services. But I think the arrival of her father next week is an issue more vital for her to resolve than an uncertain reception by an aunt she has never met."

The Traveler nodded. "Have it your way, Lord Paladín, but once this wedding of yours is done, me service with ye is ended. I will be leaving ye."

So, once again, I will stand alone. Not that I do not deserve the fate.

ENGLER MANSE, MATAMOROS, MEXICO
CHRISTMAS DAY

Sprigs of mistletoe Paladín had brought back from his San Patricio land grant festooned the Engler doorways. The parsonage, a small two-story clapboard house close to the *mercado*, was decorated for Christmas with evergreen boughs and holly. The parson's sister, Charlotte Madison, had baked mince pies and prepared plum pudding.

Hoisting his pewter wassail cup of hot spiced ale, the rangy, hatchet-faced Reverend Daniel Engler told his guests, "Be well!"

Over the rim of his cup, Paladín's gaze scanned the guests present, alighting on Fiona, deep in conversation with Charlotte. Not in any room, whether graced or barren, would Fiona go unnoticed for long—her vital energy danced off her like campfire sparks. Fiona's hair, surpassing easily the luster of the holly berries, had been curled elaborately atop her head. By Rafaela, no doubt.

Where was Rafaela? Ahh yes. His betrothed was cornered at the lavishly spread table, a polite smiled pasted on her pale features, as she listened to the ever-so-gallant Magnum, doubtlessly imparting some bromide accompanied by that charming smirk. She looked poised to take flight once again.

Magnum's wife, Margarita, was ladling a slice of mince pie onto a plate for Liam. Paladín had managed to tame the lad's raggedy straw hair into a semblance of tidiness just before they all had left by the coach for the Christmas party.

The kid, his eyes old beyond their years, had startled him by asking, "If ye dunna marry the lady Rafaela, ye give up the San Patricio land grant, do ye not?"

Paladín had released the boy's pugnacious chin and straightened. "I never give up what is mine."

With that in mind, Paladín glanced toward one corner, where Niall was talking to the shorter, olive-skinned Moses Solomon. Occasionally, Niall's keen eyes would stray across the room to pause on Rafaela. Paladín knew that, unlike Liam, Niall need never ask that question regarding Paladín's claim on lady Rafaela's hand in marriage.

Moments later, Niall took up his guitar. Spurred boot propped against one stucco wall, he began to strum softly "God Rest Ye Merry Gentlemen." All the guests paused what they were doing and turned to listen, expressions rapt.

Fiona's taut expression once more drew Paladín's attention. What devious plot was she now concocting?

"Captivating, is she not, Alex?" Therese asked quietly, standing beside him.

"Whom do you mean, *chérie*—Charlotte Madison?" He managed to recover himself with what he hoped was a diverting parry.

"You know very well whom I mean." From behind her lace fan, Therese's dark almond-shaped eyes watched him intently. "Besides, Charlotte does not have your creative range of passion." With a snap, Therese closed her fan. "I have… missed your late-night visits."

"I shall remind you, Therese, I am betrothed, but—" he nodded toward the lanky parson, "—Charlotte's brother may surprise you with his untapped fumbling passions."

Therese's laughter erupted, and she rapped his shoulder with her fan. "By all that's holy, *mon amour,* you are incorrigible!"

Hearing her chiming laugh, all eyes turned to her and Alex. When he spotted the dismissive expression in Fiona's green eyes, his coming wedding grew even more imperative. Those vows would be the one and only barrier between Fiona's virtue and his conquest of her.

As if he believed that blithering lie. As if anything, or anyone—holy or not—had ever kept his selfish soul from whatever it wanted.

11

MATAMOROS
STATE OF TAMAULIPAS, MEXICO

As soon as the mast of the brig bearing Rafaela's father was sighted off the Port of Matamoros, Moses Solomon relayed the news to Paladín in person, arriving by horseback.

With a heart that felt it was being squeezed dry of her life's blood, Rafaela stood at the *presidio*'s massive gateway, shivering in the blast of cold wind that whipped her hair from its lace cap and about her face, nearly blinding her.

So much was left to do in preparation for the wedding festivities, but she stood watching Niall as he drove the coach carrying Paladín and Moses to the wharf, Solomon's tied horse trailing the coach.

From Liam, she had learned Niall was leaving the day after the wedding, only a short two days from now. She knew there would be no words of farewell from him. No goodbye kiss, not even a "Best Wishes" or a "Happy New Year."

She backhanded a tear off her cheek. No more tears. No more tears draining the life from her. No more tears shed for any man—not for the man who had despoiled her and stolen her savings, nor for her father who had bartered her for a title, nor for her betrothed who had encumbered himself with her for money and for land.

Niall would be out of her life after the wedding… and after the wedding, Don Alejandro de la Torre y Stuart, Baron of Paladín, would be her husband. He was beyond a doubt handsome in a dangerous way, but only if one considered features chiseled from cold rock anywhere capable of expressing normal human emotions. What did it matter that her future husband had no heart?

Niall had a heart, a heart that thudded hard and fast when holding her. Even so, the Irish Traveler's will to roam held more influence over him than did his desire for her.

One man who would not be out of her life following the wedding was Cavett Magnum. Within the Matamoros community, he evidently was held in high esteem by everyone. No doubt then, that Cavett's word would be believed before hers.

The bastard had been nauseatingly congenial at Reverend Engler's Christmas gathering. Would Cavett dare to press his attentions on her again? With Paladín sending Fiona away, her only friend in Matamoros, Rafaela felt achingly alone.

Feeling a greater chill than the weather had ever perpetrated, she picked up her wind-lashed skirts and turned back toward the mission. Decorations, food, invitations, and other arrangements all awaited her attention.

Fiona was waiting for her outside the double doors. Her brows knitted over those brilliant green eyes that probed her own. "Ye're all right?"

"I will be." She blinked and forced a smile. "Shall we get started on the wedding preparations?"

For a while, they tried to help in the kitchen, but, at last, an exasperated Winnie shooed them out. The two fell into step, heading toward the commandant's office and the invitation list Paladín had prepared and requested Rafaela review.

"Ye are going through with it then?"

"What can I do?"

Fiona's gaze drifted. "Aye, I suppose 'tis your duty."

"And yourself? What will you do when you return to New York?"

With an impish grin, Fiona glanced at her. "I have been giving that considerable thought. I will not be going back there. I am staying right here to fight for me land."

"I expected as much." How Rafaela envied Fiona, just a year older than she. Resilient, brave, and blessed with a liveliness that was so attractive, Fiona seemed a heady mixture of sunshine and champagne and warm honey.

"You do realize, Fiona, that, should you win your claim to the land grant, you will be preempting my husband and myself of our future home."

They had reached the door to the commandant's office and Fiona stopped short. "I had not taken that into account." She shrugged her narrow shoulders, her lips curving into a broad grin. "Well, then ye can come and live with me and Liam in San Patricio."

"And my husband, Paladín?" She followed Fiona inside and crossed to the desk he used. Yes, there was the wedding list, scrawled on fine parchments with his heavy, looping penmanship. "What of him?"

"The devil takes his own." Something in Fiona's normally lilting voice hinted that her feelings for the Lord Paladín were not entirely indifferent. She was poised in front of the fireplace's smoldering embers, hands outstretched toward the remnants of its heat.

Momentarily, she braced her palms on the desk. Her taxing trip back from San Antonio de Bexar, her subsequent illness, her apathy now—she supposed all were taking their toll of her energy.

"Thank you for your offer, Fiona. You are the only bright light I have encountered in this blighted land."

Fiona knelt to stir the peripheral embers to life with a poker. "Oh, Tejas itself is not so bad. Everything blooms here with profuse ease and everything here is on a larger scale—and with little grime and uncrowded streets. Besides, Rafaela, the opportunities offered in Tejas are far beyond anything I might have ever dreamed of in County Kerry and not at all back in Five Points."

"You are right, of course." She glanced at the list with its illustrious names of Matamoros's finest citizens, including one not so fine, Cavett. "I fancy I should consider myself fortunate."

"Rafaela, look ye over here at this!" Fiona was pointing at a bronze statue beside the hearth. Lingeringly, her fingers traced the curves of an entwined couple.

Flushing at the "art," Rafaela moved closer to it, drawn by the blatant eroticism of the nude couple.

Fiona breathed, "Exquisite, is it not?"

Rafaela recalled bitterly the benumbing time spent at the hands of Cavett, who, she suspected, delighted in controlling other people's fate, their money, and their property. Her frightening sense of danger, the loss—no, it had been nothing like the impassioned loving embrace of the bronzed couple.

She wadded the wedding list, and hurled the vellum into the fireplace.

Fiona rushed to the hearth to rescue the parchment. "Little good it will do to destroy the list, Rafaela. The invitations are already delivered."

"What if I refuse to go through with the ceremony?"

"If it is not Paladín, then, like ye told me, your father will only locate another titled suitor for you to wed, maybe even a worse candidate than Paladín."

Rafaela sighed deeply. "You are right. The parson has been retained for New Year's Day. Whether the date is tomorrow or a week later, my fortune is cast. A healthy deposit of four thousand pounds to Lord Paladín's account and a title of nobility ensured for my father's descendants has been done."

"And what of your Irish Traveler?" Fiona's small hands smoothed nearly flat the wrinkled parchment. "'Tis plain to see ye have strong feelings for Niall."

Rafaela could feel her damnable tears welling. "Whatever Niall feels for me, that feeling will never be as strong as mine for him. What would you do, Fiona, if you were I?"

"Well, that is easy for me to say. I want me land I was promised. To get me land, I would marry that beast Paladín in a heartbeat, if he would have me." She looked over her shoulder and grinned merrily. "Then I would poison the blackguard's tea—and, most likely, once married to me, he would be eager to drink me tea."

As Fiona's fantasy concluded, Rafaela broke out in such hearty laughter she had to wipe her eyes. Whether the tears were humorous or sourced by a badly broken heart, she did not know for certain.

Fiona shrugged her narrow shoulders and turned her attention to the task of setting to right the singed parchments. "Alas, Paladín wants the land as much as I do and does not need the pitiful likes of me to claim it." Her mouth crimped tight. "How twisted is fate, Rafaela. Our destinies should have been just the—"

The sound from outside as the mission's double doorways swung wide interrupted Fiona's melancholy speculation.

"Rafaela?" boomed a masculine voice.

Stricken, she glanced at Fiona's back. "My father... he has arrived!"

"Go on with ye, then. I shall finish up here."

Chin squared for combat, Rafaela headed down the corridor toward the vestibule. Her father had always been a taskmaster. Invariably, his letters to her exhorted the need for the perfection of her efforts—whether she was trying to master the pianoforte, converse fluently in French, Flemish, or German, or was focusing all her effort on the Royal Stock Exchange.

Not once had he so much as hugged her or told her he loved her. She had often wondered what her life would have been like had her mother lived. Perhaps her feminine nurturing would have pre-empted Rafaela's erroneous conception of what love was.

Breathless, she stared at the two impressively tall men who stood forefront and center, her father and Paladín. Behind them, weight braced on one foot, hand hitched at his holster, Niall watched dispassionately.

With a tremulous smile, she held out her hands, feeling once again the little girl.

"Father, I am glad you could attend my wedding."

He removed his top hat and embraced her, his arms rigid and awkward about her shoulders and waist. Quickly, he released her and stepped back. "You have grown into a beautiful young woman, Rafaela. How long has it been? Three years or more since last our visit?"

"Four years, eight months and two weeks." She forced a smile. "And you still look the same. Dashing and *soigné.*"

In truth, he had grayed considerably. Even his goatee was now completely gray. Pouches beneath his glistening eyes bespoke of excesses in libation and too little sleep. His stature seemed thin to her, almost brittle.

Before now, his presence had always overwhelmed her, because he had been larger than life and seemed so worldly wise to her. Juxtaposed with Paladín, her father appeared a faint and flat two-dimensional rendition of his former self.

"*Señor* Carrera." Paladín smiled, ever the gracious host. "I realize you must be tired. My housekeeper has prepared a room for you where you may refresh yourself before dinner. Rafaela can show you the way. I am quite certain you have much to talk about."

Rafaela took her cue and linked her arm with her father's. Heading toward the cloister rooms, she stole a glance at him. Looking at her, his expression was of a man immeasurably pleased with himself. "I have missed you, my child."

To her dismay, she found herself quaking. She glanced away, experiencing, possibly for the first time in her life, anger in place of her usual anxiousness for his affection. That anger was building within her so rapidly her voice, when she was able to speak, sounded in her ears like the feeblest of whispers, her words punctuated, One-At-A-Time, with extreme difficulty.

"I have never been your child, father. Only your pawn."

"A pawn?" Beneath his graying eyebrows, his hooded eyes widened. "My every action has been with your best interests in mind. As a parent—"

Now her words burst forth like booming rifle shots. "Parent? A parent nurtures a child. You, you simply got rid of me. Shipped me away from you as soon as Mother died!"

He stiffened. "That is not the way it was. You cannot even begin to know how much I missed you all that time. Guatemala was in a state of riot for years, fighting first against Spain for its independence, then suffering from a series of dictators. I wanted you to be safe, wanted you to have the best. The best education, the best—"

"So now you believe Paladín is the best husband for me?"

That frown she so dreaded appeared. "Don Alejandro is a man of principle."

He had assumed that, as well, about Cavett Magnum.

Bile rose into her throat.

"Paladín's title will give you everything I cannot." Her father continued, unaware and unconcerned he was shattering her life. "And the proximity of Matamoros to Guatemala City means I shall be near enough to see you more often."

"All I have ever wanted from you, father, was your love!"

He placed his veined hand over hers. "I love you more than I can ever tell you, Rafaela. I only want the best for you, and in spite of rumors, I feel Don Alejandro is the best marriage prospect."

Suddenly, drained by the lava-like fury of her anger and the scorch of her hurt, lassitude overcame her. At this point, what had she to gain with the revisiting of past hurts? She must go forward.

With a resigned sigh, she managed a similitude of a smile. "I love you, too, Papa." And she did. Perhaps the marriage he had arranged would prove, over the years, to be one of surprising fulfilment? "Let us begin our grand adventure, shall we, Papa?"

12

Exhausted from two busy days of cooking and decorating, Fiona retired to her room to ready herself for the New Year's Day wedding. The water in the two buckets she lugged was already tepid. Worse, the galvanized hip tub leaked like a Dutch dyke. Knees drawn up to her chest, she sat there, dejected, without any clear idea why.

Aye, in truth, she did know. She was a weakling, a simpleton, when it came to Paladín. Most certainly, it would not do for her to be anywhere near his disturbing presence once he and Rafaela were married.

He was right to try and send me away.

The sooner she and Liam left after the wedding, the better. She had been so eager to strike out on her own, and now she reluctantly faced the morrow.

The nuptial festivities would begin within a few hours, yet she performed her ablutions lethargically. At last, with damp hair wrapped in a linen towel, she began to dress for the party.

Listlessly, she shrugged into her chemise and corset, then paused, her gaze falling on the parchments she had rescued from the glowing embers of the commandant's office fireplace two days before.

She had tried to smooth out the wedding list Rafaela had wadded and realized she had collected, in addition, another sheet from amid the cinders. Harried and distracted by the nuptial's preparations, she had not bothered with that bit of foolscap.

But now, she idled to the chest, as if stalling could eliminate the inevitable wedding, and picked up the second sheet of foolscap. Its edges were charred, the parchment itself slightly smoke-stained, but the writing on it was legible. If she squinted a bit, she could just make it out.

Headquarters of the Army
Camp east of Nacogdoches

Grant has marched away from Bexar with 200 volunteers—this after having despoiled the handful of courageous men left at the Alamo of ammunition, blankets, medical stores, and everything else of any worth has proceeded to San Patricio. Here, he is expected to be joined by Colonel Fannin and others to descend by month's end on Matamoros to capture and loot the place. This foolhardy expedition, which has paralyzed our Provisional Government, can only prove disastrous. The only thing we can do now is make certain word of it is not carried to Santa Anna. To that end, it is imperative we identify as soon as we can and eliminate the Chaparral Fox.

S. Houston.

Her lips formed a silent whistle.

General Sam Houston.

Apparently, Paladín had counted on the hot coals destroying this incriminating bit of evidence.

Well… this message clearly identified Paladín as a secret agent for the rebels. That explained his absences from *Presidio* La Espada and his attendance at gaming houses and saloons and, aye, mayhap even brothels.

She grinned. After all these weeks of anxiety, she might have drawn an ace in the hole to guarantee her land.

———————————

CARRIAGES, COACHES, CURRICLES, AND CHAISES, pulling up inside the *presidio* compound kept Liam busy at the task Fiona had assigned him. Fortunately, the weather was cooperating, and only a mild chill was ushering in the year of 1836.

By late afternoon, guests comprising of Matamoros's elite social class spilled over from the parlor onto the mission terrazzo. Its high walls offered some protective warmth that made the pungent mesquite fire in a huge *chimenea* mostly superfluous.

Fiona shouldered past the throng on her way to Rafaela's room, but paused at the parlor entrance just beyond the kitchen. With some satisfaction, she surveyed the terra cotta jars and pitchers of orange blossoms and dried lavender scattered throughout the room, providing a festive touch.

Winnie had set out savory platters of meats and some lentils for good luck, while Frederick had filled glasses with the mission's cache of Criollo grape wine.

Satisfied all was in order, Fiona set off down the open colonnaded corridor leading to the rooms next to the courtyard. She stopped short when she noticed a figure cast into shadows by the sun's lingering rays.

The silhouette leaned against the hallway arch. Arms folded, the man appeared to be staring past the terrazzo's wrought-iron gate toward the revelers gathering there.

Warily, she drew even with Paladín. Now was not the time to use the leverage of the General's missive. But sound Paladín out, she might.

He was dressed almost regally in a black flared frock coat with pantaloons and a gold-trimmed, finely woven waistcoat. Without looking at her he said, "You did well with the wedding arrangements, given the short notice."

She peered up at him. Nothing in his carved expression ever betrayed his thoughts. Still, she detected a sense of unrest about him. "A compliment coming from ye, me Lord, is most unexpected."

"You know me oh, so well, Fiona."

She ignored his unusually mild sarcasm. "No. No, I do not. Me thinks ye are one thing and then, like a chameleon, you change to another."

He glanced at her, slightly and obviously amused. "What precisely do you wish to know about me?"

Several questions leaped to the forefront. Would he decide to return to England once she took possession of the mutually exclusive land grant they both claimed? Did he desire her still, even though he found her so lacking in integrity? And blackmailing most certainly would add to her lack.

"Why does yuir voice always sound so… so rusty?"

His measured response was interrupted only by the conversational hum of the guests on the terrazzo. "Do you mean hoarse? Raw?"

She nodded.

"'Tis from screaming."

She frowned. "Somehow, me Lord, ye do not seem the shouting sort."

The edgy lift of an eyebrow altered the appearance of his features, as did his full lower lip compressing the bowed upper one into a blade-thin line and the muscle flicking in his jaw. "I said 'screaming.' There is quite a difference between the meaning of that and shouting."

Head canted, she raised her own brow.

His eyes held hers in a tense bond. "Sometimes a man screams when his pain of loss feels unbearable. Unending."

"Yuir wife's death?"

"Yes."

"I thought…." She felt uneasy standing alone before him in the cold dark corridor. Unconsciously, she hugged herself. "I heard there was gossip that says ye killed yuir wife."

"I did. And my mother. And my sister."

Her jaw went slack and her gasp almost made inaudible to him her next question. "Why?"

"Why? And I ask you, why are you not afraid of me?"

That question threw her completely, but she answered without pausing. "I do not know."

"But here, you stand beneath mistletoe." He pointed upward.

"What?" She tilted her head back. Looking upward, she saw the glossy thatch of green suspended from the apex of the arch.

"Remnants of the mistletoe I brought back from *our* land grant."

She could not ignore his emphasis on that one word. "I had Liam hang it above the doorways as wedding decorations." She swallowed. "And… uhh… that reminds me, I must see to Rafaela. To help her get—"

"Kissing is a prescribed activity when one is encountered beneath a sprig of mistletoe. That is, of course, unless you were lying to me when you said you were not afraid of me."

When his bleak gaze settled on her mouth, she felt her lips soften. What compelled her, she could not say, but she leaned closer to him. Why not? She would be lying to herself if she said she did not want to kiss him—an intimate act of which Rafaela had admitted to Fiona she wanted no part.

After tonight, he would be married. And shortly thereafter, she would be on her way. Why did she feel as if she were betraying the knave?

When he made no move, only watched her like a tutor did a student processing cyphers, she took the initiative upon herself.

Standing high on tiptoes, her neck arched, her eyes closed, she splayed her hands against his lapels and offered him her lips. A moment passed. Nothing. Her lids snapped open. He was smiling down at her. The first sign of genuine amusement she had ever known him to offer her. "What?"

He clasped both her shoulders. His face descended toward hers. "This." He drew her up against him so tightly her hands were pinned between her shoulders and his chest, the tips of her slippers barely grazing the tiles. She had not realized the immense power of his strength. She sucked in a taut breath. Inhaling his scent of bayberry and burning lust worked on her like alchemy.

It seemed an eternity passed before his lips reached hers. Her pulse was racing in anticipation. His features were blurred. Her eyes drifted shut.

Not so suddenly, but totally, he was kissing her, slanting his mouth against hers. His kiss was a blazing hearth fire imposing itself upon the dark winter without.

"Hmmmm." Could that sound be her... *purring?* Oh, sweet Jesus! Scooching her arms up to curl around his neck, she sagged from the slamming impact of so much never-before-felt pleasure.

When he paused, she breathed, "No."

"No?"

She buried her face between the folds of his lapels and mumbled, "'Tis too pleasurable."

"Dios." He lapsed into a spate of Spanish. *"Qué maldición me visitará después!* You do walk directly into my very soul, Fiona!"

Shaking his head brusquely, as if to clear his senses of her, he set her away from him. As he did, a rueful smile tugged at his ever-expressive mouth. "How ironic. A kiss to begin the year 1836—and a kiss that ends... all else."

ONLY HALF-LISTENING, CHARLOTTE STOOD on La Espada's terrazzo with her brother, Daniel, Margarita Magnum, and Burt Beamon, the watchmaker, as they discussed future plans for the parsonage renovation.

"I am grateful for your offer to help raise funds for our parsonage and church, Mrs. Magnum."

"Our pleasure, Reverend Engler."

Then, turning to the balding and paunchy watchmaker, who hooked thumbs inside his web suspenders, Daniel added, "And, Mr. Beamon, your assistance with winding and cleaning our church clock would be greatly...."

From the corner of her eye, Charlotte watched a barn cat weaving among the wedding guests' feet, heading toward the corner where Moses Solomon and Niall Gorman were holding forth quietly, almost secretively. About what?

"Kindly excuse me, Daniel, Margarita, Burt."

She slipped away from the three and shouldered past Mrs. Beamon, talking volubly with the Land Commissioner and Therese del Valle. With trepidation, Charlotte approached Moses and Niall.

Charlotte was a large woman, afraid of nothing—neither varmints, human or otherwise, nor public opinion, such as it was applied in Matamoros, but she felt perspiration beading her upper lip and beneath her underarms as she drew closer to Moses Solomon.

Shorter than she by several inches, one of his most prominent facial features was a flattened nose. She ignored that dubious distinction, noting that Moses possessed a calmness of purpose within his quiet and private manners. His dark brown passionate eyes truly unnerved Charlotte.

No, hardly *unnerved* her—instead, he made her feel quite lightheaded. A most agreeable sensation. His deep stare and aroma of fresh tobacco also affected her senses, a stark reminder of the male companionship missing from her life.

Her former husband had found her lacking, although she had never known precisely what he desired of her that she did not freely offer him. A softer, smaller woman? A more subtle woman? A more seductive woman?

Seduction. She was not certain exactly what that term required of her. Her upbringing had never included any clarifying directions on that arcane topic.

The times she and her husband had coupled before he deserted her, well. Those couplings had seemed to her somewhat brisk but... productive to him, if groans of release were any measure. Like her, he spoke his mind, and she had thought that mutual trait made them perfect mates.

Too clearly, he had thought otherwise, bluntly stating as he gathered his clothing to leave that morning long ago, "'Blimey, ye are about as warm in bed as a day-old fish!"

Because of Charlotte's all-too-brief marital experience, she had come to the firm conclusion that where there was no difference, there could be no spark. Like flint and tinder.

And like that barn cat, she halted herself before Moses and Niall. While the cat began to rub its length against Niall's leg, Charlotte gathered her gumption.

Moses Solomon's gentle brown gaze fell on her, warming her. "Good evening, Mrs. Madison."

"Evening, ma'am."

"Gentlemen." She nodded at each. "I shall come directly to my point."

"You always do, ma'am." The Baron's hired hand's mustache curled faintly up at one corner with a kind smile that she noticed did not quite reach his eyes.

Trying to still an unfamiliar edginess, she turned toward Moses. "You were at the Magnum's gala in honor of General Houston."

"I was."

"You danced with the Lady Rafaela Carrera's companion—Fiona."

"I did."

"Then you must have also watched when she was in the accompaniment of the Baron. And, if so, you cannot have missed the way the nobleman was looking upon her."

She glanced from Moses to Niall Gorman and back to Moses. "Both of you are friends of the Baron. It is my opinion that he and the Lady Rafaela are not a suitable match for one another. You simply must stop this wedding."

Niall bent over and picked up the cat, cradling it in one arm, stroking it. "Mrs. Madison, I would fling myself head first from the bell tower before I would stop this wedding."

"And I," Moses told her in his warmed-wine tone, "would be interested in how you arrived at your opinion. I would like to know what you believe makes one person a proper match for another."

She might well speak her mind about a multiplicity of topics, but this was not one of them. And most certainly she would never speak her mind to this man.

That he was not of her faith, but a Sephardic Jew, bothered her not so much as the way he made her feel when she was close to him. Solomon had the power to elicit a weighted yearning from her, a yearning so puzzlingly complex, so unlike the uncomplicated young woman she had always imagined herself to be.

And thus, her coquettish reply also was so unlike her nature. Could that be her, batting her lashes at the little man? Astonished, she heard her voice lighten to a crooning. "I would be delighted to share my observations with you Mr. Solomon. So, please, do call upon me soon."

RAFAELA STOOD, AS STIFFLY AS a statue, while Fiona tied the sashes and ribbons, fastening the multitude of satin-covered buttons that closed the back of her wedding dress. Of rose lace over cream satin, the dress had accompanied Rafaela all the way from London on her most reluctant journey to her fiancé.

Lastly, Fiona pinned the rose lace veil to Rafaela's burnished brown hair, arranged in a labyrinth of curls at the top of her head, and lowered the veil over her face.

The tall, pale young woman stared at the mirror inside her wardrobe's open door—and sighed sadly.

"Oh, 'tis right lovely ye are, Rafaela!"

Without responding to Fiona's observation, Rafaela paid inordinate attention to drawing on her long kid gloves. "My future husband is opinionated, extravagant, and all too complicated for my taste." Her tone had changed to a determined briskness. "And those are his better qualities. He is also a dilettante, a gambler, and a Lothario."

Her voice sounded brittle to Fiona, like the most fragile crystal.

"Nevertheless, I am quite certain we shall make a splendid go of this consignment to hell." Rafaela rounded on her. "Please, Fiona, please tell me I am doing the right thing."

She swallowed hard. She had to overlook her own misgivings. "There are worse things. Count yuirself fortunate that ye will have a roof over yuir head and food to fill yuir stomach. And I have yet to hear of Paladín beating any woman."

Though he did tell me he has murdered three.

Rafaela managed a faint smile. "Now, why do I suspect your cheerfulness is as forced as my acquiescence? You are correct, of course. These are only nerves I am experiencing. Now, the rouge pot, if you please. Do apply it as thickly as you can. I want, at least, to appear a ravishing bride. Whether or not I am."

At last, the fateful moment arrived. Fiona handed Rafaela the nosegay of baby's breath and camellias Fiona herself had fashioned.

The guests were already seated in the chapel. Outside it, in the vestibule, Rafaela hesitated. Sheer panic shivered her tense features.

Fiona whispered with a feigned grin, "Ye do not have to do this—we can always offer our wares at Lady Letty's."

Rafaela's response was a raw murmur. "I feel I am already selling my wares."

Her father pushed open the chapel's double doors. The man appeared more rested than upon his arrival and was beaming with pride and pleasure. "Ready, my child?"

Lips pressed tight, Rafaela nodded.

Fiona deserted her then, joining the wedding party inside the mission chapel. The flickering of the multitude of candles she had lit earlier shimmered the chapel with eerily dancing shadows. She passed Winnie and Frederick standing in a pew to her left. Between them, a bored-looking Liam shifted from foot to foot.

Her unwilling footsteps dragged her down the aisle toward the rangy Reverend Daniel Engler and a saturnine Paladín. A carnation had been tucked into his black lapel, but his snow-white cravat was uncharacteristically knotted carelessly at this throat. So unlike his meticulous nature.

Beside him stood his best man, a stony-faced Niall, minus his ever-present revolver in deference to the house of the Lord, much as Paladín was lacking his rapier.

A smile plastered on her face, she took her place to the reverend's right. Despite Engler's rough-hewn, grave features, the smile he offered her was warm, reassuring.

His sister, the statuesque Charlotte Madison, stood in front of Fiona on the first row. Charlotte was dabbing a lace handkerchief at her eyes. Beneath her bonnet, the loops of blonde braids at either side of her ears bobbled. Beyond her, the faces of the other guests were a blur to Fiona.

Glumly, she stared as Rafaela and her father moved down the aisle at a funeral pace that seemed to take hours. The chapel was airless and warm, heated by the candles, amid the scent of a century of cloying incense. *I think I am going to be ill.* Her throat worked to hold back her bile. She slid a sidewise glance at Paladín, supposing he would be gazing at his bride walking down the aisle.

He was looking at *her!*

As Rafaela and her father reached and paused before the Reverend Engler, he cleared his throat to deliver up what might as well be the Last Rites for the wedding party.

"Uhumm. Our Heavenly Father knows the depth and breadth of our sinful selves and has lovingly provided a way to our salvation by joining us with the one our soul has the power to restore—"

13

The thunderous crash of the mission doors bursting asunder and horseshoes clattering on the vestibule tiles outside the chapel burst alike the eardrums of the guests and the honorees.

Then the chapel's double doors were thrust open.

A rider, red bandana masking his lower features, charged through, followed by two other masked riders. Screams and shouts reverberated against the chapel's three-foot-thick, pock-marked stucco walls. Guests dove behind pews.

A flash of gunfire blinded Fiona. A bullet zinged passed her head. The reminiscent stink she associated with firecrackers stung her nostrils. She saw Frederick tugging Winnie from the path of the first rider, who spurred his mount down the aisle.

"Bloody hell!" she gasped before she herself was grabbed by her shoulder and yanked backward. Her hands clawed at the iron band manacling her waist. "Ye scurvy bastard! Take yuir bloody—"

"Shut up!" Paladín's harsh growl echoed in her ears. He yanked her through the doorway at the back of the chapel into the padre's quarters.

The last thing she saw was the first two riders flinging themselves from their mounts as the bedchamber door slammed closed. Paladín was just snatching his derringer from the commode when the door in back of them banged open.

He turned to fire his derringer somewhere behind and yanked her past his bed toward the bell tower entrance. Another bullet whistled past her and plowed into that door. Wood splinters flew.

He jerked the tower door open. She scrambled up the narrow, spiral stone staircase ahead of him. At the top, outside, he caught up with her and slammed shut the staircase door.

"If yer planning on jumping from the rampart, I warn ye I am afraid of—"

"It is you and me they are after."

"What?"

"The land grant."

Behind them, the staircase door burst open, and a man wearing a concho-spangled *sombrero* came crashing through. Paladín raised his derringer to fire. She heard the empty click of his pistol and gulped as the grinning man raised his blunderbuss.

Paladín flung his pistol at the man's face. The *bandido's* flinch gave Paladín the opening he needed to dive at the man headfirst.

His Brown Bess clattered heavily onto the tiles and she scrambled to grab it. Springing to her feet, she tried to aim the heavy piece, but its barrel wavered. She had never fired a pistol, let alone a rifle. Could she possibly kill another human?

When a second *sombrero*-clad gunman lunged to the head of the staircase, she swung around. Her finger jerked the trigger. Her shoulder recoiled in a burst of pain. An explosion of smoke and sulfur enwreathed her and her eardrums fairly burst from the boom.

The man's eyes widened. He staggered upright for a horrifying second, then tumbled backward, down the stairwell.

She whirled to see Paladín plunging a knife up and under the ribs of the man beneath him. Blood geysered. The man's body twitched, then went slack.

Shock paralyzed her. Then, all her senses heightened painfully. The setting sun was a bloody blotch seeming to cover the whole sky. Her breathing felt harsh and rapid. Perspiration broke out on her temples. She felt her heartbeat thudding in her ears and she began shivering violently.

A disheveled and hard-breathing Paladín peered at her from where he was hunkered on one knee. "Do you enjoy the smell of gun powder in the evening, Fiona?"

"Ye killed him?"

"Oh yes, I most certainly did. Better his knife gutting him than me, would you not say?"

Her voice was a ragged whisper. "No, not really, me Lord."

He laughed. Then, slowly, he pushed himself to his feet. One of his coat tails was ripped off, and his long shirttail was pulled halfway from his pantaloons. A crazed expression ravaged his features, mostly obscured by the black hair tumbling diagonally across his forehead. The rapacious glint she saw in his eyes snatched her breath.

Still gripping the dead man's knife, he advanced on her.

Well, then, this must be her time. Her turn. *He is finally going to kill me as he has the other three women, so he can seal once and for all time the ownership of me land.* She backed away until she felt the parapet wall behind her.

He loomed over her. In his eyes, she saw the savagery that too often accompanied the act of defying death and devastation and annihilation. "Raise your skirts."

"What?!"

"At long last, I have won the rights to your favor." His free hand shoved her skirts above her hips.

"Ye canna be serious!" Her knees nearly buckled and only her palms braced on the parapet held her upright. His hand found the slit in her drawers and dipped inside.

"If you move even an inch, I will nick you."

Dazed and drained, her breath held so tightly not even her ribcage could expand, she complied. Then she felt it, a hard tug.

Dropping her skirts back in place, he held before her a tuft of reddish hair. He tucked his prize into his vest pocket and smiled grimly. "I have claimed a lock of my lady's hair to carry into battle."

"Have ye gone all the way barmy?!"

"Paladín!" Both their heads swiveled toward the stairwell. Niall stood framed there. Below his broom-like mustache, his lips stretched taut. Gone was his cocky grin.

Paladín stepped in front of her, as if shielding her. "The third marauder?"

Niall's gaze took in the dead body. He shoved back his cap and sighed. "It was that Mexican mercenary, Carmargo. I am dead sure of it. He rode off before I could get to him."

Rubbing her throbbing shoulder, she moved slowly around Paladín. "Is everyone all right?"

"A ricochet nicked Rafaela's arm. Winnie is with her. But Hector Carrera—he has answered the final summons. Took a stray bullet, I imagine, meant for either one of you two."

Collecting her skirts, she edged carefully past the dead man and headed for the stairwell.

Niall stepped aside for her. "Take care of her, Fiona—take good care of Rafaela. Please."

She nodded and shouldered past him. At the stairwell bottom, the marauder she had shot lay sprawled grotesquely, one *chaparajo*-clad leg jack-knifed beneath his hip at an abnormal angle, his bloodied sugarloaf sombrero crushed beneath his head.

An even more bizarre scene greeted her inside the poorly lit chapel. Moses Solomon and Reverend Engler had corralled two horses. Nickering and snorting, ears twitching, they were prancing wildly.

Cavett had shepherded some of the guests to the back of the chapel and into the vestibule, where they hovered, stunned. Many had apparently already fled for their buggies and coaches.

Frederick and Liam were picking up candlesticks that had been knocked over and restoring toppled flower vases. The bride's wedding bouquet lay trampled before the altar.

A weeping Rafaela was draped over her father's chest. A scarlet-stained swatch of cloth was wrapped around the left sleeve of her wedding gown.

"Father… Father…."

"Jesus, Mary, and Joseph!" Fiona's fingers went to her locket, only to discover it was missing and realized she must have lost it during the fray. "Rafaela." She bent over her, hands at the young woman's waist. "Come with me. Let us get you changed out of—"

"No, no, Fiona. I never had enough time with him. I cannot leave—"

"Frederick will take care of your father." She eased Rafaela to her feet as Winnie hustled through the chapel doors, bearing a brightly striped cotton blanket for covering the corpse.

Rafaela turned a wrathful expression to both of them. "My father, Paladín, Niall… this disaster is of their making. They all were so determined to have me go through with that marriage!!"

ARMS FOLDED, PALADÍN LEANED HIS shoulder against the live oak. Despite a few mid-winter falling leaves, the mighty evergreen managed to shadow the open plot. The morning was cold and cloudy with a sky forecasting worse weather yet to come.

As Reverend Engler intoned prayers for the deceased, dutiful mourners encircled the plot with heads bowed to either listen or offer up unspoken prayers of their own.

A grieving Rafaela, her arm in a sling, was supported on one side by the decorous Therese del Valle, on the other by Charlotte Madison, whose massive furred chapeau made her appear almost diminutive. Top hat in hand, a solicitous Magnum and his wife stood among the mourners.

Paladín had to admit to himself that his plans were now at an impasse with respect to Magnum, as well as to Matamoros. He was nearly bankrupt and, at the moment, his brother's San Patricio land grant was no closer to being reclaimed from the morass of rubber stamping that was prevailing. Now, he was quite certain Magnum was masterminding the deed delays. The bastard would seem to hold all the winning cards.

Until now, Paladín's gambling abilities had kept him afloat. That and the iron-clad confidence that something worth dying for might emerge from the hardscrabble colonists' battle with the Mexican dictator Santa Anna.

At the moment, it was still unclear to Paladín precisely who was in charge of the Texican army—Fannin, Grant... or Houston?

Noticeably absent from the funeral party were Fiona and Liam. Few of life's issues ever surprised Paladín, but Fiona had accomplished that feat and she went right on doing so. Perhaps that was why her appearance on the wharf the day he had awaited his fiancée's ship had nudged him into rearranging his own plans.

Thoroughly unpredictable, Fiona had proved to be a fascinatingly lethal combination of sprite and banshee.

From behind, he felt someone approaching and knew without turning it was Niall. "I thought you would be long gone by now." Paladín chose not to look at the younger man who had paused beside him, cap in hand.

"What I told you earlier was that me services in your behalf were over once the wedding took place."

"Ahh, yes. Well, until a suitable mourning time has passed, that wedding cannot take place. Meanwhile, in light of this attack, I am sending Rafaela to stay with the widow del Valle."

"And Fiona? What about her?"

"Strangling her seems a promising possibility."

—————

FIONA LEFT SHORTLY AFTER the funeral service began. Paladín knew where to find her. The Port of Matamoros was a stopover for every seaweed-covered bit of flotsam or jetsam that washed ashore on these outlaw beaches.

Wearing her shabby woolen coat tugged closely around her and her out-dated burgundy bonnet, wind-whipped, she sat on a weather-roughened backless bench in front of Chapman's Pawn Shop. She appeared to be watching Liam, who stood at one end of a dock slapped by frothing waves. He was chunking mollusks shells from a pile at his feet. Each shell he hurled radiated frustrated energy.

Loosening the buttons of his black frockcoat, Paladín sat beside her, flipping back the frockcoat skirts and stretching out his long legs. His sister had always teased him unmercifully about their spindly length. "Stilts," she had called them. He had killed her that final time she had called his legs stilts.

Fiona's glazed, empty eyes glanced up to his face before settling once more on the expanse of water that, close to the wharf, was dotted with schooners, ferries, lighters, and brigs.

The wind rushing off the rough water slithered papers, fish bones, and other trash along the rutted road running between the storefronts and the cobbled ramp that descended to the docks below. An ox cart laden with bales of cotton rolled by, heading for one of Moses Solomon's warehouses.

Paladín waited until the creaky ox cart had lumbered past. "I take it my gold watch has been converted into a sizable wad of bank notes?"

Without lifting her gaze off the churning water, she fished into the depths of her reticule and delivered over to him his watch and fob.

Tucking it into his vest pocket, he narrowed his eyes to examine her profile with its small nose, determined chin, and lips that were set firmly in a forbidding line. "Do not tell me your conscience got the better of you, *mi querida.*"

Her sigh sounded more like a grunt of exasperation. "I have taken a position at Charlotte Madison's Rio Bravo Female Seminary."

What did she say? He blinked. "As what? Scullery maid?"

She looked at him then, eyes blazing, daring him to scoff. "School marm."

He somehow managed to keep his countenance neutral. "Teaching precisely what subjects?"

"Reading and writing."

"And what credentials of past employment did you present?"

Her smile remained a wisp. "Hired by *Madame* Margie in Five Points, New York I was—to teach her and the prostitutes of her establishment to read and write and do their sums."

"I see." At least that explained her past. The least part of her past. Who had taught her and guided her mercurial mind far beyond rudimentary subjects? Some smitten youthful suitor? "Have you found a place to live while working at Charlotte's Female Seminary?"

Her chin lifted. "Mrs. Madison has offered me a room in the back."

Now there was a compatible pair, he thought. Charlotte Madison and Fiona Flanigan. The saint and the sinner.

"You are not giving up efforts to claim the land grant, are you?" It was a statement, not a question. He related to her far too well.

She switched her stony look back toward the Gulf. "Liam and me both want a place of our own. It would be a sin to abandon me aim now."

He arched a brow. "I prefer to think it would be a sin for you to take *my* land grant."

Despite her efforts to frown, the ends of her lips curled upward ever so slightly. "An absurdity on yuir part then."

Notwithstanding the events of the past few days, he saw himself relaxing into a purely conversational moment for the first time in what felt to him like eons. Enjoying the invigorating, salty wind, appreciating the elemental power of the turbulent waters and boiling gray clouds—and, yes, fascinated by the lively sea siren at his side. "How did you find your employment... at the, uhh, past establishment?"

She switched her gaze back to the Gulf, where a schooner flying a Dutch flag was putting in. "Me older sister fled County Kerry—to New York with her lover—and quite a bugger he was. Left her high and dry." She paused, lips evidencing to him only the faintest of tremors.

"And…?"

"Upon the deaths of me younger brother and two sisters that next year, I followed Peggy… and found her at Miss Margie's… slowly dying from the pox, Peggy was. After she hanged herself, I offered me services to the other whores." She slid him a sidewise glance. "Me services put food in me mouth and a wee bit of awareness into their heads."

Anyone observing Fiona at that moment might have noted an impassive countenance, heard an unmodulated voice, one bereft of its natural musical lilt, but he inferred otherwise. This sprite at his side possessed superior strength of will, all of it solely and abundantly in aid of disguising a battered heart.

"And in what manner did you come about your education?" he inquired in a deceptively disinterested tone.

She offered him a puckish grin. "'Twas not me but me mum who was the scullery maid. At the Earl of Grantam's manor house. Whenever she could, she slipped me into the master's house when the old tutor came to give the English master's son—Geoffrey—his private lessons. We both were scarcely five when our tutoring started. I would swear to ye this day that Geoffrey's noggin was only a wee bit thicker than me own."

This opening was perfect. A way to both rid himself of her claim to the land grant and to remove her as a target for hired cutthroats. "Then perhaps that noggin of yours might be open to a suggestion I could make to you?"

The wind riffled her red hair across her nose, upturned at its end, and, eyeing him warily, she tucked the wayward strand back under her woebegone bonnet. "And that would be?"

He shrugged. "That we play a game of cards. Monte, faro, roulette, or whatever. McNelly's Gambling House is only a block over. I win, I keep my claim to the land grant, and I advance you passage all the way home to Ireland. You win, you get the land grant, and I decamp back home to England."

She rolled her eyes and sighed. "First thing—yuir skill at cards is well-known. I do not trust ye… me Lord. Second, I do not have a home in Ireland to return to. Tejas is me home now. But here is me suggestion for yuir own noggin. Wed me, and we both get to keep the land."

He blinked, opened his mouth, then shut it. His eyes did not miss the wildly beating pulse at the base of her throat.

"Is that such a far-fetched idea? Rafaela would not have ye. Canna say I blame her. Would not want ye in my bed after ye have been in so many others—especially when ye would, doubtlessly, continue that habit. But separate bedrooms would easily remedy that problem, would it not now?" She looked so damned pleased with herself.

Blood roared in his ears. Sitting straight up, he turned on her. He felt a great tidal wave threatening to engulf him—one created by a monstrous earthquake, its source he could not determine. Its tremors rumbled throughout him, shaking relentlessly the very foundations of his resolve. His teeth were clenched so hard he thought tears must be springing into his eyes. He remembered precisely the moment of his disintegration at what seemed eons ago.

"If I wanted to bed you, separate bedrooms would not stop me. But the thought of your birthing a child of mine is most unbearable."

She jerked away, as if had slapped her. "Oh, 'tis the likes of me that shames ye, does it?" She jumped to her feet, eyes hurling daggers at him. "That, ye would never need worry yuir head about. I would sooner take a knife first and rip yuir bairn from me belly!"

With that, she yanked something else from her reticule—a charred piece of parchment and flung it at him. Then she spun away, her furious stomps taking her down the cobbled ramp onto the wharf to retrieve the boy.

Should he have expected any the less of a reaction from her?

Blankly, he stared down at Houston's missive and realized what she had offered him—the protection of his identity as an agent for the Texican rebels.

And what could he offer her? Why, her life, of course.

He could feel his temples pounding. He squinted his eyes against the chilling wind. When he had offered her his proposition—knowing her loss at gaming would mean her safe return to her Ireland, putting her at a safe distance from him—he realized he had blundered, and badly.

Yet he would so dislike having to deal out yet another death.

14

MATAMOROS

STATE OF TAMAULIPAS, MEXICO

Casamata—the Killing House.

Though not the precise, literal translation of the name attached to the massive thirteen stone armories rimming Matamoros, that was how the locals referred to it, followed by genuflections.

The Chaparral Fox thought *Casamata* most appropriately symbolized his intentions for the fate of the rabble of rebels who would dare thwart his empire, modest though it might be when compared to... well, compared to Alexander the Great's.

Brigadier General Urrea was no idiot. He had accumulated a string of victories, among them the recent ruthless squashing of the uprising in Zacatecas. Last August, he had met in Matamoros with three hundred Comanche to form a treaty. Anglo settlers had seen it as a conspiracy to use the Comanche as allies against Tejas—a conspiracy that had been widely reported in the United States.

As Santa Anna's most capable general, Urrea had been sent once more to Matamoros, specifically for this clandestine meeting within the *Casamata*.

Since Matamoros's polyglot population gave additional value in intelligence gathering, the Chaparral Fox had been commissioned for a fact-finding mission by the Mexican government and given secret instructions—seek with greatest prudence all news you can regarding the affairs in Tejas.

The Chaparral Fox followed the guard along one of *Casamata's* underground tunnels, leading past prisoner's cells and a torture room, and then up out its bowels by a narrow stairwell to the commandant's office.

Here, Urrea awaited, having arrived with some of his staff after a long ride from Saltillo the night before. Born in *Presidio* de Tucson of *hidalgo* lineage, Urrea was of the same age as the Chaparral Fox and had evidently once been handsome, but a double chin now detracted from his otherwise patrician profile.

"General." The Chaparral Fox took the empty seat opposite the absentee commandant's desk.

Urrea did not turn from where he stood, perusing the wall map. "You bring information?" His voice did not hide his contempt for a spy, a position that implied a lack of principles and integrity.

The Chaparral Fox saw his position as one of providing needful information, regardless of non-military loss of life, in exchange for consolidating the creation of his kingdom there in Tejas.

The revolt of its colonists had offered him the perfect opportunity. The revolt had started as a civil war between the Federalists and Santa Anna's Centralists within Mexico and had developed into a war for independence in its province of Tejas—even as the civil war continued elsewhere in Mexico.

He settled back in the chair, his forearms on the arm rests. "The Texican's government is in disarray. Factions subverting each other. No one knows who's in charge. The only one among the council members worth his salt is Sam Houston. But I have managed to see that their worthy general has been dispatched to the eastern portion of Tejas to deal with the Cherokee Indians."

Urrea turned now to face him. "Then the way has been paved to retake San Antonio de Bexar."

"I do not think that would be a wise decision."

Urrea's brows lowered like a cur bristling. "Why, precisely?"

He placed his fingertips together and stared over them at the general. "General Cos failed to hold Bexar, as will you in retaking it—because of men who have seen military action like Bowie, Fannin, Crockett, Travis, and others."

"Bahh. Everyone knows the superiority of our Mexican soldiers over those backwoodsmen of Kentucky and Tennessee."

"That may be true, but your Mexican officers also know that the Brown Bess muskets your soldiers tote, despite their attached bayonets, lack the range of the Texican long rifles." He leaned forward. "Nevertheless, the Texicans can be defeated—with their forces divided."

Now Urrea leaned forward, palms braced upon the desk and a sarcastic smile on his lips. "I am certain you have a suggestion as to how that could be accomplished."

The Chaparral Fox's smile was smug. "I set the stage several weeks ago at a secret meeting of theirs held at San Felipe de Austin. Matamoros is our bait."

As if taking new stock of the double agent, Urrea's stroked his double chins. "Hmmm. Go on."

"Fannin and Dr. Grant—a Scotsman who fancies himself as self-appointed Commander-in-Chief for the Texican forces—march in two weeks from separate localities. Each leads an expedition of a hundred men or so, bent on capturing Matamoros, thereby creating a neat trap for you to spring. We will draw the Texican troops far from their base at Bexar. Then, while you take them by surprise, Generals Cos and Almonte can easily defeat the negligent number of volunteers remaining in the upper part of the Colonies."

Now he had Urrea's respectful attention, and he proceeded to give the position and numbers of Texican rebels at Bexar, Gonzales, and San Patricio. He also provided vital information that Houston was sending Bowie to Goliad to attempt to halt Fannin's march to Matamoros and then to head southwest to put a stop to Grant's movements that had been synchronized with Fannin's.

After he finished, Urrea's dismissal of him with a careless flick of his hand bothered the Chaparral Fox not one whit. He knew his next step would assure the consolidation of his own personal empire and the obliteration of the insurgents who threatened it, regardless of which side of the fracas they placed their allegiance.

"YOU SIMPLY MUST GET OUT of the house for a while, *ma chère fille.*" Tea cup and saucer in hand, Therese swept into her dimly lit parlor. Clouds, blowing in from offshore, had been threatening rain all afternoon. "Having lost my husband, I can tell you that confinement is a recipe for depression."

Rafaela repressed a sigh and, despite the lingering tingle in the fingers of her injured left arm, continued her stitching. The tablecloth she was embroidering mirrored her rather disastrous life—a porcelain vase containing vibrant garden flowers except for the single common dandelion that had been discarded at the base of the vase.

"I cannot impose on your hospitality forever, Therese. Once the solicitor has put my father's affairs in order, I should have more than enough funds to join my aunt in Savannah."

"And do what?" Therese took a sip of her tea, liberally laced with brandy. "Live out your days in a staid old town as a staid old spinster?"

Her needle pricked the tip of her forefinger and she thrust it between her lips to soothe the pain. But she couldn't soothe the pain that beat behind her eyes when she struggled out of bed each morning and squeezed her heart all day long. Twenty-seven days since her father's burial—twenty-seven days since last she had seen Niall.

"Well?"

"Perhaps I prefer to be a spinster."

"Bah, I do not believe that. Besides, how would you support yourself?"

"If need be, I could take a position as a governess."

Therese made a scoffing noise and set her saucer and empty cup on the elaborately carved pine sideboard. "Ladies of quality do not work, my dear. Besides, outside the walls of my house, excitement awaits you."

"I have had enough excitement for a lifetime."

"*Non,* you may have had enough difficulties—teething troubles, I call them—but excitement, it is a different thing. It is exhilarating, whether it is a challenge or a bonanza. This town is throbbing with excitement. Capitalists, adventurers, hidalgos, smugglers—they are flocking here to reap the profits that are the benefits of, not a staid old town, but of the doorway to the frontier and adventure itself."

Rafaela's lips compressed, her needle flashed in and out of the hoop's tautly stretched cloth. "Capitalists like Cavett Magnum?"

"You have met?"

She expelled a breath of frustration and laid her embroidery hoop in her lap. The possibility of a chance meeting with Cavett Magnum was one of the reasons she did not wish to venture from Therese's house, just around the corner from the plaza and the Land Commissioner's office. "He attended the wedding ceremonies."

"*Mais oui, bien sûr.* Not a house nor a business in Matamoros has not been a recipient of his largess. But I digress. Back to the discussion of excitement. A fandango is excitement." Therese grabbed the hoop from Rafaela's lap and tossed it on the settee. "And that, my dear, is where we are going this evening."

———

THE MAGNIFICENT CATHEDRAL OF OUR Lady of Refuge shared the west side of Matamoros's beautiful garden plaza with the stately two-story government building, known as the Municipal Palace. One of its reception rooms opened weekly for the fiesta of quadrilles and the more popular *fandangos,* along with the obligatory gaming tables on the second floor.

The Irish Traveler wended his way through the revelers. Niall had occasionally attended the *fiesta* for its *fandango* music, joining his guitar with a violinist and accompanied by castanets and tambourines. Associated with the gypsies, the music had found appreciation among the aristocracy.

Most often lively and gay, the fandango sometimes could also be expressive of painful and powerful emotions. Death, desperation, imprisonment... and lost love, which could bruise like death itself.

Tonight, he was here not so much for the music but for information. Sooner or later, Carmargo would show his face in Matamoros again. What better place to ferret out the man? A place where Matamoros's aristocracy and commoners mixed with Mexican officers from Fort Guerrero and *vaqueros* in from the *rancheros*.

A pretty, dark-eyed Mexican maiden accosted him, hoping to sell a cigar, candy, or perhaps other favors. He waved her away.

At the far end of the room, a table was set with coffee urns and little cakes. On a dais, a Mexican in a food-stained white pajama shirt was playing a brassy coronet. An elderly woman wrapped in a black *rebozo* perched on a stool beside the musician and clicked her castanets with regal grace.

Niall reclaimed his guitar from the adjacent cane-bottom chair and, taking the seat, balanced the guitar on his crossed leg. Alternately strumming and tapping the instrument, he joined the other two. Raspy harsh chords played out his frustration, his longing, his malcontent.

Braving the cold, drizzly night, the patrons had come to relax and enjoy the coffee and cakes, as well as the *pulque, mescal,* beer, and other spirits. A couple of drunken soldiers took little notice of the performance, but other revelers listened and clapped after each song. Later, some of them might venture dancing the wild and rowdy *fandango* in the room's center, which had been cleared of furniture. Regardless, practically everyone attended the weekly *fete*.

So, he should not have been surprised by the entrance of Therese del Valle, followed by Rafaela. Still, he couldn't help but be caught off guard. Her long hair was caught up at her nape in a sequined net that twinkled like diamonds. After she shed her rain-damp cloak, a wide, low neckline with long sleeves of some satiny blue material drew his eye to the small rise of her breasts.

He felt as if his insides had been kicked out. He missed a note and the coronet player flicked him a sidelong glance. In the next chord progression, his fingers stuttered badly over his fretwork. The coronet player finished the melodic-like passage and leaned over to him. *"Su mujer está hermosa."*

"She's not my woman." But she *was* beautiful. Maybe not a bold, forceful beautiful, but a classical, cool beautiful that caught you unawares, that tripped you up if you were not careful. Even as he made love to his guitar, he watched her from beneath his lashes.

She and Therese took one of the benches that banked the reception room's perimeter. Throughout the rest of the evening, he pointedly ignored Rafaela—or tried to. But the occasional sound of her lovely laughter made his breath catch oddly, and the candle lights playing over her bare, alabaster shoulders did strange things to his gut.

Grace, intelligence, kindness, and quality. She deserved a life that did not include a mere horse trader with no significant family background.

Then he sighted Paladín coming down the wrought-iron staircase from the gaming room above. Quitting the tables early was unusual for him. Had he left heavy losses on the green baize? He made his way toward Rafaela in that natural, commanding way he possessed.

Niall was startled by his proprietary reaction at the sight of Paladín talking to her. Niall's creed was you own nothing, you lose nothing. Yet steam burned through his lungs, his fingertips rubbed against his thumbs, and everything in the room blurred but that of the singular couple.

Abruptly, he set aside his guitar. *What in the bloody hell am I doing? She's not mine but my friend's.*

Former friend.

He lurched to his feet, abandoning his guitar and grabbing his sheepskin coat, and headed outside into the sleet. His three-inch rowel spurs jangled on the cobblestones. Mist curtained his vision. Behind him came the muffled liveliness of the fiesta. Ahead of him the dead of night.

He threw back his head to let the freezing mist sheen his cheekbones, seep into his slitted eyes, soak his mustache, and refresh his senses. With that, he laughed at the absurdity of it all, for there was nothing else for him to do.

THERESE DEL VALLE THOUGHT THE performance that night at the provincial Municipal Palace rivaled anything produced by New Orleans St. Charles Theater, the striking and most expensive theater built in America.

As she and Rafaela had spread their crinoline skirts on the bench, Rafaela's hands had been noticeably shaking. Following the direction of her stunned friend's gaze, Therese at once comprehended the scenario.

It was not Rafaela's fiancé with whom Rafaela was in love, but the young man, Paladín's hired hand, playing the guitar. She had eyes only for him. Her face came alive, her features vibrant with a desire that made her breathtaking.

Of course, Niall Gorman was handsome in a rough, cocky sort of way and, with his steely temper, was said to be a dangerous man to cross. Therese's own preference had always leaned toward the self-assured Alejandro de la Torre y Stuart, with his strong sense of will and indomitability.

Alas, she suspected the arrogant, irresistible Baron had no inclination for a relationship with her outside that of an occasional dalliance.

She watched the *bon vivant* move now toward Rafaela and herself with that easy, fluid grace that breathed a danger all its own. If Rafaela was grimacing because she might find him cold and impersonal, that was not Therese's take on the man. He was that rare type who burned with passion.

Besides, she was not one to cut off her nose to spite her face. After all, he *had* insisted on reimbursing her for sheltering Rafaela after the murderous attack by Mexican marauders at the wedding. And Paladín *was* a baron.

He made a leg, then stood. "I take it the pair of you are here to relieve your boredom?"

"As are you?" She sent him a flirtatious smile from beneath her widow's black ribboned cap, tied beneath her chin at a saucy angle. "Though I would think squalid Matamoros might be beneath your station, monsieur, when it comes to relieving one's ennui."

"My dear, you have no idea the places I have visited that are considered beneath one's station."

The scandalous admission, rather than appalling her, alleviated her tedium, as Alejandro always managed to do.

He turned his singular attention to Rafaela, inquiring, not about his fiancée but about her effervescent companion, Fiona Flanigan. "You have spoken with her?"

"At mass last Sunday." Rafaela broke out her folding fan that dangled from her wrist by a cord. "She seems to be settling in."

At the Spanish court, fans were used in a more or less secret, unspoken code, a way to cope with the restricting social etiquette. To Therese, the message Rafaela was sending was clearly one of agitation. It could be the Baron who so agitated her, but Therese suspected it was the presence of the Irish Traveler—or, now, absence—which agitated Rafaela.

She glanced past the Baron to espy the Reverend Daniel Engler now at his elbow, and her brows shot up. The *Fandango Fete* was a most unlikely venue for the Presbyterian minister to attend.

His rangy frame was clothed in black broadcloth with a puritan's white bibbed collar and a black hat with a high crown topped his abundant brown hair. True, he had the distant gaze of a hermit, but *ooh-la-la, a roué's* mouth. She had to repress a smirk. For all their piety, these Presbyterian parsons with their puritan streak lived with gusto.

Nevertheless, compared to Alejandro, the Right Reverend Engler would be deadly dull and was most likely here as a spoilsport this evening.

He bowed curtly, surprising her by sparing the Baron a warm nod. Then, in reply to Alejandro's inquiry about Fiona, he addressed the three of them. "My sister tells me Fiona is splendid with the children she teaches and that she misses you all."

Therese was of the opinion that Fiona missed the Baron most of all, though the Irish lass might not even realize it. To the righteous reverend, Therese merely said, "And what in God's good name brings you, Reverend Engler, to this licentious place?"

He smiled gently. "Rounding up sheep, of course." He glanced around the crowded room. "Occasionally, Beaman is apt to fall asleep either here or in the alley back of the Municipal Palace, much to the angst of his wife and six children. I am searching for him now."

"I shall go help." Therese heard herself and was as astounded by her offer as was Daniel Engler. Even the Baron raised a brow in mild amusement.

"It is not the most pleasant of tasks."

"Even frivolous pleasures grow tedious. I assure you I am up to this."

"Humor her, Engler. She can be most unpleasant when bored. I shall attend to my fiancée."

Therese rose, extending her hand to the lanky parson. Nonplussed, he offered his arm, leading her toward the rear of the Municipal Palace. With every step she took, she became increasingly aware of this odd man. He smelled of lime cologne, and he walked loose-limbed, as though he were at ease, despite the den of inequity in which he found himself.

"When inebriated, Beaman can curse a blue streak, *Señora* del Valle."

"So can I, even when *not* inebriated."

At this, he grinned, and his countenance changed unbelievably into that of a strikingly good-looking man. "Still, I must caution you, he can be prone to retching up his entrails."

"I cared for my husband as he lay dying." Her somber tone was so unnatural for her reputation. "I can handle retching and much worse."

The parson's hazel eyes appeared to measure her stamina, or was it her worth he was measuring? Then he nodded.

Accepting his arm once more, she followed him out back, where the light sprinkles had increased to a steady bone-chilling drizzle. If the temperature dropped any lower, it would likely snow, a rarity for the Rio Bravo river valley. This had to be one of the wettest winters yet.

As the parson had predicted, Beaman was huddled with an empty rye bottle in the litter of trash behind the building.

The watchmaker snorted as Daniel and she hoisted him erect. "Whaz—whaz this?" His breath, reeking of alcohol, frosted the air. He then sagged and would have collapsed on broken bottle shards had Daniel not supported his weight.

"Bugger, you tryin' to pick my pockets, are you?"

Together, she and Daniel hauled him to Daniel's buggy, waiting out front of the Municipal Palace.

By the time she and Daniel returned Beaman home, she was thoroughly drenched by the rain.

By the time Daniel escorted *her* home, she was thoroughly in love with the oblivious parson. Surely, she must have come down with the local swamp miasma.

———————

AFTER THE DEPARTURE OF REVEREND Engler and Therese, the trumpet player ended the intermission by resuming the gay *fandango* music and Paladín waited for Niall's return. Moments later, he appeared, taking up his guitar, his features composed. The evening's rain had cooled off his hot temper.

Well, time to ignite it again—and keep him downstairs.

Paladín startled Rafaela by holding out his hand. "Shall we dance?"

She snapped shut her fan. "There is no need to be courteous. Everyone knows you are not enamored with me."

"Rafaela, I never bother with such civilities. I am being wily."

"Wily?"

His hand about her wrist, he pulled her up into his arms. "Merely goading our Irish Traveler a little closer to the edge."

"Oh?" She looked askance at him, her gaze one of concentration, as if she were tallying on an abacus. "You… you are no longer desirous of marriage?"

"I have never been desirous of marriage. To you or any unfortunate female within my proximity."

"But my dowry?"

Her back was stiff where his palm pressed, but she followed his lead easily. "It's yours to keep—and Gorman's, once he comes to his senses."

Confusion knitted her brows. "What about San Patricio…? The land grant's taxes and upkeep?"

"I have plans that will take care of that most tidily."

Indeed, casting his lot with the winning side would assure San Patricio was his. However, to his deep disgust, he more times than not sided with the underdog. And if ever there was an underdog, it was that motley group of foolhardy Texicans, lacking a government to coordinate them, lacking supplies for what promised to be the worst winter in memory, and lacking weapons for the coming Armageddon.

Well, Carmargo was still upstairs at the gaming table. When he deserted the green baize, Paladín meant to dog him.

15

MATAMOROS

STATE OF TAMAULIPAS, MEXICO

The Rio Bravo Female Seminary's curriculum was generally not very demanding of Fiona's students—reading, writing, basic arithmetic, and a smither of geography and history.

She had for books Webster's blue-backed *Speller*, simple moral tracts, and primers of childish virtues. A last resort was the King James Version of the Bible—last, since she wasn't even sure God cared if the children learned or not. The Bible was incomprehensible to most of her students, comprised mostly of fortunate daughters of Matamoros tradesmen.

Liam, who could barely decipher to the rule of three, was not so fortunate. The only school in Matamoros was a private one run by a student at the university in Mexico City who had returned home to Matamoros when Santa Anna had closed the university the year before.

She couldn't afford to send Liam to the private school, but she continued to teach him at night. And now, he was even more unfortunate.

In the midst of winter's wrath, he had come down with the measles. Rather than expose her students, she had packed him up and sent him to Charlotte's until after the outbreak.

Fiona's salary of fifteen dollars a month in pesos plus boarding for the five-month school term was a boon that would end too soon.

And then what?

All she had in the world was that piece of paper that was her legitimate—or perhaps illegitimate—claim to the San Patricio land grant. A claim that awaited an approval from Mexican authorities in San Antonio de Bexar. A most uncertain outcome what with the state of anarchy and the Texicans now in control there.

If possession of land had meant everything in the world to her before, the possession of it now meant both that and something not of this world, namely the despicable Paladín and his forfeiture of the land.

That afternoon, she finished cleaning the slates and straightening the chairs in the classroom, which had once been the small adobe's sitting room, with hand-planed mesquite beams and wooden floors. The single bedroom and kitchen were equally austere, discounting a wood-burning ten-plate stove in the kitchen.

Nevertheless, the adobe, rubbing shoulders with other Easter-egg painted ones, was not far from the main road leading past Fort Guerrero's iron-gated walls into Matamoros. That location, just inside those gates, gave her a window to the bustling world that was the international city. This was stimulation she loved.

She set a tea kettle on to boil. From the pie safe, she took out leftover fried corn cakes and sliced goat cheese from a small block she kept in parchment paper. Then she settled into the rush-bottom chair to read the latest issue of *The Telegraph and Texas Register*.

The most recent decree of the Provisional Government, January 2nd, 1836, warned that Santa Anna was headed toward Tejas with 10,000 men, "*… his purpose is to leave nothing of us but the recollection we once existed.*"

She got up to measure out the paltry cache of tea leaves. Brewed, the tea would taste like weak, brown bog. She eyed the bottle standing next to the Speller and Bible, stacked on the sturdy solid pine table.

Earlier that afternoon, Burt Beaman had come to inquire about the slow progress of his daughter, the adorable but stuttering seven-year-old Priscilla. Rather than participate with the other girls, Prissy would retreat to a corner and play her silent, solitary game of cat's cradle. As partial payment for Fiona's after-hours tutoring of Prissy, Beaman had left the *aguardiente*.

Against her better judgment, she uncapped the brown bottle and took a restorative sip, then a deep swig. Heat roared up through her that staved off the chill of the February afternoon.

She tugged off her lace cap and was unfastening a couple of the top buttons of her high-neck bodice, when a rap at the front door spun her around. The visitor could be anyone… more than likely a parent of one of her students.

Yet somehow, she sensed her visitor could be only one person. Things like this were inexplicable—intuition, sixth sense, that invisible Ariadne's thread which connected two people—abstractions that counted for nothing. Unless she believed that life was more than a string of coincidences, that she and Paladín were meant to cross paths. Time and again.

She placed her hand on the door's iron latch, hesitated a fateful moment, then pushed down on the latch and opened the door. But, of course, the imperious Adonis, Alejandro de la Torre y Stuart, Baron of Paladín, filled the door frame.

Booted, spurred, rapier at his side, he let his appreciative gaze sweep over her in a proprietary fashion. He nodded, as if satisfied with his findings. "Good afternoon." Ducking his head to clear the door jamb, he entered without her bidding, forcing her to move aside.

"It *was*." But her heart was racing like a horse crossing Londonderry's finish line. Damned, but the Devil was beautiful. Strange how, at first, she had thought him too full of hard angles and harsh lines to be handsome. His was an aggressively sensual face with, God help her, a carnal smile that vowed fulfilment.

"With your recent independence, I must confess I miss your addressing me as 'my Lord.'"

"I doubt ye have ever even been to a confession, a brigand such as yuirself."

That garnered a slight smile from those disturbing lips. He raked a hand through his glossy black hair. He looked uncommonly uncomfortable for the briefest of moments.

She said nothing, only waiting for him to state the purpose of his visit. He was not getting off this easy.

He planted a fist on one hip, the other on his rapier's hilt, then emitted a half-sigh, half grunt. "I have come bearing a gift."

"I am no Helen of Troy. If I remember me Greek mythology correctly, she was the most beautiful woman in the world."

He opened his mouth, as if about to say something, then closed it, and she felt cheated. He moved past her toward the kitchen, where the steaming kettle was whistling.

Following him, she continued. "Still, ye can understand then why, as Virgil warned, I beware of one such as yourself bearing a gift."

"And I am no Greek." He set aside the whistling kettle and glanced at the plate of cheese and fried corn cakes on the table. "May I?"

Without waiting for her assent, he removed his rapier, draping its scabbard belt across a chair, and turned another chair to straddle it backwards. He helped himself to a slice of cheese. Deliberately, infuriatingly at ease, he stretched those lengthy legs out close to where she stood.

He bit into the cheese and his eyes lit with the simple pleasure. At that instant, he looked like an innocent youth rather than a jaded young man. Why could she not fall in love with a decent chap? Someone like Cavett Magnum?

With that thought, her mouth dropped open then clamped shut tighter than a clam. No, it could not be. It was not possible. She simply could *not* be in love with a man as contemptible as Paladín.

Stunned, she dropped into the other chair, collected herself, and folded her arms over her chest. "So, what is this so-called gift?"

His hand dipped into his vest pocket and produced her locket, like new. "I found it on the bell tower. I had Beaman repair the clasp."

She picked it up from his large palm and fought off tears. "'Tis all I had left of me family."

Studiously, he selected a square of corncake. "Well, they do say the good die young."

Abashed by her earlier softening toward him, she straightened her back. "I suppose ye be wanting tea with yuir food?" Still clutching the locket, she banged first one tin cup then a second on the table. "Or perhaps ye are still wanting me to give up me claim to the land?"

"Right now, I would prefer silence to snippety retorts and the *aguardiente* to tea." He proceeded to uncork the brown bottle on the table and slosh the strongly potent brew into each cup. "So, you really did abandon your life of crime for providing Matamoros's young females with education and virtues?"

"Me life hasn't been *all* about crime… exactly." She took a fortifying swallow of the *aguardiente*. When dueling with the Machiavellian Paladín, she'd need something strong to gird her loins. She coughed, blinked back tears, cleared her throat, then wheezed.

He smiled. "Oh? Then you pilfered my gold watch merely with the thought you might return it to—"

"'Twas Liam who—" She bit her lip. Could so little *aguardiente* loosen her tongue to run riot?

Something in Paladín's features changed, though she could not quite say what. He leaned forward, forearms braced on the chair's top railing, his tin cup fully swallowed by one palm. "I see. Well, if your life has not been all about crime, what has it been about?"

She tossed down the remainder of her cup, coughed violently, and held it out for more. "What has me life been about?"

Paladín obliged and set the bottle back on the table without recapping it. She took another swallow of the raw courage, this one measured—no need to act as if she were paddy at the pub. "About keeping me and me family one step ahead of starvation."

He studied her with what appeared to be casual regard. "Tell me about your family."

"Not much to tell." Still gripping the locket as if it were a lifeline, she managed an indifferent shrug. "Me parents, like most of us Irish, had no security of tenure on their land. They could be turned out whenever the middleman chose—he worked for the English Lord who owned our land." She swallowed another nerve-numbing dram of the *aguardiente*. It burned like the fires of hell.

"Go on."

Instead of her family, memories of Grantam Manor's Little House filled her field of vision… of walking down a shadowy green avenue of tall elms and chestnut trees, of passing through a stone gateway and walking along a cobbled drive that led to a small courtyard. That two-story limestone cottage known as the Little House was home to the staff. On Sundays, her mother would leave it and walk the long road back to the family's sod house.

Later, Grantam Manor itself, a seventeen-room house across a bridge over a trout stream, had become Fiona's own refuge from the stench and poverty that was her life. On days the tutor came, her mother would sneak her inside. Turf fires burned in every room, and the tutor, she in her rags, and Geoffrey in his velvets were served rich tea from cups borne on heavy wicker trays.

"When it rained, our sod house leaked like a sieve."

"What else?"

So many questions. Answering them required concentration from a brain that was not spinning. "Well, me family would dread when the middleman came calling for rent. One time… me oldest sister offered herself in order to keep the sod roof over our heads. The middleman had wanted me. I was thirteen at the time and Peg persuaded him to take her instead."

She didn't like the blistery look in Paladín's eyes. Or maybe it was her eyes. They felt blistered, indeed, as if bathed by the stinging *aguardiente*.

"Your father?" He quaffed the last of his *aguardiente*. "Did he do nothing?"

"He died of lung rot six months before that. Mum's health was not faring much better. She lost her job as scullery maid the next year and died three months later. So Peggy continued to whore, and I applied for me mum's position as scullery maid. Me hiring depended on giving meself to the middleman."

She had often wondered if that, also, had been the price her mother had paid for the plum job.

Fiona was not sure, her eyes were still watering from the *aguardiente*'s burn, but she thought she saw Paladín wince.

She must have been mistaken, because he said in that sandpapery voice of his, "But you did not, did you, my little virgin?"

She reached for her cup and took a deep draught of the eye-watering, throat-burning brew. At least it eased her heart's thudding. "I passed on the opportunity to work as a scullery maid. Took in washing from Kerry, seven miles away, I did. Managed to find me own tutoring jobs there sometimes, as well. But the townspeople were nearly as poor as meself. Left with raising me younger brother and sisters, I turned to thievery."

She paused, flashed him a breezy grin and drained her glass.

He poured another round. "Do enlighten me about your thievery."

"Oh, that came easily enough. The house staff had been used to me presence the days the Earl's son was being tutored and gave me no thought."

She took another gulp of her libation. It no longer burned as badly, but the room spun a little more wildly. "Still, I always had to stay one step ahead of the middleman. The Earl never missed the two items I pilfered. A silver thimble, then a snuff box. No, wait… I forgot the piece of silverware. It helped purchase me passage to America. Ye see, after I lost the last of me brothers and sisters to the Grim Reaper, I headed for New York and Peggy."

She hiccoughed and went to clap her hand over her mouth to stifle the next hiccough. That was when she felt the wetness on her cheeks. Surely, she had not been tearing up?

Before she could brush the dampness away, Paladín leaned forward and did it for her. "I must say, you are an adventuresome lass."

Then he was tugging her to her feet, trapping her between him and the table. He took the locket, still dangling from one hand. "Turn around."

She eyed him askance, then did as he bade. As she turned, the room seemed to turn as well, but in the opposite direction. Her gaze fell on the bottle, tin cups, and books. They shifted in and out of focus. That blasted *aguardiente*. She blinked several times, trying to restore some thought of sensibility.

His forearms encircled her neck. As he fastened the clasp, the pendant dropped into her décolletage to lie coolly against her heated flesh. His hot hands cupped her shoulders.

She went absolutely still. His chin rustled the hair gathered atop her head. When his arms enfolded her against him, her head lolled to one side on his chest. Lightheaded, she sighed and gave herself over to the comfort his body afforded. Her cheek against the smoothness of his fancy woolen blue waist-coat with its silk piping, she could feel the thudding of his own heart.

She twisted in his embrace and peered up at him. Above the hard line of his jaw, he watched her much as the seducer *Vicomte* de Valmont must have eyed the hapless *Madame* de Tourvel. She gulped. "An adventuresome lass I am, ye say? 'Tis me adventuresome spirit that has landed me in trouble far too often."

She should politely thank him for the return of her necklace. Should show him to the door…. If she could find it. She should hurl at him contemptible, disagreeable, and disgusting epithets and call upon all the saints in the Roman calendar to curse him. If her tongue were not so furry.

The saints help her. After all this time, the truth of it was quite obvious to her. She wanted him to stay, wanted to bask in the warmth of his heated gaze, wanted to seek the safety of his invincible strength.

Her heart warned the untouched treasure of her body would be plundered and squandered by the roguish baron. Yet every beat of her heart kept drumming out that she wanted him, muffling all effort at sensible thoughts.

The knuckle of his forefinger cupped her chin, tilting it so he could better see her features. "Landed you in trouble? Such as?"

All hope to hate him was vanquished. Transfixed, she murmured, "Such as now."

He lowered his head until it was mere inches from hers. His voice was both quiet and rumbling. "Such as since that damnable day I first set eyes on you."

"Meself? Ye were the one who insisted I serve as Rafaela's—"

His lips shut off her protest. Without volition, she stood on tiptoe, her arms entwining around his neck. One of his large hands splayed across her arse. Shocked, she stiffened. His other cupped the back of her head, his clever fingers weaving into the careless knot of her hair. From a distance, she heard the loosed hair pins clicking on the floor, felt her untamable hair tumbling over her shoulders.

As his lips covered her willingly parted ones, she fought against his raffish charm, fought against the sweet lassitude pervading her... and lost.

She had been kissed before—one, a rather apathetic kiss bestowed by Geoffrey. Later, there had been a few snuck from her unwitting lips by a lad from Kerry and then, several times more, kisses pressed upon her by a New York cooper.

None of those kisses had been arousing enough for her to take a chance on encumbering herself with yet again more children for which to be responsible. But Paladín's kisses... ahh, they were demanding, possessive, deliriously inebriating.

She returned his passion with an urgency unfamiliar to her. He tasted of *aguardiente* and lust. Disorientation distorted the remnants of her resolve to withstand the onslaught of his extraordinary maleness. Still, she made a feeble attempt. "Please, I am not...."

"Not what?" he inquired in that corroded, yet alluring voice.

"Not... not sure."

He released her, looked at his hands and flexed them, then leveled his gaze on her. "Your ardent return of my... passion... led me to believe otherwise."

She could sense his gathering withdrawal and blurted her weakness. "… not sure how to go about this…. I feel so lost."

"We go about it slowly. Savoring each delectable moment." He lowered his forehead to rest against hers. "And I fear we are both lost, *mi querida.*"

———————

HE WANTED THIS EXCEEDINGLY FRUSTRATING sprite, regardless of who she was or the fact she sought to take what was his. It seemed those days of making do with other women would no longer suffice. He wanted to find redemption in the renewal offered by her small, innocent body.

So, it has come to this. Preserve her virginity or satisfy my lust.

He wanted to be the one who initiated her into this supreme rhapsody. He tilted his head back, eyes closed, teeth gritted.

Honor be damned.

He rose and scooped her small, lax body against his chest.

As tiny as the adobe was, the bedroom was not hard to find. Moonbeams peeked through the slatted shutters. The rag-stuffed mattress on the rope-slung bed was not the down mattress with fine linen sheets he would have wanted for her.

If there existed an ounce of integrity in him, he would tuck Fiona into bed and take his leave. If he stayed, it was either spill his seed like a callow young man or take her chastity.

Awaiting his attention, her sweet body lay trembling and compliant on her bed. He had waited for her for far too long. Nothing could keep him from her, neither his conscience nor her resistance.

His hand braced at either side of her hips, he leaned over her, staring down into the glittering green pools of her eyes. Her freckles were lost in her heated blush and her curling hair was spread fanwise, tumbling over the bedside in a bright red waterfall. At that moment, he couldn't recall anything more beautiful.

"Alas," his voice grated, "it would appear 'tis I, not you, who is the thief, robbing you of what belongs to a loving husband."

The tremulous smile curving her lips would have daunted a better man, but his desire for her blotted out all consideration of decency and right and wrong. Hell awaited him upon his death, but he would, at least, find heaven now in pleasuring Fiona. Momentarily, he closed his eyes once again against the temptation.

When he opened them, she was curling her body into a languid slumber, unaware of how close she was to being deflowered. Moonlight glinted off the tawdry pendant laying in the valley of her bodice's *décolletage*.

With an oath, he turned from the bed and left the room.

Closing behind him her adobe's turquoise-painted door, he made his way into the depths of night back toward Lady Letty's House and the person next on his agenda that night.

Carmargo would be secluded in one of her upstairs rooms, either taking his own pleasure or sleeping off this evening's hard round of drinking, which usually lasted a good twenty-four hours.

Pausing to look up at star-spangled sky, Paladín felt that he would have been wiser had he partaken of those pleasures offered by Lady Letty's girls rather than haunting Fiona's home like some love-struck youth. A youth he was not, but he could no longer deny he was love-struck.

16

MATAMOROS
STATE OF TAMAULIPAS, MEXICO

The Irish Traveler had nothing of substance to offer Rafaela and clearly, he did not want what she had to offer. At least, not on a permanent basis.

For her, his easy smile, his restless energy, his protective stance, were all she now wanted from life... and as habit-forming as opium. She would gladly suffer an opiate's withdrawal symptoms—the stomach cramps and vomiting and crawling skin—if she could but rid herself of her incessant, clamoring desire for him.

If that meant gouging out her heart, losing her mind, and peeling off her skin, then so be it.

That morning, she sat, dazed, in Therese's parlor, reading the elaborate scrawling of her father's solicitor. Basically, he had deposited in her account just enough to sustain her... *if* she was frugal. Otherwise, she faced the debtor's prison. Apparently, she was not the only one to have squandered money. Her father had squandered his on everything from wine and women to bad investments.

Yet another ending in her life, another lifestyle to which she must readjust. Madrid, Spain…Valenciennes, France… Mayfair, England… Guatemala City, Guatemala… back to England, this time London… Matamoros, Mexico… and dare she leave out the days spent with the Mexican military in San Antonio de Bexar? Next Savannah, Georgia, and her only relative—an indifferent old aunt.

She would purchase passage today. The quicker she put the Irish Traveler behind her, the easier it would be to go on with this new phase of her life.

Her reflections were interrupted by the conversation going on in the hallway. Rafaela had not even realized the plump house girl, Isabella, had admitted a visitor. Leaning forward slightly in her arm chair, Rafaela could see Parson Engler.

Therese descended the stairs to greet him and Rafaela watched the interplay going on between the French Widow and the pastor.

Pilgrim's hat in hand, long eyes narrowed skeptically, he was quizzing her. "You are certain you want to accompany me, *Señora* del Valle?"

"Therese, please."

"Where I go to find lost sheep, one also finds the dregs of humanity. It is no place for a lady."

Therese delivered a waspish smile. "I am not a lady, but a woman, Parson Engler."

The man—Rafaela had not decided if he was handsome—blushed. "Daniel." He offered his arm. "Then it is off to the seedier side of life we are bound—Baja Matamoros."

Therese turned toward the open parlor doors, calling out, "Rafaela, won't you go with us?"

Rising, letter of transmittal still in hand, she shook her head. "Thank you, Therese, but I need to go to the bank."

"Then take my carriage. We shall not return until late."

Pedro, a gnarled old man with a ready grin that displayed missing teeth and a sombrero that had seen better days, perched on the carriage box. With a pair of horses at his command, he drove Rafaela to the bank and from there to the Port of Matamoros to purchase her passage to Savannah.

A brisk wind blew in off the Gulf, making the drive seem colder than the semi-tropical sunshine would warrant. Somewhere there, in the back allies of Baja Matamoros, Therese and Daniel were searching for souls in need of succor.

As usual, the port was busy. The sounds of English, French, German, and Italian could be heard among the 7,000 or so people who made up the port's canaille. There was even an Anglo-American Consul posted at the port.

A commotion appeared to be astir near the wharf. Then, from among the throng of people, it was as if her musings had summoned Niall. A bloodied Niall, with eyes blackened and manacled between two gun-toting Mexican soldiers.

"Wait!"

Pedro's *sombreroed* head turned sharply to look at her and her anxious expression signaled him to yank on the reins.

With the carriage still rolling, she jumped down and, skirts lifted, ran to intercept the two soldiers. "For what is he being arrested?" she demanded of the heftier of the two soldiers.

"He is a *contrabandista.*" The soldier grinned, flashing a gold tooth. "The Commandant General's office in Matamoros will determine his fate."

Her breath drew in. The Mexican government did not take kindly to smugglers. Execution by a firing squad was the usual method of remedying the area of an apprehended *contrabandista.*

Thank God for the graft, the *mordida,* the Anglo Consul so deplored. She reached into her reticule and fished out the precious passage money. "Here," she urged in Spanish, "give him over to me!"

The pair shared a glance between them. "The Commandant General need never know."

With a toss of his head, the heftier one nodded in the direction of the alley a few steps away that ran between the two buildings. The two half-dragged their human cargo the short distance to release him in the narrow passageway's filth.

Niall staggered, half conscious, and she caught him, steadying him while shoving the paper money in the soldiers' greedy hands as discreetly as possible.

She got him back to the plaza and the carriage. "Pedro, *ayudame!*" What she really needed was Therese and Daniel's help, but only the pastor's Heaven knew where the two might be.

Next to her, Niall lifted his head from her shoulder. Blood streamed from his left nostril and from his mouth, coating the rim of his mustache. His left cheek bone was already turning an abrasive red and swelling so that his blackened eye above had a rakish tilt. "If 'tis not me own Angel of Death." His words were a file's rasp.

She flinched, recalling she had once so named him.

At last, the galloping carriage horses entered Matamoros proper, with Niall now slumped into the curvature of her arm. Between her and Pedro, they shouldered the stumbling, battered Irish Traveler up the stairs to her bedroom.

Tearing off her bonnet, she threw back the coverlet and helped Pedro lower him into her bed. Niall was mumbling nonsensically about ambushes and breasts and foxes.

Swiftly, she and Pedro rid him of his leather vest and chambray shirt, its right sleeve blood drenched. Cold morning sunlight filtered through the chintz curtains to fall across the mid-half of his slack, muscled body in a hazy pattern.

"Tell Isabella I need linen strips, boiled water, and liniment, and that bottle of cognac on the sideboard." She knew nothing about tending wounds but suspected the cognac just might fight off an infection. "And then keep a watch on the street for soldiers, at least until the *señora* returns. Just in case."

"So, you have taken to drinking?" Niall murmured, his thickly lashed lids closed.

"You would drive any woman to drink," she mustered a facade of coolness. Her lungs had never pumped as hard as they had when confronting the two Mexican soldiers. She had always known herself a timid soul. Worse, she was now also a penniless soul. All because this "love them and leave them" Irish Traveler had a lopsided smile that befuddled her imperturbable sensibilities.

Foolish, foolish, foolish. Even more foolish to cry over spilt milk. Nothing to do but face the consequences, the worst being the poor house—and a broken heart.

Waiting for Isabella, she examined Niall's upper torso. He was as still as a corpse.

Sweet Jesus, let it be that he has merely passed out from the pain.

Peering closely, she detected his chest moving in a shallow rhythm. Below, his stomach was laddered with muscles. For a fleeting second, her trembling fingers seized the liberty to track the line of dark hair running from between the lower ribs and heading southward down that taut stomach. Never had she had the freedom for such perusal of a man.

Forcibly, she collected herself and investigated for further injuries. His ribs were already purpling from a beating. A bullet appeared to have plowed through his right shoulder. Nervous, she probed the lacerated flesh for the bullet.

He winced and fixed her with an accusing gaze. "I'd rather you be fondling me cobs."

A flush of heat spread up her chest and neck to pinken her cheeks. "You should be thankful the bullet isn't buried—"

His left hand capturing her wrist, he flashed her that devastating lopsided grin. "I can arrange for that. For the fondling of me—"

Isabella's huaraches slapping against the tiles cut him short. The house maid entered with a tray mounded with torn linen strips, a pitcher of water, and the cognac along with a snifter.

"He will be all right?"

"Alas, yes. The Devil will not claim his own. At least this time. I shall let you know if anything else is needed."

After the house girl departed, Rafaela began to clean the wound, suffering herself with each of Niall's low, gritted moans. Once finished scrubbing his blood crusted nose, eyes, and mouth, she dribbled cognac into the blood-seeping hole.

He groaned. "The bloomin' stuff burns like blazes!"

"That is only a preview of Hell if you do not stop this kind of life you are living!" She grabbed the sniffer, poured a draught, and tossed it down—only to inhale with a raw gasp. Her eyes watered. "Jesus Christ!"

His sweep of mustache lifted with his grin. "I dinna know ladies cursed."

"Shut up." She began to wrap the strips around his shoulder and underneath his arm, tufted with dark hair. So as not to put pressure on his ribs, she was forced to lean across his bare chest in an awkward position. Her head swam, as if the cognac fumes had vaporized her senses. "There," she knotted the strip with a fretful jerk, "that should—"

His good arm encircled her waist firmly, giving her no squiggle room. "Rafaela, me body wants a tending of a different kind."

She froze. Her eyes slid to encounter his feverish gaze, nigh concealed beneath half-mast lids. With distraction, she noted the thin trail of dried blood trickling once more from his nose. "What you need is your mustache shaved."

"Never. But confess ye want me, too. I felt your touching me stomach—close to me knob."

As if a furnace door had opened, embarrassment blasted through her. "I was only examining your bruises and injuries."

"Were you now? Can ye not own up to wanting me, lass?"

With outthrust palms, she cried out. "And what is it you want from me?"

He captured one palm, pressing its center to his warm lips. "I want ye to show me love."

"I... I do not know how."

From above the rim of her palm, his slate blue eyes took their measure of her. Assessing her mettle? Her skill? Or her capacity to love?

"Oh, but you do," he murmured at last.

Her mind reeled. Was he giving her carte blanche? For once in her vapid life, could she forsake the years of rigid training? Could she shake off the role of the levelheaded lady? Could she let go of her inhibitions just this once? Most importantly, could she put the fear and revulsion of four years ago behind her?

Fiona and Therese would know what to do. But she lacked Fiona's pluck and Therese's sensuality.

"Follow your feelings, your instincts," he prompted in a whisper.

With hesitation, her darkened eyes found his. "What if I hurt you while I am…. What about your injuries?"

He sighed. "Me injuries are the least of me concerns. I fear most you will return to the distant, the aloof, young woman ye were."

"Not this day."

He reached up with his good arm and drew her down beside him, her head nestled into the curve of his arm. "But, most, me fears 'tis you, lass, not I, who is the Spell Caster."

"LIAM WAS A DELIGHTFUL, WELL-behaved boy." Charlotte raised the cup of chamomile tea to her soft rosebud of a mouth that Fiona felt was out of keeping with the robust lines of her face and body.

Surely men must find Charlotte attractive. At least, Moses must, because he had requested her hand for all the dances at the St. Valentine's Day ball to be held that night at the Municipal Palace. "And I am vastly comforted that the measles left no scars," Charlotte added with a relieved sigh.

Fiona would be relieved if the scamp did not abscond with all the parsonage's flatware. But then could she condemn him when she had once stolen a piece of silverware? Still, she meant to search the adobe after Charlotte left.

Fiona would be *vastly* relieved if she knew for sure she was still a virgin. Terror struck her heart when she considered that she could be with child. Painful memories of scraping to keep her siblings fed and in clothes nagged at her. She did not want the same for a child of hers. No, she just had to make good her claim on that San Patricio land grant.

What had happened with Paladín the night before last? Something so scandalously pleasurable she blushed to think about what portions she could fuzzily recall. Though dwell on those portions she did.

Charlotte was relating the Texican havoc wreaked by the *Invincible's* blockade of Matamoros. "Why, barrels of coffee from New Orleans are no longer to be found any—"

At that moment, Liam burst through the front door with the brown paper-wrapped bacon beneath one arm. Well, at least he hadn't squandered the near worthless government notes she had given him on something else at the *mercado*. Despite February's unusually warm day, his cheeks were flushed. He thrust out a hand bill. "Look, Fiona–Mam."

Squinting, she was able to make out the proclamation. The handbill had been issued by the Provision Council from their printing offices in San Felipe de Austin.

"What does it say?"

"'Tis announcing the approach of Santa Anna's army. It is calling upon the '... *Texicans to take to the field* en masse... *as an armed force to meet the enemy on the frontier.*'"

Charlotte's plump lips pressed flat. "By all that is holy, when the Provision Council's brief authority expires, in less than a fortnight, by all accounts its members will have an awful reckoning to make to the people."

———————————

EVERYWHERE IN THE MUNICIPAL PALACE'S large reception room red and white teased the eye—from the tablecloths graced with an array of foods, prepared by busy hands of Matamorosean women, to the staircase balustrade's gay bunting to the banner-draped dais, where an assortment of musicians were taking their turn at entertaining.

Despite the festive decorations for Saint Valentine's Day, a tense mood pervaded the partygoers that evening.

All sorts of rumors were flying—that General Urrea was headed from San

Luis Potosi north to Matamoros with a thousand men or more… that Santa Anna had crossed the Rio Bravo at the frontier town of *Presidio* and was marching with a sizable army of 10,000 infantry and 3,000 cavalry to San Antonio de Bexar.

Paladín did know that Sam Houston himself had met with both Fannin and Dr. Grant north of Matamoros, at the town of Refugio, to dissuade them from their foolhardy Matamoros Expedition. Houston was furious that the Expedition had left the Texicans, entrenched within the Alamo Mission outside Bexar, woefully unmanned and depleted of food and weapons.

Houston had not trained under Andrew Jackson without acquiring the ability to win a crowd. His eloquent appeals had convinced more than half of the Expedition's two hundred men to wait, at least at Refugio, for reinforcements.

From the little information Paladín was able to gather at Brown's Billiard Parlor the night before, it would seem Urrea was en route north to Goliad. If that were so, then the Matamoros Expedition was doomed.

As it would seem were his own efforts to out the Chaparral Fox—and, likewise, his efforts to put behind him the saucy sprite who had foiled his best-laid plans.

From his position at the bottom of the staircase, one arm draped over its newel, Paladín watched the revelers.

Solomon, who could not top five and a half feet, was partnered in a cotillion with the giantess, Charlotte. Sitting with punch glasses in hand were another unlikely pair, the ascetic Presbyterian parson and the sybaritic Therese, who seemed enrapt with him. Magnum was dutifully attentive to his wife, returning with a cup of punch he had fetched for her.

Conspicuously missing were Paladín's fiancé and Niall, who, according to Magnum, had been apprehended when tracking down a lead on the Chaparral Fox. A wealthy Spanish lady and an Irish gypsy-mercenary. Now there, indeed, was an improbable pair.

He supposed he and Fiona would also be considered a most implausible couple. He could not seem to take his eyes off her. She was dancing the cotillion with a handsome colonel from Urrea's blue-coated dragoons.

Something about the capricious woman elicited in Paladín an insane and inexplicable need to protect—perhaps from himself. If only he had protected all the women he had deeply loved. London's betting books would place odds against her longevity if he were to allow himself to love her, as well.

The cotillion ended and, when the Virginia Reel started up, Solomon escorted Charlotte to her brother and Therese, then weaved through the crowded room toward him. The merchant's gaze drifted idly around the large room. "I leave tonight for San Patricio with a wagonload of cotton bales."

Paladín glanced down at him and grinned. "Cotton, you say?"

The bronzed Solomon flashed white teeth. "Firearms for Francis Johnson's force, most of them antiquated blunderbusses that would miss an elephant at three yards."

Paladín's grin faded. Sending arms to the Matamoros Expedition forces was like throwing bad money after good, but what else could the idiocy of an ineffectual Provisional Government do? "You know what will happen if you're caught in the crossfire between Johnson and Urrea's soldiers, Solomon?"

Solomon cocked his forefinger and thumb and aimed at his own chest. "Adobe walled. And you?"

"It would seem I have a kinder fate. To Washington-on-the-Brazos."

"For?"

"To draft, with Magnum, Houston, and other delegates, a constitution for Texas. Though only God knows what personal benefits Magnum will manage to squeeze into the draft of the constitution—our official declaration of independence from Mexico, if you will."

He watched the merchant, carefully. Many settlers in Texas, Mexican and immigrants alike, were all for deposing Santa Anna, who had seized power and overturned Mexico's Constitution of 1824. But not all were for separating entirely from Mexico to establish a republic. Was Solomon?

Then there was the Chaparral Fox, another formidable foe, who could be in actuality someone as congenial as Solomon, as corrupt as Magnum—or as innocuous as Engler.

Solomon rolled his raisin-brown eyes. *"Ejoli, mano!* Santa Anna's horde is headed in that direction, Washington-on-the-Brazos. By far, you have the worse fate."

His gaze caught sight of the fiery Fiona, winding through the press of dancers toward him, her eyes ablaze. "Yes, that I do."

———————

FIONA'S EMOTIONS TEETER-TOTTERED BETWEEN fury and futility with each step that took her closer to the imposing, sartorial figure that Paladín cut. What made her think she had a chance of winning the land grant, much less his sincere affections? When in the same room, she was the powder keg and he the igniting heat.

"If you'll excuse me," Moses bestowed her with a short bow, "I am off to pursue the pleasures offered in San Patricio."

San Patricio, where she should be going… if the land grant was but hers.

"By all means," Paladín stepped forward to place his hand at the back of her waist before she could protest. "Miss Flanigan is here to importune me for a dance."

"What?!" But he was already sweeping her out onto the dance floor.

"A waltz. You dance it so beautifully, Miss Flanigan."

He knew she danced like a wooden soldier and cared not a whit. What had happened to the Spanish endearment of *my dear* that he had lavished on her after bringing her to the combustible point, where she thought she had, indeed, died and gone to a heaven?

"What happened the night before last?"

"Well, let me think… we spent a while in agreeable conversation, you drank a little too much *aguardiente,* and then I spent the rest of the night indulging your ardor."

Words of outrage corked at the back of her throat.

"You see," he went on blithely, while his eyes watched her intently, "in India, I learned the art of exquisite pleasuring—the *kama sutra* positions—and now I find myself hopelessly habituated to exploring the intense sensations I can provide my partners."

Red heat flooded her face. "Oh! Oh!" She halted abruptly and stamped her foot, her skirts backlashing around her ankles. Another couple almost collided with them.

He drew her out of the path of the waltzing partners and into the alcove created by the curve of the stairwell. Backing her against the peeling stucco wall, he anchored her waist between his long hands, preventing her from twisting away. "But you, Fiona, rendered up the most extraordinary responses to my lovemaking, so that I find myself aroused like that with no other partner. I find you addicting."

Her stomach plummeted, her knees went wobbly, and if he had not been supporting her, she would have fallen. "Try abstaining." Her voice was as wispy as his was raspy. "'Tis said to cure the craving."

"Alas, that is indeed what I intend to do. Divert my lust for you to absorption with keeping my family land grant. I am joining up with General Houston at Washington-on-the-Brazos."

He was leaving? Leaving her? The realization hit her like a bucket of ice water. He was watching her expression for… what? Waiting for what? For her to grovel? Her lips tightened. "Then I pray a bullet finds your black heart!" Let his other partners surrender to his sensual expertise.

With that, he kissed her. A sweet brushing of her lips with his, then more intently. Such a honeyed sensation flowed through her and her arms came up to slip beneath his frockcoat and encircle his back, needing to draw his honed body closer to her. She found herself rubbing against it like a slatternly cat in heat.

He stepped away, setting her from him, and made a leg. "Farewell it is then."

Stunned by his abrupt withdrawal, she could manage not a word.

Turning away, he looked over his shoulder and flashed her a heart-tripping smile. "By the way, my love, you are not cursed with carrying my child. You are still as much a virgin as Mexico's *La Virgen de Guadalupe.*"

17

BAJA MATAMOROS
STATE OF TAMAULIPAS, MEXICO

The Chaparral Fox sat in a ramshackle room of one of Baja Matamoros's backwater hostelries. Across the small, rickety table from him, he had positioned the weather-beaten Carmargo, who lounged in a chair tilted on its spindly back legs. Cold sunlight from the single dust-filmed window somewhat blinded the Mexican bandit.

An illiterate rabble-rouser, he was too easily ruled by his emotions, which the Chaparral Fox could usually manipulate.

What had once belonged to Carmargo's family had fallen into the hands of strangers. Dimly, the man understood that somewhere in the political center of Tejas—San Antonio de Bexar—land grabbers were slowly but steadily converting traditional Tejano proprietorship to new Anglo proprietorship.

The means employed could be intimidation, technicalities, or simply untiring maneuverings by shrewd lawyers. Carmargo, like many other *Tejanos*, felt powerless, dispossessed. To them, it was the *gringos* who were the outlaws.

Because Camargo knew the Chaparral Fox could affect changes he himself could not, he followed instructions implicitly.

"I can understand your frustrations, Carmargo, and I promise you, once these interlopers are driven out of Tejas, all that has been appropriated from you and your family and your friends will be restored."

"But, this last raid, on La Espada." He spread leathery hands and grumbled. "I do not understand your reasoning, *mi amigo.*"

Up until that last utterance, the Chaparral Fox had held out hope to find the man of continual use. But once questioning of authority began.... A pity that Carmargo had outlived his usefulness. The Baron was too close to making the connection. The revolver the Chaparral Fox held just beneath the table discharged a blast that tipped the chair opposite him.

The Chaparral Fox sighed and tucked away his weapon. He had yet another appointment to keep, but he paused long enough to note, with satisfaction, that the glassy eyed Carmargo was quite dead.

Within the hour, the Chaparral Fox was once again passing through one of Casamata's tunnels on his way to meet with Urrea a second time. Due to the vital information the Chaparral Fox had provided, the Mexican general was about to march with eighty of his dreaded lancers and a contingent of Yucatan infantry on San Patricio to take by surprise the imprudent Dr. Grant and his measly force.

No wonder Santa Anna was heading to San Antonio to personally finish off the rebellious Texicans at the Alamo mission there. His motives were personal and political.

Of a political nature, the unstoppable Urrea was getting all the headlines and would be seen in civil-torn Mexico as a more popular figure.

On a personal level, there was Santa Anna's embarrassment over the military disaster of Cos, his brother-in-law, at the Texican's siege of San Antonio back in December.

For Santa Anna, it was either win Tejas or lose Mexico.

"I understand you have more information—vital information, according to your missive." Standing behind the commandant's desk, Urrea planted his fleshy palms atop it. His ruddy face betrayed his exhaustion, with eyes darkened liked a raccoon's from lack of sleep and several days of beard growth shadowing his face and double chins. His enforced journeys south, to and from San Luis Potosi, were taking their toll.

Without requesting permission, the Chaparral Fox dropped into the chair opposite the desk. "Your military career is on the chopping block, General. Grant and Fannin are but small fry. However, if Santa Anna fails to take down General Houston, you can be sure Santa Anna will lay the blame at your feet."

"Houston? A backwoodsman with a penchant for drinking too much."

"I do assure you that Houston is a most worthy strategist. Which is why his scruffy volunteers will best your drill-ordered soldiers. They know how to use the terrain to their advantage, and they do not wait for time-wasted decisions. They use their own initiative."

Leaning forward, forearms propped on his knees, the Chaparral Fox introduced for the first time a persuasive tone into his voice. "Look, General, both sides know a climactic duel is coming. But when that time comes, provide Houston with wrong information about his opponent—the size of the armies, their armaments, their positions—well, the battle goes to Mexico."

"You are suggesting that Houston could be fed that fodder?"

"Yes."

"I doubt you are doing this out of loyalty to Mexico. What is it you want?"

"Santa Anna's signature deeding one million acres—all of the land between the Nueces River and the Rio Bravo—to me upon the successful disposal of Houston and his forces."

Urrea's brow shot up. "Impossible!"

"My fee is astronomical because I am jeopardizing all—and because I shall accomplish that which no other can do."

"Santa Anna would never agree to it."

His charismatic smile was a slit in his face. "It is in your best interest, General, to assure he does."

"STOP FIDGETING!"

"Ach, Fiona, 'tis scalping me, ye are!" Liam rubbed the back of his head.

Fiona hoped he didn't have lice. "Your hair gets any longer and ye could pass for a girl." She clapped a palm on the crown of his head, anchoring it, as she snipped the rat's nest into a straight line at his nape.

Sitting forward on the tall three-legged stool, he swiveled his head around. "Niall says that yellow locks are—"

"Lucky, I know. Superstitious Irish claptrap." The Irish Traveler, according to a forlorn Rafaela that morning, had left two days ago for San Antonio de Bexar. "And if that were so, Niall's ribcage would not have looked like a trampled birdca—"

At the shouts outside, she tossed the scissors on the kitchen table and, crossing to the door, flung it wide to the chilling wind. Outside, people jostled each other as they hurried toward the town's entry gates.

The carnicera laid aside his cleaver, the blacksmith dropped his bellows, the milliner yanked the pins from between her clamped lips—all were curious as to the cause of the commotion.

The watch repairman, Beaman, was dashing by, and she grabbed his arm. "What is it?"

"General Urrea's prisoners. Survivors from battles at Agua Dulce and San Patricio." Then, he was swept away by the tide of the curious.

She waded into the flood rushing toward the city walls and Fort Guerrero. The spectators watched as perhaps two dozen captives hobbled past in shackled pairs. The prisoners were a shabby, maltreated lot, some without even shoes—all showing signs of injuries.

If the rumor running rampant among the onlookers was correct, the prisoners had been marched afoot a hundred miles or more in the wintry blast. How ironic that the captured survivors were the only members of the Matamoros Expedition to reach a destination that was to have been one of glorious victory.

Then she saw Moses among the prisoners. Without thinking, she elbowed through the press of people and ran to him. Startled, his drooping head jerked around. One eye was swollen closed. His lip was split and puffed. "Fiona," he rasped.

"What happened, Moses? How can I help?" Her thoughts flew to Therese. Surely, she knew someone at Fort Guerrero, some soldier who had influence, who could intervene on Moses's behalf.

"Magnum," he choked out, "Urrea. Chaparral Fox!"

One of the Mexican soldiers shoved her aside with his Brown Bess. She would have stumbled backward had Liam not propped her up from behind.

"Out of the way."

That afternoon, she sat in Therese's parlor and, over steaming tea, shared with her and Rafaela the news of the arrival of the prisoners taken at both San Patricio and Agua Dulce Creek—and finding Moses to be among them. "'Twas a fright to God."

Therese sipped at her tea, her expression pensive. "So many of my late husband's old guard have probably moved out with Urrea. I only hope that...."

Her words trailed off and Fiona knew what she was not voicing—Santa Anna's proclamation that no quarter was to be given to prisoners. Execution was to be their fate.

Therese set aside her cup and saucer, laying a hand over hers. "I will find a way to get Moses released."

Fiona paused, hesitant to share the rest of what bothered her. After all, she was not clear what Moses had been trying to tell her about Urrea, Mangum, or the Chaparral Fox. "You may, also, want to let Charlotte know about Moses. I need to get back to the academy. I set Liam to cleaning the slates, and he has most likely scrawled, instead, all sorts of obscene drawings."

When she took her leave, another ferocious torrent had begun, sluicing the streets with freezing, ankle-deep water, its wind driving the rain in an eyeblinding horizontal force. Her pitiful umbrella's ribs were flayed. The sheltering warmth of her little schoolhouse could not come soon enough.

She should be dancing a jig in the adobe's kitchen. But no, Paladín had seduced her there. In fact, over the past six months, he had seduced her everywhere from the confessional to the ramparts. Made a gam of her. Well, no longer would she be a fool. Now she knew what she needed to do.

She sat aside the cinnamon sticks she had taken out for the Mexican hot chocolate. "Liam!"

Yawning and rubbing his eyes with his fists, he appeared in the doorway. "Wot, Fiona?"

"Mam, ye eejit."

"Eejit, ye say?" He rolled his eyes. "'Cause I dinna have yuir grand luck to be educated with an Earl?"

"For all the good it did. Now, listen. Pack your bundle. Ye are off to stay with Therese and Rafaela for a short while." She knew they wouldn't turn him away.

He scratched behind his ear. "Wot for?"

"Because I am off to claim me pot of gold. Tell them that with the luck of the Irish, or without it, I hope to be back before St. Paddy's Day."

His mouth stretched like India rubber. "Bring me some doubloons, will ye?"

After packing her own valise, she prepared a hamper of food for the road—boiled eggs, fried pork, and cornpone. Then she began the task of closing the school.

She was leaping without looking and the chasm below her was great—she was off to the certain danger and probable death to be found on a war front. But the war front was also where the right to her land grant was to be claimed. Whether it be the Texicans or the Mexicans who won, she meant to be there to battle for it.

Less than an hour later, as she closed her overstuffed valise, she heard the front door bang open and close.

She whirled around. Looking like a drenched cat, Rafaela stood at the bedroom doorway. In one hand she carried her portmanteau and in the other, a rifle. "I am going with you."

"Have you taken leave of yuir senses?"

She shook her head, her bonnet spraying water. "No, I just found them."

"So, Niall succeeded in charming ye, he did? Liam tell ye I was leaving?"

Rafaela raised her eyes to the rafters. "As if Paladín isn't in your blood."

"Ye do not even know if Niall is with Paladín, for sure."

Her chin shot up. "I know Niall, for certain—I know his loyalty is as good as his aim. He will be with the Texicans, just like your Paladín. Besides, I have Therese's carriage—and Charlotte's flintlock. We shall be needing both."

Fiona hefted the valise. "Then we're both gams. I'll lock the door behind us."

THE MEMBERS OF THE FIRST Presbyterian Church had been meeting in a blacksmith shop until the small white clapboard building on Calle Real was completed, three weeks earlier. Inside, Therese could still smell the newly constructed church's pine shavings and fresh paint.

"Daniel carved the pulpit himself," Charlotte bragged.

At the moment, only she and Charlotte occupied the church. Services were due to start within the hour. She had known she would find Charlotte here. The young woman had just arrived to open its doors and play its harpsichord.

Therese's practiced eye perused the beautifully carved mahogany stand. Was there anything the parson could not do?

"Charlotte, can we sit a moment, please?"

Puzzled, Charlotte nodded and seated herself close to Therese on the front pew.

Slipping her hands out of her beaver fur muff, Therese shifted on the pew's hard seat to face Daniel's sister fully. "I have bad news, Charlotte."

The young woman's gloved hands tightened on the handle of the umbrella, the tip of which was placed between her kid boots. "Yes?"

"Mexican forces at a battle in San Patricio killed all but a few of our Texicans and *Tejanos*. After a forced march—"

"Yes, of course. I heard about the captives' arrival here yesterday."

"Moses was among them. Their fate... well, I do not have to tell you what it will be."

The small, pretty mouth—the only delicate feature about Charlotte—tightened into a surprisingly obdurate line. A far-off look appeared in the flinty gray eyes. "Prayers first, of course..." talking more to herself than Therese, "... then, I shall immediately gather a committee of our congregation to prepare a petition. And I shall contact the American consul—"

Therese reached out and touched the other woman's large, clasped hands. "The captives are not citizens of the United States. The consul's hands are tied."

Charlotte drew a reflective breath. "All right, if that is the case, then I shall write—"

"There is no time for letters. Execution could be tomorrow... maybe a couple of days at the most. I have what I think is a plan that may work. I still have occasional contact with members of my late husband's staff. With luck, we may be able to get Moses transferred from Casamata to a Mexico City prison. There, mandatory execution might be delayed. Maybe even a pardon could—"

"Maybe's are not an option," came a male voice from behind her.

She turned around to see Daniel, standing at the church's back door. Shaking the rain from his ulster cape, he walked toward them in that purposeful stride peculiar to both him and his sister. One look at his rough-hewn face, and for some ridiculous reason, Therese began tingling, starting with her toes and working all the way up to her hair follicles.

Now, is this not a novelty! "And you have a better suggestion, Reverend?"

"Yes. As a man of God, I will simply appeal to the guards at the Casamata for the opportunity to pray with Moses."

"But how will you then get him out of the Casamata?"

He shrugged, but his slow smile changed his countenance to one of angelic beauty. "I shall let the Lord's miracles deal with that matter when the time comes."

Therese rose to face him. "Your Lord is dealing with that matter already. I am accompanying you—as your wife. I assure you, the diversion I will create will provide plenty of opportunity to spirit our Moses away."

The same flinty eyes Daniel shared with his sister gazed upon Therese with great respect and evident admiration, but her suggestive choice of words, designating theirs was to be a spousal relationship, had perhaps introduced another element as well.

Charlotte insisted on accompanying them and, after church, the three of them approached the Casamata an hour later with pious, concerned expressions. They passed through the door to the left of the outside stone staircase, rising to the slitted lookout parapet. Inside, they met with the captain in command of the garrison.

Clinging possessively to Daniel's elbow, Therese batted her lashes at the young officer and chattered gaily. "Why, I do not remember you when last I attended an officer's ball, *Capitan* Morales. My late husband, *Capitan* Miguel de Valle—did you know him?—he served here two, or was it three years ago? We met in New Orleans, and he brought me as a young bride to Matamoros. He was not as tall, nor as handsome as you, but I was smitten by him, nonetheless."

With an adoring expression, she turned her face up to Daniel's stern one and patted his arm. "And my new husband—oh, this is Reverend Daniel Engler, and his sister, Miss Madison—well, anyway, he has captured my heart when I had thought it impossible ever to love again."

By that time, she had completely beguiled the soldier.

Daniel stepped in. "To my sorrow, I have heard the San Patricio captives are to be executed within twenty-four hours."

"No, no, Revered Engler. Our law allows all persons under sentence of death three days' grace—a respite called *capilla.*"

"Ahh, yes. The grace period giving all criminals time to make religious preparation for death. As parson of the First Presbyterian, I have come for just that reason. May we spend some time in prayer with one of the captives—Moses Solomon, my sister's husband?"

Theresa suppressed a grin. So, the good parson could lie as facilely as she.

At once, the bemused *Capitan* Morales made arrangements for the visit and the three followed a musket-wielding guard along a corridor that led to but another door, down a staircase, and into a tunnel with cubicles branching off it.

Each cubicle was entered by a solid, barred door. Moses, sitting in a corner of one cubicle with knees drawn up, looked up at the three with astonishment.

Pushing past the waiting guard, Charlotte lifted her skirts and rushed to kneel before him. "Moses, my love, what have they done to you?!"

"Tienen cinco minutos," the burly guard growled, his back planted solidly in front of the closed cell door, his eyes narrowed on the four of them.

Therese stepped nearer the guard and gazed up at him, her lower lip half quivering and half pouting. "Only five minutes to repent for a lifetime?"

While she remained chatting charmingly with the flustered man, Daniel brushed past to kneel alongside Charlotte. "As a good Christian, Moses, I exhort you before you die to forgive all your enemies."

From beneath her skirts, Charlotte slipped Moses the Bowie knife.

"Reverend, I have none to forgive—for I have killed them all. Or soon will have."

With that, Moses sent the knife spinning, hilt over blade toward the guard standing beside Therese. Within an instant, Moses had one less enemy.

18

GONZALES

REPUBLIC OF TEXAS

Niall took off his rain-soaked beret and beat it against his thigh, showering the sawdust-covered puncheon floor of DeWitt's Tavern.

In answer to Colonel Travis's urgent plea for help, Niall had conducted thirty-two Texicans from Gonzales to San Antonio de Bexar. The Alamo mission was under siege, and he didn't hold out much hope for its Texicans and *Tejanos*.

After riding furiously all night, he had his horse give out beneath him and had ended up walking, leading the horse. At last, he made it back to Gonzales, capital of the DeWitt colony, for however many more volunteers he could conscript and head back to the Alamo mission.

He took a seat at the board in the taproom. The tavern was the only place in the settlement where he could get fodder for his horse. A large, wretched structure covered by clapboards, the tavern sported two big fireplaces and lodging for seventy-five cents a night. At that time of morning, the place was nigh empty.

"So, you returned." The comely Naomi Dewitt set a tankard of rye whiskey in front of him.

He winked. "Aye, that I did."

The blue-eyed lass and her mother, the widow of the founder of the colony, ran the tavern. According to Naomi, her mother—whose Virginia family was quite wealthy and had contributed to her husband's endeavors—was selling off some of her property in Missouri to help finance DeWitt's *empresario* venture in Tejas.

With the back of his hand, Niall nudged aside the tankard. "I do not suppose ye would be having any coffee to keep me peepers propped open, would ye now?"

She laughed and leaned forward, displaying her ample cleavage.

He would bed the lass, if he were not so tired… and if the disturbing image of a tall, cool Spanish maiden did not dampen his ardor that morning. And every morning.

"Coffee is as scarce as hens' teeth. As will everything else be by tonight."

"Why is that?"

Lowering her voice, she leaned entirely across the board now, so close he could smell the scent of her lilac water and sweat. No, her scent did nothing for him. "Talk is General Houston has up and left Washington-on-the-Brazos in a tearing hurry—jest after he put his John Hancock on the declaration of independence. Talk also has it that he and his staff are due to arrive here sometime tonight to organize forces against Santa Anna."

Then so, too, would be arriving Rafaela's fiancé. With Niall's exhaustion and his Irish temper, he might succumb to killing a man he sincerely liked. "Thank ye, lass. I had best be on me way." He plunked down seventy-five cents. "Keep the rye for Houston and his entourage."

But he had walked no farther than the plaza when two Mexicans rode in on burros, shouting and gesturing wildly, drawing a crowd. Niall ambled nearer. One of the poncho-clad Mexicans, the scout Juan Seguin, had tears in his eyes and was talking rapidly in half English, half Spanish.

"All of them *muertos*… Santa Anna, he sent one of his *jefes* with an order for us to come with *carretas* to carry his dead to *el campo santo* for burial. Then we were ordered to bring wood and seco branches to a *lugar* just outside the mission—*hijole*—we hauled there the Alamo's dead bodies. *Dios, nos perdone,* we were ordered to light it!"

Within minutes, the fall of the Alamo spread. Gonzales had been the only town to send aid. At that moment, there was scarcely a family in Gonzales that was not mourning the loss of one or more of its members.

So, Niall thought, the final siege had occurred not long after his departure. He should have stayed instead of going for reinforcements.

He listened to the frenzied shrieks of the women and the heart-rending crying of their fatherless children… and he thought about the thirty-two ill-fated but heroic volunteers he had helped escort to their deaths at the Alamo.

He pivoted and strode back to DeWitt's Tavern. He meant to drink the rye for which he had paid and all the whiskey the tavern had until he was thoroughly drunk, and the mercy of the brew blighted his mind.

THE RAIN POURED, THE TEMPERATURE dropping drastically. The barouche Therese had spared Fiona and Rafaela, not the most sturdy form of transportation, sloughed north through the mud toward Washington-on-the-Brazos.

Despite Rafaela's skill with horses, the lightweight carriage often became mired. Fiona would have to climb down from her seat beside Rafaela on the driver's perch, slosh through mud and icy water to the carriage's rear, and, with frozen, mittened hands, heave her weight against it.

"Crikey," she muttered, trying this time unsuccessfully to rock the carriage from its mud-lock. Next, she slipped, flailed, and fell face first into the mud. Hands levering herself to her knees, she wiped the black slime from her face, then let loose with a volley of oaths.

"Fiona?" Rafaela shouted over her shoulder from the carriage bench. "Are you all right?"

"Dancing on sunshine, I am." And she was, because at that moment a flatbed wagon came racing around the bend of pines. Someone to help!

Instead, she was splattered with a fresh coat of mud. The driver, an old farmer in a soggy, wide-brim felt hat, and his stick of a wife appeared too frazzled to notice. "Better git going, girl," he called out, reining in. "The devils are hot on our heels."

Fiona wiped the mud from her face. "What?"

Rafaela twisted around on the front seat. "Who?"

"Ya haven't heard?"

Fiona shook her head.

"The Alamo's fallen. All the defenders massacred."

"And 450 more Texicans and *Tejanos* lined up and executed as pirates on Palm Sunday, along with Fannin, at Goliad." The old man tugged the edge of his hat brim to sluice off its accumulated water. "Santa Anna's killing everything in his path on his way to catch up with General Houston. You'd better skedaddle while you can."

He lashed his whip over the horse's rump, and the wagon shot forward, spraying Fiona with yet another coat of mud. "Bloody hell."

The rest of the day, she and Rafaela crossed paths with, and eventually joined, a stampede of fleeing settlers, many on foot, as their draft animals had already been requisitioned by the Texican army.

Heading east, the prairie had given way to timbered lands, but the stands of trees did not protect the fleeing colonists from the elements. The skies opened up and torrential rains fell throughout the bitterly cold day, making the wagon trails a quicksand and filling rivers from bank to bank. The refugees repeatedly found themselves at uncrossable fords.

The next day, snow began to fall. Huddling next to Rafaela, Fiona could not remember ever being so cold. The wind whipped their sodden, frozen cloaks. At midday, Therese's carriage started to wobble out of control, and both Rafaela and Fiona had to grab for support to keep from being thrown from the carriage.

"A wheel must be coming loose." Rafaela passed the reins to Fiona. "Keep a firm grip while I inspect the wheels. I may be inept at the pianoforte, but I excel at all things horse related."

Nervous, Fiona accepted the reins. "Ye know me and horses are not bosom friends."

"Everyone is your friend." After a moment, she came around Fiona's side of the carriage.

"I see. A linchpin is loose." She headed toward a pile of debris left from a creek flood.

She returned, lugging a snow-flecked stump the size of a mallet. Gripping the reins and hardly daring to breathe lest she excite the horses, Fiona could hear Rafaela pounding at the linchpin.

Several families afoot, one with a strapping son, streamed by the carriage, unwilling to take the time to help her.

After a few minutes, Rafaela climbed aboard the carriage, her cloak, skirts, and gloves mud-and snow-caked, her hair straggling from her bonnet a matted mess. "I think the linchpin will hold for now, anyway."

Grateful beyond words, Fiona passed her back the reins. Because of her statement about everyone being Fiona's friend, Fiona's words tumbled out unplanned. "Truly, ye are the one who is a friend. My valued friend."

Rafaela smiled sweetly. "Who could not want to be your—"

Fiona cut her off while she still had the courage. "I am ashamed to confess, when we met on the wharf there at the Port of Matamoros, when ye dropped your reticule, I stole pounds from it just before I returned it to ye."

Rafaela's smile tweaked a dimple below each cheek. "I knew that."

"Ye did?"

"Yes, later—the day I fled from La Espada, I counted the pounds and realized several were missing. It did not take long for me to make the connection."

"Why, that rotten whelp. I instructed Liam to return all of them."

Maybe it was their exhaustion, their lack of meals, their private fears, but both women erupted into laughter that allowed much needed tears to spill, and they hugged one another in consolation.

Sometime toward the middle of the day, the hovering blue-gray clouds stopped snowing. At last, trailing in the wake of a flight of settlers, she and Rafaela arrived at the Guadalupe River, its banks overrunning with the continual rain. A crowd waited their turn ahead of the carriage to board a now fully loaded ferry.

While it braved the turbulent water, a young pregnant woman squatted off to one side, amidst the rushes, and panted out a groan. Hunkered next to her, her frantic husband was arranging his wet and shabby brown coat around her shoulders.

Fiona twisted on the carriage seat, dug into her valise and found her only petticoat, one saved for a special occasion. At the inquiring lift of Rafaela's brow, she explained, "The babe will be needing swaddling."

Kneeling on the sodden, matted rushes with the worried husband and shrilling wife, Fiona began to assist in her seventh child birthing. Four had been those of Madam Margie's prostitutes and two had been younger siblings.

"Not here…. Not now."

"What a story ye will have to tell your grandchildren. Pausing to give birth with Santa Anna's horde of ten-thousand hot on yuir heels." Fiona turned to the husband, who had the face of a baboon. "Ye have a knife? A hatchet? Something for cutting the cord of the wee-one?"

Twenty minutes later, the young woman held her blood-dappled, wailing infant girl, wrapped in Fiona's petticoat.

Tears welled in the eyes of the grateful husband. "Fiona, you say your name is? The lass will be named for you."

Grinning, a blood-smeared Fiona returned to the carriage. That made three more Fiona's that she had helped introduce into the world.

With the gray shrouded sunlight fading in the west, their carriage was, at last, loaded onto the ferry along with a cart, a saddled horse, and a dozen more passengers. The wooden-planked barge bobbed perilously in the rushing muddy water. Debris collided with the ferry, and she and Rafaela latched onto the carriage to keep their balance. An uprooted tree, a wooden churn, and a cradle swept past.

Then the swollen carcass of cow sideswiped the ferry, causing the carriage to skid violently. Passengers staggered to keep their footing, and a mangy mongrel was bumped overboard. As it bobbled on past out of reach, the doleful howls of a boy to save his dog were in vain.

While waiting in the near dark for their turn to be unloaded on the left bank, Fiona overheard a wizened settler. "Gonzales, but a score of miles, has a public house—DeWitt's Tavern. With God's providence, we may find food and shelter there."

A Mexican woman, carrying a baby in a red rebozo wrapped around her shoulders, genuflected and said in broken English, "*Sí,* and the Texican army, it is there. Weeth it, we will be safe."

But with Paladín, will I ever be safe?

With that uncomfortable thought came an explosion that lit up the night sky a brilliant orange.

GROCE'S FERRY
STATE OF TEJAS Y COAHUILA, MEXICO

A heavy gloom fell over the Texican army, which was capitalizing on the line of defense afforded by the swollen Brazos River to drill and train. Mutterings and arguments broke out as to the tactics the army should take.

Many wanted to stand and fight—some spoke for retreat. A sizeable number of men deserted, fearing for the welfare of their families now in the destructive path of the bloodthirsty Santanistas.

With Raj and Saracen, Houston's gray stallion, hobbled nearby, Paladín sat beneath the stand of pines on his saddle. His Wellington boots were propped on a log and a blanket covered his head and body in a futile attempt to avoid the pitter-patting rain that puddled in the stand's carpet of brown pine needles.

His thoughts turned to Fiona. Was the feisty fairy still a virgin? At that thought, he had to grin. And was she safe there in Matamoros now that Urrea's army had taken to the field? Paladín's grin crumpled into a grimace. She would be safe anywhere, as long as he did not let himself fall in love with her.

A few feet away, Houston sat on his own saddle, likewise enshrouded in a blanket. After having been ferried across the Brazos by the steamboat *Yellowstone*, seven hundred men—including a small cavalry unit of sixty—camped in the cotton field beyond. Only a few tents were to be had, but Houston had eschewed the privilege of such quarters.

Camped along with the army was the first wave of panicked emigrants, with hundreds upon hundreds more expected to arrive daily. Two weeks before, after ordering first Gonzales and then San Felipe de Austin to be burned—as well as their wells poisoned, boats sunk, and anything destroyed that could be used by the enemy—Houston had retreated to just outside Groce's plantation.

The Groce women made sandbag fortifications for the army and old man Groce himself was melting his lead pipes for bullets.

At the moment, Paladín knew that Houston was more concerned about helping the fleeing families evacuate the country. The General looked up from the express that had arrived that morning. "It seems our illustrious government of the Republic of Texas wants me to stand and fight."

The majority of volunteers from the United States had been killed either under the ill-advised Matamoros expedition led by Grant, Johnson, and Fannin—or had met their deaths with Travis and Bowie at the Alamo. So, the Texican army now consisted mostly of colonists.

Paladín nodded out toward the rain-soaked field. "A few muskets, no kegs or gun powder, mostly knives, canes, and clubs to do battle with. We may be the only force left to deal with Santa Anna's legions, but I would think it's prudent to wait for a more favorable occasion to decide the fortunes of our infant republic in a battle."

Applying pencil to the missive, Houston wrote his usual salutation. Headquarters of the Army… Camp West of Brazos. "Ahh, but we soon are to have two six-pounder cannons—the Twin Sisters—donated by friends in Cincinnati."

"And you have my Colt revolver," came a familiar voice from behind Paladín.

One forearm braced on his thigh, Paladín turned to look over his shoulder. "Well, what took you so long?" His voice held its usual grating rasp, but his heart was now as light as the turtle napping on the fallen pine just beyond.

Niall shrugged and grinned. "Had to file for a homestead."

"Then you are staying in Tejas?"

"If you'll have me as a neighbor—and if Santa Anna will turn tail."

"That's about as likely to happen as my giving up drinking." Houston's grin was just visible from beneath his sopping blanket.

———————

SOMEWHERE UP AHEAD WAS GENERAL Houston, his ragged army… and Paladín.

In its retreat, the Texican army had been moving eastward in a zigzagging pattern that the hasty flight of settlers followed.

And chasing them, flush with their string of victories at the Alamo, Goliad, San Patricio, and Agua Dulce, came the three prongs of the enormous Mexican army—with Santa Anna's force the middle prong.

Fiona and Rafaela had fallen in with the slew of other fleeing settlers. They passed a desolation of the countryside that beggared Fiona's imagination. Houses standing open with beds unmade and breakfast plates still on the tables. Pans of milk left molding in the dairies. Cribs full of corn. Smoke houses full of bacon. And nests of eggs found in fence corners.

All abandoned... as Paladín had abandoned her.

Yet, gam that she was, she traipsed along in the fleeing army's wake like a Mexican *soldadera*. A very knackered *soldadera*.

A day out from the Texican army's last camp, Groce's plantation, she and Rafaela came upon the picket guard of Houston's army, Texas Rangers—although she suspected scouts had already forewarned the Texas Rangers of this latest arrival of emigrants.

Next to her on the carriage seat, Rafaela stared through the morning mist at the miserable mass of humanity, most afoot, trudging along the quagmire of a road. Heavy frost covered what patches of grass lay untrampled. "Well, now what?"

She shivered. To come all this way, lured by the promise of land.... "If neither Paladín nor Niall is here...."

She couldn't bring herself to finish the thought.

"If Paladín is here, then Niall will be here. As I told you, he is loyal."

She envied Rafaela's tender image of Niall. For herself, Fiona had no illusions about Paladín. He was crippled by his arrogance, but love him, she did. "Then find General Houston, and we'll find them both."

With a click of her tongue, Rafaela nudged the horse forward through the crowd—a slave leading a pack mule by its collar made of braided corn husks, a father with his son straddling his shoulders, a soldier with carpet for shoes, a wailing baby slung in a shawl from its mother's back.

One gaunt ruffian toting a knapsack grabbed the reins Rafaela wielded. "You don't need this here carriage, lady."

Rafaela tried to snatch the reins back, but the man shoved her hard. Bypassers, laden with their own troubles, took no note of this scuffle, just one among hundreds occurring in their headlong flight to the U.S. border.

Fiona reached beneath the carriage seat and hefted the rifle to her shoulder. "She may be a lady, but I am not."

One look at the determination in her face and the scruffy man released the reins, stepped back, then whirled and made his getaway.

Rafaela threw her arms around Fiona and began laughing, then weeping. On her part, Fiona sat rigid, appalled by what she might have done, once again. Brigands or barons—they were all the same. They took what they could.

By noon, the weak sunlight had scuttled the clouds, but the day had grown colder, and they had drawn only a little closer to the army's front. When the close order formation of the soldiers—few who wore any semblance of a uniform—became more apparent, she knew they were nearing the core that was left of the army.

She called out to one young soldier, scarcely more than fourteen or fifteen, in a blue wool short jacket with wrinkled trousers that looked like old elephant legs. "General Houston, where can I find him?"

The kid had the spunk to wink at her and Rafaela. "As bonnie as you two are, the general will find you, ma'am."

The general did not, but toward sundown, a furious Paladín did. She should have known the charging steed parting clusters of sojourners could only be Raj. Word of their presence must have been passed forward.

Gone was the dapper dresser. Clothed in dingy buckskins, Paladín reined abruptly alongside their carriage on her side. Beneath the wide-brimmed hat, his black eyes blazed. "What in hell are you doing here?"

Her ribs became a drum against which her heart was pounding. Around them, curious refugees this time paused to stare. "I have joined up with the Texicans, and there's nothing you can do about it."

"The hell I cannot!" With a modicum of effort, he leaned over, swept her from the carriage seat, and deposited her in front of him on Raj. "Stop squirming, or I shall give your fanny the thrashing I have been wanting to."

Then, in a kind voice to Rafaela, "Ask for the quartermaster, my lady Rafaela. He will take the carriage and horses as war material—but he will also take you to Niall."

With that, he spurred Raj away. Sitting stiffly while her insides quivered like quince jelly, Fiona rode in silence with Paladín to a camp a short distance from the hundreds of puny fires sparking the dark.

The camp itself was little more than a tarp. A tall man mantled in a Cherokee blanket, and a man she recognized as Deaf Smith, the frontiersman she had danced with at Cavett's party, were poring over a tattered map.

With courtly manners, the tall man rose from the crate that served as a chair. "So, you are the termagant Fiona Flanigan."

"So, ye are Sam Houston."

At that, he chuckled. "I see what you mean by feisty, Paladín."

She vaguely recalled seeing the inordinately tall man at Cavett's dinner party—perhaps vaguely, because every particle of her body had been entirely focused on Paladín that night and every night since. She flicked him a baleful glance but said to Houston, "Whatever he has told ye sir, 'tis not true."

"I sincerely hope it is, Miss Flanigan. Join us while we plot tomorrow's route, ma'am. It seems we have come to a fork in the road."

She stepped closer, and he pointed a hoary finger at the map. "The left fork—here—it leads due east to Nacogdoches and safety inside United States territory. The right fork, veering to the southeast, leads toward Santa Anna and certain confrontation."

"With your permission, Sam," Paladín's voice came from behind her, "I would like to send Fiona by way of the left fork—on to Nacogdoches—with your aide-de-camp."

Houston grinned. "You'll have to clear that with the lass here."

19

Sitting very straight like a lady, with her legs folded beneath her spread skirts, Rafaela nudged the wormy biscuit to the side of the tin plate. Only after taking a deep draught of the brackish water from Niall's canteen did she allow herself to relax, oh so slightly, against her portmanteau. Nevertheless, she felt giddy, and the fine hair on her arms were electrified by his proximity.

They sat on his saddle blanket, rolled out beneath a deep, black velvet sky streaked with occasional meteor showers. A soft southern wind warmed the air. Wherever groves of pine and oaks offered shelter could be found hundreds of huddled bodies of both soldiers and settlers.

Niall had selected their site for the small privacy afforded by a tall stand of grassy tussock, somewhat away from Houston's central camp… and perhaps too near alligators and bats and other fearsome creatures, such as Niall himself.

She knew marriage was anathema to him—a saddling his soul would never tolerate. Yet he was her universe, and she would settle for whatever crumbs of affection he might dole out.

He sat less than an ell's bolt distance, with one leg out stretched and his forearm resting on an upraised knee. His eyes watched her pensively. "Why did ye come, Rafaela?"

She shoved back a tangle of hair that had fallen from the plaits at her nape. Tidiness was not a luxury in the wild flight of the last few days. Dirt was encrusted beneath her fingernails and needlelike pain was shooting along her spine from the many days of sitting on the carriage seat's hard board.

She took a deep breath. Her next words would decide her future. "You know that bullet you had planned to use on me, if necessary, when you rescued me in San Antonio?"

"Aye."

She leaned to one side to withdraw his revolver from its holster, draped across his saddle, at the edge of the blanket. "It would take that to stop me from being with you, whether you want me or not." She held out the gun to him.

A too-long moment crept by, and she knew not what was going through his mind. At last, he reached out, took the revolver, and replaced it in its holster. "Come here."

His square hand caught hers and tugged her forward onto her knees, then both hands slipped beneath her armpits to pull her into the hollow created by his broad chest and upraised knee. His callused fingers tipped her chin. "Ye have come this far, across an ocean to a wilderness, and ye have waited this long since you were duped to come to me. 'Tis time you replaced the bastard's face with mine, if I am, indeed, what ye truly want."

Her fingers intertwined with his vest's leather fringe. "There has only been your face since first I saw you, on the Port of Matamoros landing. Cavett's face has long since—"

"Cavett? Cavett Magnum?"

She could not believe her slip up! At once, her palm shot up to cup one side of his face to distract him, and a convincing smile of playfulness tipped her lips. "Since I saw you at the Port of Matamoros, gentling the horses, I knew I wanted you, gentling me. If you make me wait one more minute for your—"

He sealed her mouth with a fierceness that stole her breath. His fingers twisted in her hair and his hitched leg, cradling her, gave way to roll her beneath him. "Holy Mother of God, Rafaela, I canna believe ye are here. Needing me."

Her trembling fright ebbed. "Yes, yes, Niall. I need you now. And always." God help her.

Tenderly, his mouth settled on hers, and he whispered words that gentled her love-starved soul. His enforced leisureliness of claiming her would live in her memory as long as she lived, melting the chill of Cavett's despicableness that had frozen her in time. From her narrow feet—blistered by the wet leather of her shoes—to her chilblained and reddened hands to her grimy, lank hair... not a particle was left unworshipped.

And afterwards, toward the cold depths of morning, he held her tightly against him. "I fear 'tis the stallion who has been gentled and not the mare."

"IF THE ONLY WAY I can lay claim to me land is by dogging yuir steps, then I will." Fiona was determined she would never let Paladín know how his heartless smile stole her heart—she would never give him that power over her.

"And I keep what is mine."

They lay beneath a supply wagon contributed by the felicitous arrival earlier that day of two-hundred well-armed deserters from the U. S. Army of Observation, poised at the U. S. border of the Sabine River.

After she and Paladín had supped with General Houston and Deaf Smith later that night, Paladín had grasped her elbow and steered her from beneath the tarp off to the shelter of the supply wagon, parked by a small lake with encircling carts, flatbeds, and two brass, small-bore canons.

Spreading his bedroll, he had stretched out like a lazy lion on his back, hands clasped behind his head. She lay on the edge of the stinky woolen blanket and stared up at the ceiling of wagon slats. Their bodies were separated by inches and conflict.

"And if dogging my steps means forever, would you?" he asked without looking at her.

"Aye." If she could but douse this bonfire of desire she felt when with him. "Unless ye murder me first." After all, three women in his past lay dead. But she knew there was more to their stories. More morality to Alex's personal code than he let show. She could wait.

In the sudden silence between them, she could hear the mournful plucking of a banjo, the burping of frogs, and an occasional chorus of crickets.

"Open the locket," came Paladín's rusty voice.

"What?"

He rolled onto his side, facing her, his head propped in his palm. "Look inside your locket, Fiona."

She had not bothered to open the locket in years. Supporting herself on one arm, she grasped her four-leaf clover, laying between her breasts, and gingerly pried the top open. For a moment, she squinted in the darkness, not comprehending what it was she saw—not a portrait miniature but... her breath wheezed with her sharp inhalation.

"I told you in feudal times that a knight wore a lock of his lady's pubic hair into battle. I am going into battle soon. I seized this boon from you before. What I want is for you to give it to me freely now."

Her gaze skittered from the locket's contents to his face. What she was seeking there, she knew not. Certainly not love, for he had made that plain he could never come to care for someone of her ilk.

So many levels comprised their relationship. Servant to master. Maiden to beguiler. Claimant to claimer. She realized she wanted not just the land but a husband and children to be a part of it, a part of her vision for something as grand and enduring as was Texas.

And Don Alejandro de la Torre y Stuart, Lord Paladín, would never offer the lowly born Irish wench, Fiona Flanigan, that holy state of matrimony.

With a sigh as heavy as regret, she knew she would settle for any kind of relationship he wanted from her. She also knew that, in acceding to him, she was forfeiting all hope for realizing her vision. All that she had undergone, all that she had toiled and suffered for, would be for naught.

The plague take the rogue.

She pinched the red tuft between her thumb and forefinger and held it out to him. "That ye may return safely from battle, my knight."

He grasped her wrist and the tuft fluttered between them. "You are the boon I want, Fiona." Tugging at her wrist, he pulled her half-beneath him, his lower torso pinning hers, his upper supported over hers by one forearm.

His face was a black wrath above her own, his heated breath a warmth against the cool of the night. His bone and flesh and muscle and sinew—the strength she so craved. "Want or need?"

"Both." He angled her chin to better answer with the kiss his lips slanted over hers, a kiss for which she had been waiting weeks. Maybe forever... because, for once, his lips were tender, giving, moving over hers in a way to suggest that all he desired most was to love her. "Ahhh, Fiona, my little termagant," he muttered against her temple, "if only I could rid my mind of you."

She smiled against the darkness and inhaled his scent. She loved the essence of his maleness—the old leather, the woodsy smoke, the muskiness that betrayed his want of her. "Not yet, me Lord. Not until ye have rid my body of its want of ye."

With a heavy groan, he held her closer. "Dawn is near... and possible death. Whatever passion we are to share should be something better than a hasty coupling now. It should be a splendor or nothing at all."

She rose on one arm, her hair a cascade of fire around their faces. Her fingers cupped his beard-stubbled face. "If ye think to rid yourself of me, forget it. Ye are cursed with me presence... me Lord."

His long fingers capped the back of her neck, pressing her head onto the cradle of his shoulder and encompassing arm so that she could not see his features.

When at last he spoke, his words were muffled. "It is not your presence but my love that is cursed. I have brought about the death of every female I have loved. My mother died giving birth to me. I pushed my sister, who had been teasing me about my spindly legs, and she tripped... ironically impaling herself on the stake used in our family's game of horseshoes."

Jesus, Mary, and Joseph! Fiona could sense something remained unuttered—something even more terrible that was chaining him to the past. "Go on, me lov."

Another long silence filled the dead of night. "I was a fledgling assigned to Bombay.... Within the year, I saw action in the Third Anglo-Maratha War in India. Winning it sealed East India Company's absolute rule of almost the whole of India... and sealed my absolute command with the Company. But the price was costly. After my Punjab wife was raped, and our baby ripped from her stomach, I put a bullet to her head and solved that rather indelicate problem."

There was no further sound, but the great heaving of his chest told her of emotions choked back. Softly, her fingers stroked his chest where the dark hair whorled. So, that explained it. Never would she or any other woman be the recipient of his request for a hand in marriage, nor carry his child within their womb.

She stifled the sigh prompted by her heavy heart and pushed upright on her elbow once more. "Well, the problem with us Irish is that we are a hardy lot. I may have to kill ye before ye kill me." Her free hand latched into his hair and she lowered her face over his, whispering, "And bedding ye tonight as I intend to, me Lord, may bloody well kill ye first if I have me way about it."

20

The next day, valises in hand, Fiona and Rafaela fell in with the rest of the Texicans' rag-tag army and remnants of accompanying refugees as they sloughed afoot on toward the southeast and the inevitable showdown with Santa Anna.

The scent of horses was high in the warm, humid air—the smell of wet leather, bits, bridles, and other items of saddlery. Occasionally, Fiona caught sight of Paladín up ahead. Sometimes he would be listening to a scout's report or talking to an officer. At other times, he would be riding alongside Houston and deep in discussion.

Men seemed drawn to Paladín's insight, his dry wit, his inner strength. She suspected that he appeared to them the swashbuckler they wished they had the audacity to be.

Toward midafternoon, somewhere near the hamlet of Harrisburg, a couple of well-dressed soldiers, lonely and eager to talk, caught up with Fiona and Rafaela. The two young men were New Orleans Greys, fresh volunteers with dapper uniforms, well-maintained rifles, adequate ammunition, and some semblance of discipline.

One, a toothpick of a young man, offered to carry Rafaela's valise, but she demurred.

The other, scarcely more than twenty and with a thick accent, smiled at Fiona. "In New Orleans, ma'am, snow is unheard of. Last week was the first time I've seen it. I never figured I would—"

He broke off at the sight of the mounted Paladín, who had abruptly dropped back to ride alongside of them. "Afternoon, boys." He braced a forearm on his saddle horn.

Both young men looked up at his fierce countenance. The first Grey's Adam's apple bobbed uncontrollably. "Well, I guess we ought to be moseying on—"

"Oh, but I want to hear more about New Orleans," the perceptive Rafaela said, drawing abreast of the two. "And I do need help with my valise, after all." Passing it over to the skinny Grey, she linked her arms in the arm of each young man, nudging them on ahead.

Paladín dismounted and, reins in one hand, relieved Fiona of her own valise. She was pleased to think he might just be jealous.

Dropping into pace beside her, he peered down at her, his expression almost solicitous. "You are all right?"

She thought her ridiculous grin had to betray her light heart. "Dancing on sunshine, I am." Before he could suspect that he had won her heart, after all, she hurried on. "I have been thinking, me Lord, about me land grant. Me instincts tell me that cash crops like corn and cotton— or sugar cane and rice—anyway, they would go a long way toward making me a wealthy land—"

"No, you are quite wrong. When I lived in India, I noticed how the Brahman cattle fattened the profits of the landowners. My gut tells me that if I import the Brahman and crossbreed them on my land grant with the feral cattle already here, I could become richer than my forebears ever were."

Grinning, they both slid sidelong glances at each other, neither about to surrender in the war of wills. Despite their stand-off, Fiona recognized that magical thread of communication that existed between them. He and she did not need words to understand their feelings, however tumultuous they may be, because there existed an empathy binding them as strongly as a chain.

And she was counting on that to win her heart's desire—a league of land in Texas.

———————

RAFAELA RECOGNIZED THE ROAN CANTERING toward her at once and felt a heady excitement. "If you will pardon me," she smiled at the two Greys, "I see an old friend—a horse trader from Matamoros." She took her valise from the clutch of the skinny Grey. "I need to speak with him about finding a mount for me."

"But, ma'am, there are not any horses to be—"

Skirts lifted in one hand, she was already moving toward the rider and horse. Niall should have been a centaur—that mythical being that carried off women—for he had certainly carried off her heart.

He leaned over, extending his hand. "Give me your valise, Rafaela."

Happily, she offered it up and he hooked its handle over his pommel. Only then, as she accepted his hand pulling her up to mount in front, did she note the difference in him. "Your mustache!" She turned sharply to look at his bronzed face. "You shaved it!"

He flushed and said gruffly, "Aye, that I have."

"Why?"

"I figured if I was planning on settling down in Texas, I would need a wife, and…." His melodic voice trailed off, and he shrugged.

"Did you have one in mind?" She scarcely dared to breathe, scarcely dared to hope. "A wife, I mean?"

"Well, the one I want… I do not think she would have both meself and me mustache."

She laughed and wept and rejoiced all in one breath, then kissed his marvelous clean-shaven lips.

SAN JACINTO
REPUBLIC OF TEXAS

Among Houston's scouts and spies, Juan Seguin and Deaf Smith were the eyes and ears of the Commander-in-Chief. Never had a more resourceful group of spies, most of them Texas Rangers, served any army. And it was obvious affairs had reached a crisis point for the Texican army, a hasty collection of poorly armed farmers and frontiersmen paid and fed upon promises.

All day and night, the army had marched to reach White Oak Bayou, eight miles north of Harrisburg. From there, it had crossed Buffalo Bayou on a raft built of flooring ripped from a nearby farm house.

A bearded and ragged Deaf Smith, after forty days in the field, sat upon a keg under the tarp that morning, April the nineteenth, and shared what he had learned in laconic sentences to the big, shaggy commander in his mud-stained unmilitary garb.

"News ain't so good. 1,700 hostile Indians are massing in East Texas. Meanwhile, President Burnet and our ad-interim government has fled in a tearin' hurry from Washington-on-the-Brazos with a trunk of our land-office documents—and the Santanistas are in hot pursuit."

Well, Paladín thought, that trunk of land-office documents Fiona would find worth pursuing in a tearin' hurry. But that pursuit was an impossibility at the moment.

He had seen Burnet's frequent and caustic letters, ordering Houston to stop retreating and fight. Houston had continued to retreat. Settlers jeered Houston as he passed, and officers had threatened to seize command, to which Houston had invariably responded he would have any shot who tried.

Now President Burnet himself was in retreat, and Houston was standing firm.

Smith turned his head to spit a stream of tobacco juice in the dirt. "Burnet and the cabinet are hoping to set sail from Galveston for New Orleans before the Santanistas catch up with them."

Houston sat opposite him, one gnarled hand braced on his knee, his other holding a soggy, tattered map. He had celebrated his forty-third birthday six weeks before, on March second, the very day he signed the Declaration of Independence for the Texas Republic, but he looked much older. "Where are the Santanistas camped now?"

"Took two Meskin prisoners who say Santa Anna just burned Harrisburg and is on the march again. With combined armies of 1,400 strong."

"So," Paladín paused in his measured pacing, hands clasped behind his back, "Santa Anna's objective is to secure the seaports."

Smith pinched another plug of tobacco from his rawhide pouch. "One of the prisoners referred to a visit from a spy of the Santanistas—The Chaparral Fox. Don't seem to know anything more about him, other than he's an American."

"Then it looks like we, at last, cross paths with the Napoleon of the West…" Houston's long finger jabbed at a point on the map, "here, where Buffalo Bayou merges with the San Jacinto River. Here is the Crossing of the Rubicon, our point of no return."

"*Alea iacta est.*" Paladín quoted Julius Caesar. And was the die cast as far as Fiona was concerned?

Only she, Rafaela, and a few other camp followers had separated from the flight of settlers who had gone on east toward the safety of the Sabine River and U.S. territory. Even then, Houston had ordered all the runaway settlers' powder, lead, and horses to be confiscated for the coming battle with the Santanistas.

Paladín massaged the bridge of his nose. His thoughts should be on the coming battle. Yet he could only worry, could only wonder, if his love for the lass with freckles that glinted like halfpennies be the death of her? And her feelings for him…. Did she want him because she loved him—or did she want him for the land grant?

The unanswered question was a twisting in his gut—that reliable instinct that told him that he, too, had reached his point of no return.

———————————

APRIL TWENTY-FIRST DAWNED A beautiful spring day—a glorious day for so many about to die.

From her position beneath the live oak, an exhausted Fiona could see Santa Anna's flags floating over the Mexican camp three-quarter's a mile away. She could hear the enemy's chilling bugle wafting *Deguello* in the muggy morning air—the same dismal fanfare of "No Quarter" that had been played at the Alamo the previous month.

General Houston had ordered all remaining colonists to cross the bridge at Vince's Bayou for safety's sake. Those remnants of the refugees left tracking the path of the Texican soldiers, realizing a battle, the battle, was eminent, had hastily complied.

A German woman had all her possessions in a bundle on her head, a sucking babe in her arms, a little girl leading and a small boy following.

Rafaela and Fiona's bags were already stowed away in a waiting buckboard Niall had commandeered. Yet here Fiona stood, rooted beside the buckboard, even with the taste of her fear so powerful it stung her throat.

Less than fifty yards away, the Commander-in-Chief rode along the lines of his men, shouting to them that they would soon get some action. "The victims of the Alamo, the names of those murdered at Goliad, call for cool, deliberate vengeance."

Until this event, Santa Anna's reputation had been that of a cunning and crafty man, rather than a cruel one. But with the chilling news of the fall of the Alamo and the massacre at Goliad, both Santa Anna and the Mexican people had gained a reputation for cruelty. The two monstrosities had aroused the fury of the people of Tejas, the United States, and even Great Britain and France.

Those soldiers fortunate to be in possession of long rifles had cleaned and oiled them. Only the New Orleans Greys and one other company—Colonel William Wood's Kentucky Rifles—wore uniforms.

Her eyes scanned the assembly of close to nine-hundred men but did not see Paladín's unusually tall frame. Then, at last, she spotted him, striding toward Houston's tarp with Chief-of-Staff Major Hockley, Lieutenant Colonel Sydney Sherman, and Colonel Mirabeau Lamar.

She pointed them out to Rafaela, who stood busily securing her long brown hair into a braid. She had, early in the flight, lost her bonnet. "What do ye think is going on?"

"This morning, Niall said that Houston would be holding a Council of War." From under her arm, she turned to look at Fiona, saying softly, almost shyly, "Last night, Niall told me he wants to stay and fight for the land... and for me. Stay, I would, Fiona, if Houston would only let us."

She wore that look of a woman who has been well-loved—a glowing look with eyes sparkling, cheeks beard-reddened, and lips slightly swollen.

For Fiona, it reminded her of her years at Grantam Manor. Of being an outsider looking in at the grandeur that could never be hers. As Alex would never be hers. Lust after her, he may. But love her, she knew he would never risk it. And go on, she must.

She tore her gaze away from Rafaela's love-burnished face to watch Houston. The way he carried his extraordinary height, his humor, his magnanimous power, his wisdom—it was no wonder men looked to him to lead them.

He dismounted and, passing his reins over to Patton, his aide-de-camp, strode toward the shelter of the tarp. Then her eyes widened, and she stiffened at the sight of the man accompanying him. *Cavett Magnum!*

"Ma'am." She whirled around to see Deaf Smith ambling on bowed legs toward her, his long rifle cradled in his arms. With him were a detail of men, each carrying pine-knot staves. "Time for me to escort you two and the others back across the bayou."

She hesitated, her gaze still locked on Cavett Magnum's back. Moses's words flooded back to her. What if the Land Commissioner worked for Santa Anna and the Mexican government?

Smith's gruff voice addressed her adamantly. "Paladín said to tell you to skedaddle now, ma'am."

Given no option, she and Rafaela, along with the six mounted soldiers and Smith, hastily made the twenty-minute return trip in the buckboard past the prairieland and marshes and stands of arching live oaks.

A massive wooden bridge spanned the bayou, its roiling water also out of its banks. But when the seven men dismounted and began to light the staves, Rafaela gasped. "What are you doing?!"

"Sorry, ma'am," Smith called out, "my orders are to burn the bridge. Take the road to the right. It'll lead you to Nacogdoches as straight as a compass."

Now Fiona realized Houston's strategy. With the bridge burned, neither the Texicans nor the Mexicans could retreat from the battleground, practically encircled as it was by Buffalo Bayou, Vince's Bayou, and the San Jacinto River. The losing side, whichever it turned out to be, would be given no quarter.

Already the Texicans were moving along the bridge with their torches. Everywhere, flames sparked. Rafaela glanced at Fiona and she saw desperation written all over the young woman's patrician features. "It cannot end like this, can it, Fiona?"

"Never worry." She hoped her voice sounded more assured than what she felt. "Alex always wins—at cards and everything he sets his intention on."

Hot cinders were beginning to rain on them, and reluctantly, Rafaela snapped the reins, nudging the whinnying horse on toward the bridge's far side.

Fiona turned in her seat to look back one last time. Alex, with his far-fetched idea of a separate country—under-financed and under-manned as the Republic of Texas was—had brought them to this. The scoundrel had sent her packing, with himself now standing alone with his vision of an unimaginable amount of four-thousand four-hundred and twenty-eight acres in sight.

Yet Cavett Mangum's presence continued to nag her. What if he was, indeed an agent provocateur for Mexico? What if he was, even at that moment, misleading the Council of War with false intelligence?

What if this time, Alex does not win?

She grabbed the reins from Rafaela's lax hand. "Get out of the buckboard. I am going back."

Rafaela grinned at her. *"We* are going back."

She took control of the reins again, flicking them over the horse's back and sharply wheeled the wagon around. As the blazing fires began to devour the bridge, the forefront of its incinerating heat and black smoke engulfed them. The horse balked. *"Vaya!"* she shouted.

Fiona could hear Smith yelling at them. Tongues of red flames leaped high into the midday's blue skies. Suddenly, a fiery timber toppled in front of the carriage and the horse reared, refusing to advance any farther. Rafaela lashed the whip again and again.

Fiona jumped out of the carriage to try to kick the beam aside. She almost succeeded when her skirt caught fire. Rapidly, she ripped away at its sparking hem. She gave the truss a final shove, barely feeling the heat searing her hands and cleared the bridge.

Within a quarter of an hour of frantic driving that threatened to overturn the buckboard at hairpin curves, they reached the Texican campsite. The hour was nearing three o'clock, and the War Council must have just concluded, because the men, ducking their heads, were exiting from beneath the tarp entrance. Niall sat on a cartridge crate, cleaning his revolver with a sock.

Magnum had his arm around Major Patton's shoulders. Behind them trailed Alex, Houston, and the other officers of the War Council.

Fiona flung herself from the wagon and, hefting her skirts, dashed to Alex. His expression thunderous, he gripped her shoulders and shook her so hard her head bobbled. "What the *hell* are you doing here?"

She wrenched half wayaround, with his hands still gripping her, and pointed at Cavett's back. "Cavett Magnum—*he* is the Chaparral Fox!" She might be wrong, but she was not going to risk that chance.

At the sound of his name, Magnum whirled. *"What?"*

Upon hearing the name 'Cavett Magnum,' Niall, too, looked up.

"Ye're the Chaparral Fox!" she charged, her breath hammering against her ribs. "Moses Solomon saw you in the Mexican camp at San Patricio—with General Urrea.

Niall sprang from the crate, upsetting it and the sock-wrapped revolver atop it. "Magnum, ye perverted bloody bastard!"

At that same moment, Alex released her and also lunged toward Magnum.

Faster than the eye could track, Magnum whipped a pistol from inside his frockcoat and took dead aim.

"No!" Fiona cried and threw herself between him and Alex.

The shot, its bright red-orange, ear-shattering blast, echoed in the camp, the first shot announcing the two-hour carnage that was to come.

UP AND DOWN THE LINE, Houston rode the magnificent white stallion he had just acquired from Travis's law partner. The commander-in-chief slipped his sword from his scabbard. "Trail arms forward. Now hold your fire, men, until you get the order!"

Paladín cocked his long rifle, waiting…. and knowing that without Fiona to bedevil him, life had no purpose. But with Fiona, he knew his purpose would have been to defend life, family, and land.

Once again, Death hounded at the heels of those he loved.

At Houston's command of "Advance!" Paladín charged with the other patriots out of the treeline and over the swale. Silently and tensely, the Texicans sprinted across the high grass plain that was No Man's land. Bending low, he hear a soldier's fife piping, "Will You Come to the Bower."

Now at close range, the two donated cannons, drawn by rawhide thongs, were wheeled into position. The Twin Sisters belched their charges of iron slugs into the enemy barricade.

Then, Paladín, with Niall at his side, charged forward with the entire front. Men yelled freely, *"Remember the Alamo! Remember Goliad!"*

Paladín began firing away at the surprised and panic-stricken Mexicans. Running zig-zag, he and Niall stormed over the breastwork and joined in hand-to-hand combat.

With a savagery of which he had not thought himself capable, he emptied his long rifle, then began swinging its stock as a club. At one point, he risked a glance at Niall. The young man was slashing right and left with his knife.

The enemy fell by the scores under the impact of the Texicans savage assault. Here and there, he heard the wailed, *"Me no Alamo!"* and *"Me no Goliad!"*

But their pleas won no mercy from the other revolutionists, nor from him—not with Fiona's mite of a body lying on Houston's pallet, that firefly of a frame lacking its exuberance and animation that had so powerfully attracted him from that first moment there on the Port of Matamoros docks.

At that death-knell of a moment, it seemed to him that skin without freckles was like a night without stars.

Suddenly, a blue-coated Mexican aimed his musket and fired at him point blank.

Nothing. The Mexican's gun was empty.

As he drew his musket down to lunge with his bayonet, one of his own comrade-in-arms ran directly between, and the bayonet was driven through the Mexican comrade's body.

The jab was given with such force, that in falling, the impaled soldier twisted the bayonet, preventing the other soldier from withdrawing it. He anchored his boot upon the fallen soldier in a frantic attempt to extricate it.

With cool precision, Paladín extracted a rapier from a dead Mexican officer and ran the blue-coated soldier through, from navel to spine. The man gaped at him with surprise, then, bloody hands clutched at the blade, he toppled.

With the rest of the enraged patriots, Paladín grabbed up the musket, reloaded rapidly, then chased after the stampeding enemy. The fugitive

Mexicans ran in headlong retreat over the open prairie and into the boggy marshes surrounding the San Jacinto plain.

But the avengers of the Alamo and Goliad followed and slew them outright or drove them into the waters to drown. Men and horses, dead and dying in the morass to the rear and right of the Mexican camp, formed gory stepping stones for the pursuing Texicans. The swampy water ran red.

The breeze changed direction, smacking Paladín with the scent of spilled blood and guts and spent gunpowder. Mid-stride, he halted, appalled by the carnage around him—a carnage triggered by the fury of Texican patriots well beyond the least civilized restraints.

Turning, he realized he was about to pay a fatal price for his careless pause. That one imprudence on his part allowed yet one more Santanista to rise before him in the pall of smoke, his escopeta cradled against his shoulder, its site on Paladín himself.

THE NIGHT WAS A BOWL of blurred, swirling stars. Arms looped around her updrawn knees, head thrown back, Rafaela wept silent tears that seeped into the hairline at her temples. Her calico dress was wet with perspiration.

She sat with her back against a tall oak, far from the night's maddening melee—but close enough to the tent should Fiona make any sounds, show any indication of living through that night.

Shuddering, Rafaela closed her eyes against the slow-motion images of Niall, weaponless.... His explosive fury overwhelming all caution upon seeing Cavett, the man who had damaged the heart of the girl she had been.

Then Cavett had cocked his pistol.

And, with that, Rafaela had taken her first life with her rifle.

She shuddered, knowing this was something she would have to live with for the rest of her life—killing another human being. The horror of literally blowing out a man's brains. Her nails dug into her arms.

And yet, she wasn't sorry. The danger was dead.

She had equated danger with affection. Niall, too, represented danger. Perhaps that's why she had been drawn to him. But he had let her choose whether to accept his affection.

From behind, she heard the clink of spurred boots approaching over the carpet of dead pine needles. Hunkering beside her, Niall scooped her up into his arms. "We're going home, lass."

SAN JACINTO
REPUBLIC OF TEXAS

A sickle moon rose over the vast wildflower-carpeted prairie and the soft southern wind carried the floral scent to tickle Fiona's nostrils. Somewhere in the distance, she heard a bugler playing, surely the loneliest sound in the world.

Her lids flickered and a weathered gray canvas ceiling gradually coalesced into view. She blinked, flexed her fingers, felt the discomfort in her lower back that was followed by the acute pain in her upper arm—a wave of agony so intense that her head spun with a sickening swirl.

A familiar face coalesced above her. "Fiona!"

The voice was so faint, but she recognized its gravelly tone. She seemed to remember feverish kisses snatching her from oblivion. Her palm slipped up to align with one side of the man's jaw, stubbled with a days-old raspy beard, and she winced at the movement the effort cost her. "Alex?"

His long fingers smoothed back her sweat-dampened hair. "You are awake!"

She frowned, hearing something in his voice that she could not identify… and tasted something she could. Laudanum.

"How long have I been sleeping?

"Nearly twenty-four hours."

And by the look of his red-rimmed eyes, he appeared to have gone without sleep. "What happened?"

"Magnum shot you in your shoulder. It would seem you and Rafaela have a penchant for getting in the line of fire. And for firing at men, when necessary."

With fuzzy recollection, she saw again Magnum's burst of gunfire meant for Alex. "How did Magnum, I mean what—"

"He's dead. Seems Rafaela had a score to settle—or it might have been worse. And had it not been for Niall, I would be among the dead littering the battlefield."

"Neither the devil nor meself," she managed to get out, "is ready for yuir brigand's soul to depart just yet."

His smile was sober. "So many dead, it is unimaginable. And you. It seems you are not safe anywhere near me. For too many God-awful hours, I feared you would not make...." He made a choking sound, then said gruffly, "But we *won*, Fiona. Santa Anna surrendered!"

She heard something in his voice, something never present before. Humility. She reached up to caress his beautiful face and her shoulder screamed in protest. Her forefinger detected the suggestion of moisture. "Ye are crying?"

"No, merely perspiring. The tent's damnably hot."

Now she understood the depths of fear from which his love was coming. But her heart did not think it could stand the strain of both a wounded shoulder and a wounded heart, if he was hell bent on keeping her safe from him. "In the confessional that day... ye... ye told me ye'd never deprive me of heaven."

His head canted with a puzzled scowl. "That I did."

Her voice cracked, and she took a breath to steady it. "'Tis not heaven without ye—I mean, without me land grant." Then she summoned the strength to add, "Me Lord."

Something like what the saints called salvation glimmered in his eyes, and a wide smile broke the severity of his stubbled jaw. He bent over her, his long black hair that smelled of campfire smoke and gun powder and fear-rooted sweat tickling her temples. He cradled her face with his hands. "Oh, my dear scamp, by loving you, I thought I had lost you, too."

She grinned up at him. "Oh no, we leprechauns are invincible."

His face moved closer, and his features blurred. It seemed forever for him to close the distance between their lips. Forever, while her heart thumped excitedly, and her breath caught in anticipation. His lips brushed hers—a soft, lingering kiss that felt like fire in the middle of the harshest winter.

At last, he raised his head slightly, but between them still sparked that current of two people finely in tune. "And no more 'my lord.' Alex will do quite fine for a spousal address."

"What?" She was not quite sure she had interpreted correctly what she had heard.

He lifted his head to look at her again. "A priest has arrived to administer last rites to the fallen. Since I, too, have fallen, been tripped up by one of the wee people, I was thinking maybe the priest could administer either our last rites—or our wedding vows."

She grinned. "We will let him administer our wedding vows. After that, the next time ye bedevil me, I will take care of the last rites meself."

AUTHOR'S
NOTE

THE MATAMOROS EXPEDITION WAS NOT only a military disaster but also was a major contribution to Santa Anna's defeat of the Texicans and *Tejanos* at the battle of the Alamo a couple months later by having siphoned their forces of both manpower and firepower.

However, the Battle of San Jacinto was one of the decisive battles in history. For nearly two hundred years, the saga of the Texas Revolutionary War has been retold until it ranked with the ancient lore of desperate courage and great adventure—of grim deprivation and unimaginable tragedy.

During the eighteen-minute battle, nine Texicans were killed. The Santanistas lost 630, while 730 were taken as prisoners. The following day, Santa Anna, dressed as a common soldier, was captured at Vince's Bayou and later recognized when his soldiers saluted and addressed him as El Presidente.

According to legend, Santa Anna was sequestered with a mulatto woman named Emily Morgan at the time of the Texicans' opening salvo. A song titled The Yellow Rose of Texas was later written about Emily Morgan's purported role in the battle.

The freedom of Texas from Mexico, obtained at San Jacinto, led to the creation of the Republic of Texas. A decade later, the country's agreement to annex with the United States resulted in the carving into the additional states of New Mexico, Arizona, Nevada, California, Utah, parts of Colorado, Wyoming, Kansas, and Oklahoma. Nearly one-third of the present area of America, nearly a million square miles of territory, changed sovereignty—from the Republic of Texas to the United States of America.

Sam Houston became the only person to have become the governor of two U.S. states through direct, popular election, as well as a U. S. senator and a foreign head of state—the President of the Republic of Texas.

IN RESEARCHING AND WRITING *The Brigands,* I gratefully acknowledge use of *The War for Texas Independence* by Ruby Cumby Smith and *Matamoros and the Texas Revolution* by Craig H. Roell.

PARRIS AFTON BONDS IS THE mother of five sons and the author of more than forty published novels. She is the co-founder and first vice president of Romance Writers of America, as well as, co-founder of Southwest Writers Workshop.

Declared by ABC's *Nightline* as one of three best-selling authors of romantic fiction, the award-winning Parris has been featured in major newspapers and magazines, in addition to being published in more than half a dozen languages.

The Parris Award was established in her name by the Southwest Writers Workshop to honor a published writer who has given outstandingly of time and talent to other writers. Prestigious recipients of the Parris Award include Tony Hillerman and the Pulitzer nominee Norman Zollinger.

She donates spare time to teaching creative writing to both grade school children and female inmates, whom she considers her captive audiences.

CPSIA information can be obtained
at www.ICGtesting.com
Printed in the USA
FSHW011411210920
73927FS